ON THE SIDE OF THE

Francis de Belvoir, the "Ba... handsome, urbane, a man of daring and bri... ination, and a legendary figure in the Paris underworld.

ON THE SIDE OF THE GERMANS

Rudolf von Beck, decorated warrior and superb *Abwehr* officer, deeply involved in the growing plot against Hitler.

AND IN-BETWEEN

Michèle, a beautiful Jewish Parisienne commanded by a man she cannot resist to make love to a man she hates, and discovering with horror her weakness as a woman.

THE ENIGMA

"Action-packed . . . double-dealing, cold-bloodedness and violence . . . it would make a great movie!"—*Booklist*

"Taut, daring, authentic . . . heartstopping and exciting . . . a gripping story of terror . . . MICHAEL BARAK IS THE NEW MASTER OF THE SPY THRILLER!"
—Ladislas Farago

bestselling author of *The Game of the Foxes*
"YOU'LL KEEP READING WITH GUSTO!"
—*San Francisco Chronicle*

Big Bestsellers from SIGNET

PROLOGUE

THE
DECISION

A THICK JET OF ORANGE-WHITE FLAME FURIOUSLY SPURTED from the tail of the huge cigar-shaped rocket. The powerful engine roared angrily as a mixture of liquid oxygen exploded in its combustion chamber. When the thrust of the motor reached 55,000 pounds, the missile shivered and slowly rose from its launching pad; up and up it soared, its tail blazing red, climbing beyond the evergreen tops of the slender Pomeranian pines, heading for the low, gray sky. After four seconds of vertical flight, the thirteen-ton rocket slowly started tilting to horizontal position. Within fifty seconds it attained an angle of 49 degrees and crossed the belt of sand dunes rising on the coast; soon it was far away in the sky, gliding over the murky waves of the Baltic.

On the desolate beach, two men were following the rocket's flight through powerful binoculars. One of them looked like a product of the "pure German race" as depicted on the propaganda posters of the fanatic Reichsminister Dr. Alfred Rosenberg. He was young, tall and fair-haired, and his handsome face was illuminated by a pair of blue eyes and an easy, confident smile. He wore a tweed jacket, a white roll-neck pullover and casual slacks made of expensive wool. But his easygoing outward appearance was misleading: At the age of thirty-two, he was Germany's wonder boy, and her foremost rocket scientist—Dr. Wernher von Braun, the master brain behind the huge rocket research and development base of Peenemünde. The other man's appearance offered a striking contrast to von Braun's: He was small, ugly and narrow-chested, clad in the uniform of a general of the Wehrmacht. He was Major-

3

General Walter Dornberger, commanding officer of the Peenemünde Rocket Research Institute.

Both men followed the rocket flight with wonder and excitement. Von Braun had been launching rockets ever since that day in his early teens when he had slipped from the Baron Magnus von Braun's house and joined the Verein für Raumschiffahrt, an amateur association for space flight that fired rudimentary missiles from the Raketenflugplatz in the outskirts of Berlin. He had been conceiving and building more and more sophisticated rockets ever since, but he never succeeded in suppressing the deep emotion which overtook him each time a new engine would roar, spit smoke and flames and head toward the skies. And today it was the gem in the crown—his latest, most powerful rocket, which would soon turn out to be the deadliest weapon of the Third Reich: the V-2.

His enthusiasm was visibly shared by General Dornberger, who repeatedly uttered sharp cries of excitement. Cheers echoed also in the clearings scattered through the thick pine forest, where hundreds of scientists, engineers and technicians had come out of their camouflaged labs and hangars to watch the V-2's flight.

However, not everybody in Peenemünde took part in that morning's jubilation. In the underground control room, several men in white smocks were clustered around a row of radio transceivers and other control and guidance instruments. The worried expression on their faces showed clearly that something was wrong. "It doesn't respond anymore, damn it!" a white-haired engineer growled while frantically activating the remote control switches. "It's completely out of control!"

"What kind of gyroscope did you put in, Wolfgang?" inquired an SS colonel who was standing close by, watching the scientists but not mixing with them.

"It's not a matter of gyroscopes," the white-haired scientist answered with slight contempt. "The rocket carries the remote control equipment of the Wasserfall anti-aircraft missile. It's a test flight."

"You'd better find a quick solution," the colonel said icily. "If anything happens, they won't like it in Berlin."

His veiled threat was received in silence. Everybody knew what it meant. Since the overall supervision of Peenemünde had been assumed three months ago by the

SS Reichsführer Heinrich Himmler, chief of the State Secret Police, fear had crept into every lab on the site.

But even fear couldn't prevent the forthcoming catastrophe. The V-2 disappeared into a cloud, and that was the last the Peenemünde people saw of it. The rocket continued its lonely flight north, over the Baltic Sea, overflew the tiny island of Greifswalder and crossed the dented coastline one hundred and eighty miles away. Ten minutes after takeoff, the rocket dived sharply and crashed in the marshes of Kalmar, in neutral Sweden.

That same evening an old shepherd, Olof Gerhardson, reported to the only policeman of the hamlet of Hovmantorp "the fall of a star" in the very midst of his flock.

The policeman's initial disbelief quickly faded away when old Olof produced a chunk of charred, twisted metal from his leather sack. The officer mounted his rusty bicycle and furiously pedaled to the county town of Växjö, twenty miles away to alert the authorities. The next morning the marshes were surrounded by special police and army units; the army engineers succeeded in retrieving most of the rocket, which had broken into several pieces during impact. There could be no doubt about the origin of the strange device: The German inscriptions and abbreviations on the fins and cone were eloquent enough. Late in the afternoon, the German ambassador in Stockholm was summoned to the Foreign Ministry to hear a strongly worded protest by the minister himself, who severely condemned "the brutal violation of Swedish neutrality" and demanded "swift clarifications" from the government of the Reich. The ambassador's detailed telegram arrived in Berlin two hours later. Joachim von Ribbentrop, the Foreign Minister of the Reich and Hitler's old crony, read the text carefully; after a slight hesitation, he reached for the red phone that connected him directly to "The Wolf's Lair," Hitler's advanced headquarters at Rastenburg, East Prussia.

The strident ring of the telephone, perched on a stand in a corner of the vast, wood-paneled map room, interrupted the Führer in the middle of a tense discussion with some of the most notorious warlords of the Reich. The subject of the meeting was the impending invasion of France by the Allies, which Hitler expected for the beginning of the summer. Hitler looked older than usual tonight, and his expression was grave as he listened to the reports of his generals. He was bent over the long map table and his somber eyes were riveted on a large-scale map of the French Atlantic coast, while Field Marshal Gerd von Rundstedt, the Commander-in Chief for the Western Front, described the fortified "Atlantic Wall." On the other side of the table stood a small group of people: Field Marshal Wilhelm Keitel, head of the High Command of the Wehrmacht, Admiral Karl Dönitz, Commander-in-Chief of the Navy, and Field Marshal Erwin Rommel, who had just arrived from France. Two officers stood a little apart, each one as remote and unattainable as an iceberg: Admiral Wilhelm Canaris, Head of the Abwehr, the Military Intelligence, and SS Reichsführer Heinrich Himmler, impassive in his black SS uniform, ornamented with skull-and-crossed-bones insignia. At the other end of the room, General Alfred Jodl, chief of the operational staff, and Colonel Rudolf von Beck, one of Canaris's assistants, were busy preparing documents and air photographs for the later stages of the meeting.

It was Jodl who answered the phone and listened in silence to the slightly nervous voice of Ribbentrop. Then he tiptoed to the map table, bent over Hitler's shoulder and repeated the message to him in a low voice.

All the blood drained away from Hitler's face and a deathly pallor settled on its waxen skin. Strange flames lit up in his eyes; he remained momentarily immobile, and then, under a sudden impulse, crashed both his clenched fists on the table.

"That's treason," he shouted in a shrill, high-pitched voice. First his face, then his whole body contorted with rage. "Treason," he repeated. "Sabotage." With each word he pounded the table again and again. "My V-2. My vengeance weapon." He moved around the table, intently scrutinizing the startled faces of his generals. "With that rocket I was going to stop the invasion. I was going to turn the beaches of France into a gigantic death-trap for Churchill and his Jewish bunch. I would have fired on them hundreds of *Vergeltungswaffen*! I would have destroyed London."

He paused. His face was covered with sweat. "But now what?" His voice trembled. "Now my wonder weapon, my most precious secret is in the hands of the Swedes. Tomorrow it will be in the hands of Churchill. Who did it?" He turned to the petrified Jodl. "Who is the traitor who fired the rocket to Sweden? I want him here, Jodl, immediately. I want him court-martialed. I'll have him hanged."

Himmler said in a cold, even voice: "The man is General Walter Dornberger, *mein Führer*. We'll bring him here at once. If only I had assumed control over Peenemünde earlier, I am sure nothing would have happened."

"Dornberger," Hitler said. "Dornberger. Get him, Jodl, right away!" He turned abruptly on his heel and left the room. Jodl started to say something, then shrugged helplessly and returned to the phone.

"That is the end of Walter," whispered Rommel to von Rundstedt.

But events took an entirely different turn. Late at night, the officers were admitted to Hitler's private quarters in the west wing of the building. Hitler was sitting in his favorite deep armchair, his eyes dimmed by the lost, faraway look that his intimate aides knew so well. He acknowledged the entry of the military with an almost imperceptible nod and again sank into his brooding. Long after the officers had taken seats around him, he started to speak in a low voice, as if talking to himself. That was his habit—soliloquizing endlessly in his armchair until he fell asleep of exhaustion. "Ribbentrop called me again," he said. "The Swedes want us to apologize for violating their neutrality. Me—apologize." His voice started to gain power and intensity. "The Führer of the Reich to apologize to those treacherous cowards who didn't even dare to fight in the war. Stockholm is swarming with British spies and they want me to apologize. Every morning I hear that another Danish terrorist has escaped to London by way of Sweden—and I should apologize. We should teach them what those insults to the Reich mean. And I say: There will be no apology!"

"But, *mein Führer*," Keitel intervened respectfully, "if we apologize maybe we could get the rocket back."

"Nonsense," Hitler retorted. "That is of no importance. Germany is strong enough without that rocket. At a second thought"—he suddenly smiled—"it's very good, after all. This rocket fell in Sweden. They'll understand what challenging the Reich might bring upon them. Let them see that their neutrality can't protect them from my wrath.

Let them tremble. Next time our rockets might fall not on Kalmar, but on Stockholm, on the Royal Palace itself. Yes. That's what our ambassador should tell them. The Royal Palace." There was triumph in his voice.

"What about Dornberger?" Jodl asked uneasily. "He is flying in tomorrow aboard a special Dornier."

The Führer looked at him with indifference. "Send him back," he said. "I don't need him." His voice faded away and he closed his eyes, putting an end to the conversation.

In the corner of the room, far from the Führer's earshot, the stupefied von Beck leaned toward Admiral Canaris and blurted: "The man is insane."

Canaris slowly turned his head and looked at him. Not a muscle moved in his foxy, cunning face. He remained in that position for a long moment, until von Beck started to regret his impulsive remark, one that could cost him his life.

And then Canaris spoke. "Yes," he said matter-of-factly to von Beck. "The man is insane."

The British ambassador in Stockholm, on his way to an urgent appointment, bumped into the ambassador of the Reich on the majestic staircase of the Foreign Ministry. Both men, deeply embarrassed, drew back and looked the other way, trying to ignore each other. Continuing on his way, the British diplomat suddenly realized that the German ambassador had just come out of the office of the man he was going to see: the foreign minister himself.

As soon as the door of the minister's office closed behind him, the ambassador sensed that something was wrong. The foreign minister looked deeply shaken. Angry red spots colored his cheeks, his eyes flashed with frustration, and there was a slight tremor in his voice when he asked his visitor to sit down. The ambassador wondered what his German counterpart had said or done to infuriate this suave, self-controlled Swede. Maybe it was the same affair which had driven him to ask for today's urgent meeting: the V-2 incident.

The ambassador went straight to the heart of the matter. "His Majesty's Government," he said, "has learned from various reliable sources that a German rocket has fallen on Swedish soil." He paused. "We are at war with Germany, and it is quite certain that the rocket was intended for us," he said firmly. "Consequently, it belongs to us, and we should like to have it in the state in which it was found." The ambassador spoke forcefully, but deep in his heart he knew his request had not a chance to be satisfied. Sweden was a neutral country, and she would not dare to antagonize the Reich by handing over the rocket to its enemy.

To his great surprise, the Swedish minister didn't try to counter his argument. "Could I ask you to excuse me a moment?" he said quietly. "I have to place an urgent phone call. Please remain seated, I shall do it from my secretary's office."

Five minutes later he was back. He had regained some of his composure, and there was an unmistakable note of satisfaction in his voice when he said to the astonished Briton: "I just talked to the Prime Minister, who consulted King Gustav. We shall have no objection if the British Government takes possession of the rocket, as long as it is done discreetly. We shall deliver the rocket to you on Swedish territory and you will undertake its transport to your country. My assistant will call your office in the afternoon to discuss the time and place of the rocket's delivery."

Thirty-six hours later, shortly before midnight, an unmarked DC-3 Dakota airplane landed on an apparently abandoned airstrip in the vicinity of Stockholm. The plane was piloted by Jimmy Bradford, an American ace who had specialized in that kind of unorthodox mission. A civilian lorry emerged from the darkness; several people hurriedly loaded some heavy crates and a number of smaller objects wrapped in tarpaulin aboard the aircraft, while ground servicemen feverishly pumped gasoline into its tanks. Barely half an hour later the Dakota took off. Trying to avoid the concentrations of German anti-aircraft batteries, Bradford took the plane by an oblique route over Norway. In a Shakespearean storm, amidst heavy thunder and diluvial rain, the DC-3 landed safely at Keystone, a small military airfield on the outskirts of London.

The following night, a group of high-ranking officers and civilians entered a huge hangar a few hundred yards off the main Keystone runway. The hangar was heavily guarded by a special detachment of paratroopers. The soldiers immediately recognized among the visitors the bulky figure of Prime Minister Winston Churchill; the famous black beret, adorned with two badges, of Field Marshal Montgomery; and the perpetual smile of General Dwight

D. Eisenhower, the Supreme Commander of the Allied forces in Europe.

The visitors of the night climbed a rusty spiral staircase and emerged on a small platform which offered a fine view of the central part of the hangar. The floor had been cleared of all unnecessary equipment; powerful projectors were casting dazzling beams of light on the oblong, evil-looking object that a group of technicians was carefully assembling. They were just mounting the heavy cone on the cylindrical fuselage of the rocket.

"So that's the V-2," Churchill grunted. He had come straight from a formal dinner and was wearing a dark suit and a bow tie. He pushed his spectacles to the very tip of his nose and bent over the railing to look more closely at Hitler's deadliest weapon.

"V-2 stands for Victory, doesn't it?" asked Eisenhower casually.

"That's what some of our Danish sources say," answered V.R. Jones, the scientific adviser to the Prime Minister, "but a German source tells us that *V* stands for '*Vergeltung*' which means 'revenge.' "

"And a terrible revenge it will be if we let them fly over the Channel," Churchill said forcefully. "We should find out at all costs where those fiendish devices will be positioned, and then blast them with everything we have. And all should be done to carry out the invasion before Herr Hitler has more of those rockets ready."

A young, rosy-cheeked major coughed tactfully behind the Prime Minister. Churchill turned around. The officer kept his voice down to a discreet whisper. "The head of Military Intelligence to see you, sir. He says it's quite urgent."

Churchill nodded and took a fresh cigar out of his breast pocket. "Excuse me, gentlemen." He went down the stairs and followed the officer to the center of the hangar. There, close to the monstrous shape of the V-2, General Bodley was waiting. Without a word he handed Churchill the pink form of a telegram. Only a few words were printed on it.

Churchill examined the document thoughtfully. "This is extremely disturbing," he said. He sounded genuinely worried. "It might turn the invasion into the most humiliating debacle of the war." ·

The director of M.I.6 nodded gravely. "I think there is

a way out, sir. Maybe you remember the plan I spoke to you about in December."

Churchill looked at him with a face devoid of expression. "And you have the man you need?"

"I think so, yes, sir."

Churchill contemplated the German rocket for a long moment. "A fiendish device," he repeated. Then he looked at Bodley again, with the same blank, sealed look. All of a sudden, without uttering one word, he turned abruptly and left the hangar.

A slight shadow of a smile flashed on General Bodley's lips. He walked quickly to the emergency phone at the far corner of the hangar, and asked to be connected with General MacAlister, head of the Special Operations Executive. "I just saw him," he said softly. "I think we've got the green light. Tomorrow then, all right?"

I

THE ADVENTURER

March 18, 1944

IN THE FIRST LIGHT OF DAWN A BLACK BENTLEY LEFT LONDON and set out on a long journey through the rain-swept countryside of southwest England. The car was driven by a huge, square-shouldered Welshman who looked rather ill at ease in his black chauffeur's cap. In the rear of the Bentley were seated General Bodley and General MacAlister, both dressed in civilian clothes. But their attire could hardly fool anybody. The posture of their erect backs, their calm self-confidence, the hard, resolute glint in their eyes, didn't leave room for any mistake: These were people accustomed to command. In any other respect, however, they were utterly different from each other. Everything about MacAlister was big and heavy. He had a bulky chest, thick arms and legs, a broad face and a bulbous nose. The bulge of his belly, only partly concealed by his well-tailored blue suit, betrayed a liking for good food; the multitude of tiny red spots on his puffy cheeks disclosed a penchant for the charms of Bacchus. Those outward characteristics of a *bon vivant* couldn't affect, however, the air of power and daring that emanated from Harold MacAlister. It wasn't for nothing that he had been appointed head of the Special Operations Executive, the phantom organization that Churchill created in 1940 after the fall of France and Belgium at the hands of Hitler. The newly appointed Prime Minister had asked the Commander-in-Chief of the British Army to send him "the most indomitable and daredevil officer in the Kingdom." The next morning, fifty-year-old MacAlister had reported to 10 Downing Street. He had been flown in from Palestine, where he had been secretly training a regiment of German-born Jews, dressed in German uniforms and carrying

Wehrmacht weapons, for suicidal operations behind the German lines. Churchill had looked at the mountainous general, whose record recounted many unorthodox feats accomplished during the last thirty years in India, China, and Abyssinia.

"Hitler reigns all over Europe, MacAlister," the Prime Minister said gloomily. Then he snapped forcefully: "Set Europe on fire!"

Which MacAlister had done, establishing the Special Operations Executive, building Resistance networks all over occupied Europe, parachuting many hundreds of audacious fighters behind the enemy lines on missions of destruction and sabotage. Most of MacAlister's men didn't return, meeting a gruesome death in the Gestapo cellars. But a growing number of Britons, Frenchmen, Poles, Dutchmen, Norwegians, Greeks and even freedom-loving Germans found their way to the S.O.E. training centers and volunteered for suicide assignments in Nazi-ruled Europe. MacAlister himself, ignoring the explicit orders of his superiors, had jumped twice into occupied France, the first time to coordinate the underground diversionary operations on the eve of the ill-fated raid on Dieppe in August, 1942; the second, to confer near Bordeaux with a French general, head of a group of high-ranking French officers who intended to join the Resistance. The decisive meeting, however, turned out to be a trap set by Heinrich Himmler. Most of MacAlister's aides were captured, never to be heard of again, while he succeeded in escaping through Spain and Portugal, and returned to his office in Baker Street with a nasty thigh wound that made him limp for the rest of his life. The humid weather on this late winter morning caused him heavy pain, but nothing showed on his broad, strong face while he calmly smoked his briar pipe on the rear seat of the Bentley, to the great displeasure of his companion, General Brian Bodley.

Compared to MacAlister, Brian Bodley looked almost ascetic. He was a very thin man, with narrow shoulders, long and bony limbs, and small hands and feet. The extreme pallor of his skin indicated that he had spent most of his life indoors. The meagerness of his face accentuated the determined setting of his jaw and the hard line of his tightly pressed lips. His clear forehead was topped by neatly combed snow-white hair. Equally white and neat was his small moustache. But the most striking feature in that lean face was the eyes: big, clear, china-blue, but burning with an almost frightening glitter of sharpness and cunning. Those cold, chilling flames were the only reflection of the mind that lay behind. Brian Bodley was indeed the very image of the mystery man: sealed, secretive, never disclosing his motives, never revealing his objectives, always busy building layer upon layer of leakproof covers in order to shield himself, to protect the long, vulnerable tentacles of his secret organization. That obsession for secrecy and deception had been highly rewarding for Brian Bodley: very few, if any, of Britain's military leaders knew the true story of his career in the secret services since that day in 1904 when he had plunged, a lad of twenty, into the shadow world of espionage. Of course, there were stories and gossip where truth and fiction were tightly interwoven. According to one rumor, his mother had been German, and he spoke her language perfectly; he had spent most of the First World War in Berlin as the top British agent there, operating under the cover of a junior communications officer in the German Imperial staff. Another rumor insisted that he had been based in Istanbul, posing as a German railroad expert, and that his highly accurate reports about the Turkish Army contingency planning had enabled Lawrence of Arabia to instigate the fabulous Arab uprising. Other stories placed him in revolutionary Russia in the early twenties, in Japan during the invasion of Manchuria, in the German "Kondor" legion in the Spanish Civil War. He never tried to deny any of the rumors, and some of his colleagues suspected that he spread them himself, in his everlasting efforts to shroud himself in a veil of mystery. Since his appointment in 1941 as head of Military Intelligence, M.I.6, he would always confer with Churchill alone, stubbornly ignoring the regular channels of command. A widespread version maintained that his special relationship with the Prime Minister had started about twenty years ago when, looking for solid political connections, he had approached Winston Churchill and become his main informant in the secret services.

The two men had been in close contact for years, without becoming friends, however. Bodley was hardly the kind of man who could be friends with anybody. But he was brilliant, highly intelligent, and his piercing blue eyes spelled an overwhelming natural authority. He was deeply respected by his fellow officers. Very few ever dared to question his judgment.

MacAlister did not. Between the two of them, Bodley was the brain, and MacAlister the muscle. Bodley had the devious, scheming imagination; MacAlister was the fearless commando fighter who would never retreat before danger. They formed a good team together, and had carried out many hazardous operations in perfect harmony. Nothing, however, could match the fantastic plan which was put in motion when they set out on their present trip, this morning of March 18, 1944.

"I think what finally convinced Winston was that German rocket, the V-2," Bodley said thoughtfully, breaking the silence for the first time since they left London. "It made him realize that if we don't get firsthand information about the deployment of the Wehrmacht, the invasion of France could turn into a bloody fiasco."

MacAlister nodded. "Did you get his authorization in writing?"

Bodley looked at him condescendingly and a slight note of irony slipped into his voice: "Come on, Harold, you know old Winnie. Cunning as a fox, as always. He didn't even say yes. He just looked at me without saying no. Officially, he never approved of the operation; unofficially, I can go ahead."

"So, if we fail . . ." MacAlister's voice faded.

Bodley sighed. "Yes," he said dryly. "If we fail, we are the only people to blame. Therefore we have to succeed."

He looked through the car window at the bleak countryside that surrounded them. A drizzling rain was pouring from a dark-gray sky; nothing could suit better the desolate moorland of Devon, strewn with patches of heather and dark granite rocks. Bodley couldn't help admiring the late Arthur Conan Doyle for choosing this gloomy part of England as the setting for one of the most notorious adventures of Sherlock Holmes. One almost expected to see the horrid hound of the Baskervilles emerge from the evil-shaped black cliffs, hellfire blazing from its eyes and jaws. The moorland could also serve as an ideal hiding place for any convict who succeeded in escaping from the ill-famed prison of Dartmoor, whose massive walls loomed not far ahead against the dark background of the sky. Dartmoor prison was, in fact, the ultimate goal of the long trip Bodley and MacAlister had undertaken.

After a short stop for identification by the guards, the heavy gate opened and the car penetrated into the obscure inner court of the prison. A small, wiry man in a navy-blue uniform came to meet them. His face was blank, but Bodley detected a suppressed note of antagonism in his voice when he said formally: "I am Austin Murdoch, the warden. We've been expecting you. Would you follow me, please?"

He led the way in silence through a labyrinth of corridors. They were accompanied by an aging guard carrying a bunch of big keys, who unlocked the heavy iron doors that barred their passage at regular intervals and remained behind to lock them again. An acrid smell—a mixture of moisture, stale air and cheap disinfectant—hung all over the place. MacAlister wrinkled his nose in disgust.

They entered a small room, meagerly furnished with a rectangular table and some decrepit chairs. There were no windows and the only light came from a naked electric bulb that spread a dim, yellowish illumination.

"The prisoner will be here in a moment," the warden said.

"We'll see him alone," Bodley said. He didn't ask, he simply stated a fact. The warden frowned, but left without a word. A few minutes later, a third person entered the room. The door behind him closed at once, and a key turned in the lock.

The man was dressed in a crumpled prisoner's uniform made of rough, light-blue cotton. Nevertheless, he looked surprisingly well: he was tanned, freshly shaved, and his wavy dark-brown hair had been recently cut. He was in his early thirties, tall and well built, with a good face and intelligent gray eyes. There was something sullen and hostile in his cold look, but he quickly smiled and said, with a tinge of irony in his deep voice: "What a pleasure. Distinguished visitors from the world of the just. I am honored, gentlemen."

"Cut the crap, Belvoir," Bodley said. "Our time is short."

"De Belvoir, if you please," remarked the prisoner with the same amused smile. His English carried a slight French accent.

"I said Belvoir and I know what I am saying," Bodley

replied firmly. "You have never had any right to attach a preposition to your name, and you know it. You are no more a nobleman than I am, and if your fellow criminals find pleasure in calling you 'Baron' that's their business."

The prisoner shrugged indifferently.

Bodley leafed through a thin file he had brought with him. "Your trial is scheduled for next month," he said casually. "You are charged with smuggling gold from France into England, with desertion from the British Army and with illegal entry into this country. Well, I'd say all this will keep you as a guest of His Majesty's penitentiary system until the end of the decade."

Maintaining his even tone, the prisoner asked: "Who are you and what do you want?"

"I can offer you a way out of this mess," Bodley said evenly. "I can have the charges against you dropped, and I shall pay you 200,000 pounds if you accept my offer. I want you to go to France and carry out an operation for me. I shall pay you 50,000 pounds on accepting the mission, the rest on your return."

The prisoner looked at him appraisingly. "And who are you?"

"My name is Bodley. That's all you need to know."

"That's more than enough," Belvoir said. "I know who you are. The uniform would suit you better, General."

Bodley ignored his remark. "I made you an offer."

"What do you want me to do?" Belvoir inquired warily.

"We'll tell you when you agree."

The prisoner moved toward the door, then turned back to face the two officers. "No deal," he said. "First I want to know what it's all about, then I'll tell you if I take it."

"What the hell is the matter with you?" MacAlister intervened. "Do you want to rot in prison?

The ironic smile again touched the prisoner's face. "As you can see, I don't exactly rot here," he said. "I am well taken care of, and my good friends make my stay agreeable even here in Dartmoor. Now, about your offer. I might accept it, but on my own terms. As I told you, first I want to know more about it."

MacAlister started to reply, but Belvoir interrupted him. "And stop ordering me around," he said with sudden anger. "You need me, don't you? If you had men of your own for that assignment of yours, you wouldn't have come all the way from London. So take it or leave it."

"We'll take it," said Bodley calmly. "Tomorrow morning at eight a car will take you to London for a briefing."

"Make it eight-thirty," said Belvoir, gently tapping on the door to call the guard's attention. "I don't finish breakfast until then."

"A gold smuggler?" MacAlister asked in disbelief. "What kind of a criminal is that one?"

The two generals were seated at the "Three Feathers," a quiet pub in the outskirts of Salisbury where they stopped on their way back to London.

"The worst kind," Bodley said, sipping his brandy. "He worked for the Germans in Paris with a gang of criminals. They robbed and shipped to Germany the property of wealthy Jews and Resistance leaders who were sent to concentration camps. Then, one day he decided to go into business on his own. He succeeded in stealing half a ton of gold from the Gestapo main warehouse in Paris and smuggling it into this country. We would never have caught him if he hadn't been betrayed. He is as slippery as an eel."

"Half a ton of gold from the Gestapo!" MacAlister was stunned. "I'd say that requires some talent."

"He's got plenty, all right," Bodley said pleasantly. He looked quite eager to talk about Belvoir, like a child given an opportunity to show his marbles to a guest. "Theft and smuggling are in his blood, if I may say so. He is a real international adventurer, the charming crook you read about in the papers—the kind who drives women crazy."

"Is he French?" MacAlister inquired. "He speaks a remarkable English."

"His father was a shady character of French origin who called himself the Baron de Belvoir. He was a gambler and a thief who specialized in robbing luxury hotels and millionaires' mansions. He operated with a gang in the French Riviera at the turn of the century. Very sophisticated sort of chap, used to introduce his accomplices into the house as valets or chambermaids and glean all the necessary information before he struck. Then one night his luck ran out and he was caught redhanded by a young American heiress while he was robbing her parents' villa. Cecilia Van Damm was the lady's name."

"Van Damm? Any connection with the railroad king?"

Bodley nodded. "His daughter. I don't know what Belvoir told her that night. Maybe all that Robin Hood stuff that seems to thrill romantic rich girls. Taking from the rich and giving to the poor. . . . Anyway, the next morning she was missing. For a while her family thought she had been kidnapped. It was quite uncommon in those days, you see, and her father offered a tremendous reward to whoever might bring her back. The story made headlines all over the world. For six months there was no news from her. And then, all of a sudden, she turned up in Hong Kong, very happy, very pregnant and very legally married to the Baron de Belvoir."

MacAlister lit his pipe. "Her father didn't like that, I guess."

"He disinherited her, of course. But she didn't seem to care. The child was born in Macao. Belvoir pretended the boy was born 'on a roulette table' in the Casino there, but I guess that was just an embellishment to the Baron's legend. They called him Francis, or 'Frankie.' For some years the three of them roamed the world, leaving a trail of swindles and thefts behind them. They were never caught. After the First World War Cecilia died of yellow fever, in Bangkok. When Frankie was sixteen, his father, the Baron, was assassinated in Paris. One of his accomplices plunged a knife in his back. It was only natural that his son would carry on and inherit his phony title as well as his true profession. He grew up in the underworld of Paris, and very soon outdid his father. He speaks French and English fluently."

"You said something about desertion from the Army," MacAlister remarked.

"Yes, that's the most curious part of it. He was drafted by the French Army at the outbreak of the war, then succeeded in making it to Dunkerque and to England. Here he joined the British Commandos—not the Free French—and took part in the raid on Dieppe. But there he vanished. Some months later he was back in Paris, first mounting his sophisticated swindles, and later working for the Germans. It all culminated with the Gestapo gold affair. Scotland Yard was tipped about him, and he was arrested as soon as he landed here with his gold. The police were seriously worried he might escape again. He has quite a reputation, you see—so, as an exceptional measure, they sent him to Dartmoor to await trial. Jolly good security arrangements there, as you noticed."

"Fascinating," MacAlister said, sucking his pipe. "Absolutely fascinating." He looked a Bodley appraisingly. "You seem to know every single detail about him."

"I've been studying his file for the last six months, since he was arrested," Bodley said coldly. "You see, he is the best thief in Europe. Exactly the kind of man I need."

A THICK, YELLOW-GRAYISH FOG HAD CREPT INTO LONDON during the night and lay over it now, clinging to the wet sidewalks and the cold walls. Visibility was low, and the few people venturing into the open would emerge and disappear in the thick, murky mist, like dark ghosts. Even the sudden gusts of icy wind that whined through the desolate streets would only briefly tear the fog into trembling, shapeless patches that soon merged again into a uniform dark wall. The few cars out moved slowly, their pale yellow eyes striving in vain to pierce the heavy curtain that swayed around them.

A gray limousine whose color merged with the surrounding fog crept slowly north on Baker Street. Its driver bent forward over the wheel, intently examining the blurred shapes of the buildings that stood on his left. "Here we are," he finally said, sighing with relief. "Saint Michael's House." The driver cautiously parked by the big corner building.

The plainclothes policeman who was sitting on the left side of Frances de Belvoir gently tapped his shoulder. The officer opened the door, looked around, and then motioned to Belvoir and the other plainclothesman, who was positioned on the prisoner's right side. Belvoir, in brown corduroys and a beige turtleneck pullover, was quickly rushed over the slippery sidewalk and into a side door of the building. The sergeant on duty at the door carefully examined the plainclothesman's papers. "They are waiting for him," he said finally. "Second floor, third door on the left. You escort him to the door, he walks in alone."

In the oblong, sparsely furnished room, bright fluorescent lights were burning. Heavy curtains were tightly pulled over the three windows. Bodley and MacAlister, in full general's uniform, were sitting on both sides of a long oak table covered with charts and papers. The walls were bare, except for a big blackboard that hung opposite the windows. A young major was busy drawing a curious sketch on the blackboard, frequently consulting a blueprint he held in his left hand.

Belvoir closed the door behind him and slowly looked around. "Well, well," he said mockingly, "I didn't know that the brave British Army had taken over Marks and Spencer."

Bodley and MacAlister exchanged glances.

"I see you know Saint Michael's House," Bodley said. "Well, it still belongs to the department store company, but it was lent to the government for the duration of the war. MacAlister and the S.O.E. have established their secret headquarters here. That's why we call them the Baker Street Irregulars."

Belvoir smiled. "The last time I was here, the place was full of women's nightgowns and brassieres." He looked challengingly at MacAlister.

The general's face reddened. "Well, it's not today," he said aggressively, and added with undisguised contempt: "Ever steal anything from here, Baron?"

The cool gray eyes of the prisoner, missing nothing, noticed the quick angry glance Bodley shot at his colleague. That confirmed his impression after yesterday's meeting: Bodley was the boss around here.

"Let's get down to business," the chief of Military Intelligence said quietly, getting up. "Please take a seat, Belvoir."

He spoke succinctly, carefully picking his words. "In a few months the Allies will land in France and open the second front. This is no secret. We are getting ready, and so are the Germans. They are quite busy building their defenses. The success of the invasion will depend to a large extent on our military intelligence. We must know what the enemy's plans are, where his elite divisions are based, what is the state of alertness of his troops. Lately, Hitler is throwing new weapons into the battle—the V-1 and V-2 rockets. We must find those rocket sites and destroy as many of them as we can.

"We control a multitude of intelligence sources and spy networks in enemy territory. But they are inadequate. We

must, at all costs, break the German communication codes
and decipher their radio messages. That will assure us of
the final victory. It will also save many thousands of
lives."

He paused and looked at Belvoir, waiting for his reaction, but there was none. The prisoner listened calmly, his
arms crossed, his face devoid of expression.

Bodley went on. "The top level communications between the Oberkommando der Wehrmacht—Hitler's supreme
headquarters—and the high-ranked field commanders of the
German Army are carried out by coded radio signals. The
signals are top secret. So is the enciphering and deciphering
system. The signals are enciphered by a special electric
machine. The Enigma."

"Enigma?" Belvoir repeated. "Isn't that the Greek word
for puzzle?"

"And a puzzle it is for all of us, I can assure you,"
Bodley said forcefully. "For almost five years the best
teams of cryptographers the Allies could put together have
been trying to break the Enigma cipher. We failed all
along the line. There is no way to crack the Enigma
secret. I won't exaggerate by stating that the Enigma is the
most jealously guarded secret in Germany today."

Bodley turned to the major, who had completed his
drawing. "Will you carry on, Major?"

The young officer pointed at the blackboard with a long
thin stick. "We have here a rough sketch of the Enigma,"
he started. "It is based on information from various sources
and we believe it's quite accurate."

Belvoir stared attentively at the blackboard. "It
resembles an old-fashioned typewriter," he said.

"Yes," the major agreed, "and it is about the same
size."

The drawing on the blackboard indeed looked like a big
portable typewriter, complete with its box and cover. The
machine had an ordinary keyboard, like a standard
typewriter; but under the keyboard was a multitude of
round sockets, in which were inserted oval-shaped plugs
interconnected by electric wires. From the upper part of
the machine protruded three thin indented disks.

"How does that function?" asked Belvoir, intrigued.

"The principle is quite simple," the major said. "The
keys of the typewriter are connected to revolving drums,
or rotors, which are placed inside the machine. The rela-

tionship between the drums is changed by shifting the plugs in and out of the sockets. According to the arrangement of the drums, any letter typed on the keyboard is switched to a different one. B might become F or Z or whatever—it all depends on the combination of the plugs. The enciphering is easy: the operator types the message in clear, as if typing on a conventional typewriter; but it comes out completely garbled. It is then radioed in that form. To anyone intercepting the message, it will have no meaning whatsoever. The operator on the receiving end, however, has only to feed the message into a sister machine where the drums are set according to the same pattern—and the message comes in clear."

"Childishly simple," Belvoir murmured.

"Childishly simple," MacAlister grunted. "It might interest you to know that it would take about a month for a team of topnotch mathematicians to find out all the key combinations needed for discovering the meaning of one single message. If you bear in mind the fact that the drum settings are periodically changed, and that each military command—army, navy, air force, in each and every country—has its different pattern, you might begin to understand that the childishly simple Enigma cypher is unbreakable."

"Unless . . ." murmured Bodley, casting an oblique glance at Belvoir.

"Unless what, General?" Belvoir asked sharply.

"Unless somebody volunteers to go to France and steal an Enigma machine for us," Brain Bodley said.

For a long moment Belvoir sat completely still. Gone was the ironic smile that usually curled the left corner of his mouth; gone was the gleam of laughter in his eyes. Deep furrows wrinkled his forehead. He dug in his pocket and produced a long, thin cigar. He lit it with MacAlister's silver lighter, which was lying on the table, and inhaled the pungent smoke while an expression of deep concentration gradually set over his face. Finally he looked back at Bodley.

"This is a dangerous undertaking," he said.

"Not just dangerous," Bodley corrected. "Suicidal."

Belvoir's penetrating gaze didn't leave Bodley's face. "Why should I do it?" His tone was conversational, almost casual. "Give me one good reason why I should risk my life."

"I can give you many," Bodley said firmly. "The first is your freedom. You don't want to spend the next ten years in prison, and you know it. If you agree, you walk out of here a free man, and no charges will ever be pressed against you for the desertion and the gold affair. Who knows," he chuckled, "you might even win the Victoria Cross. The second reason is the money. You love money, Belvoir. This is the only value you are loyal to, and for which you are ready to take risks. Two hundred thousand pounds is a lot of money, and just for once you won't have to break into the Bank of England to get it.

"And there is a third reason, the most important. The thrill of it, Belvoir."

"What do you mean?" Belvoir asked, surprised.

"You heard me perfectly well," Bodley said softly. "The excitement." He bent toward Belvoir and stared straight into the prisoner's eye. "The Gestapo and the French police have not left a stone unturned anywhere in France in their search for you. They want your head. And you—you'll love to beat them again, won't you?" The general's voice went down to a harsh whisper. "You are a gambler, you take dangerous risks, you are always looking for new challenges. Remember the Fratelli affair in 1939? When you robbed the apartment of the police commissioner in Rome three nights in a row? You know and I know that it wasn't for the money and the jewelry. You had scooped up everything on the first night. It was just for the fun of it, for the risk, for the challenge, for nurturing the legend of the Baron. Well, I offer you a genuine challenge, not merely some operetta bravado. Just for once it's the real stuff, where you can gamble your own life. You'll love that, Belvoir."

A brief grin flashed on Belvoir's face. But when he spoke, his voice was cold and slightly sarcastic. "And because your analysis indicates that I am a gambler, you assume I should readily gamble on my own life."

Bodley shrugged. "I might be mistaken," he admitted indifferently. "Maybe you prefer the present state of things. You can go back to Dartmore if you wish. They'll take good care of you there, and with your connections I am sure life won't be too hard for you." A note of irony slipped into his voice. "And only very seldom, during your cozy future in a nice prison cell, will it occur to you that on the whole, even the most charming jail is a jail nevertheless."

Belvoir stared fixedly in front of him. Then he asked in a matter-of-fact voice: "How many Enigma machines are there in France?"

Bodley was his old precise self again. "Twenty-seven, tuned already to the messages of Hitler's supreme headquarters. We have obtained a copy of a top-secret situation paper of the German Signal Corps, dated February 15, in which are listed all the Enigma machines operating in France, the names of the units to which they are attached and the location of each and every unit."

Belvoir stretched out his hand. "Let me see it," he said calmly.

MacAlister shot an alarmed glance at the Head of Military Intelligence. Bodley hesitated a second, then fumbled in his leather case and took out a single sheet of paper. He handed it to the prisoner. Belvoir examined it attentively.

"And you want me to steal one of those?" he asked.

"Stealing it won't be enough," Bodley replied. "Even if you manage to get hold of the machine and get away with it, the Germans will stop using the Enigma as soon as they find out that one machine is missing. No, what we want you to do is steal the Enigma, and simultaneously blow up the building or the installation where it was kept, so that the Germans would assume the machine was destroyed with all the other equipment."

An amused smile appeared again on the lips of the prisoner.

"And you want me to do that alone?"

"No," MacAlister intervened. "The operation should be disguised as a sabotage raid by the French underground. A group of French Resistance fighters will work with you on that project."

Belvoir looked suspiciously at the two generals in front of him. "Why me?" he asked. "Why did you pick me? You have highly trained people, here and in France. Why not use them? Why take all the trouble to release me from your prison and pay me money for it?"

"Because for that job we need a thief and a smuggler," Bodley said bluntly. "We need somebody to steal the machine before he blows up the building, and then smuggle it out of France. My files show that the Baron is the best in that field. The man who stole the gold from the Gestapo cellars can steal anything."

Belvoir lapsed again into a long silence. Then, in a sharp movement, he threw his head back. "Okay," he said. "I'll do it. But on three conditions. It will cost you not two but four hundred thousand pounds."

"Three hundred thousand and not one penny more," Bodley snapped with finality.

Belvoir didn't insist. "I want half of the money now, in cash, and half on my return."

Bodley was a hard bargainer. "One hundred thousand now. The rest when you are back with the Enigma."

Belvoir nodded. "And I want a week's leave, with complete freedom of movement, starting today. No policemen, no tails, no baby-sitters." He hastily raised his hand when Bodley opened his mouth to object. "Arguing at this point will do no good, General. I shall not budge from this position. You'd better send somebody for the money, at once."

"But we can't let you go free, man," Bodley flared. "You are on a top-secret assignment."

"Then forget about it."

"What do you need that leave for?" For the first time Bodley looked genuinely alarmed.

"To see the sights of London," chuckled the Baron. "Do we have a deal, General?"

The white-haired man stared at Belvoir. Finally he sighed. "I guess we have," he said. "The major will take you to another room while we prepare the money for you. How do you want it?"

"Fifty thousand in pounds—and the balance in French francs," Belvoir said, and added sharply: "And no tricks, General. Good genuine money. I don't fancy substitutes."

Bodley looked at him wordlessly.

Half an hour later Francis de Belvoir headed for the street where the car that had brought him there was waiting. In his right hand he clutched a small leather bag. The fog had almost dispersed by now, and the streets were full of people. Before he left the building, Bodley caught him by the hand: "How shall we contact you?" He was tense and his face was worried.

"You won't," said Belvoir flatly. "Just give me a phone number where you can be reached."

He memorized Bodley's direct phone number. When he emerged on the street, he entered the car and turned to the driver: "To Piccadilly Circus, please." At the first intersection lights he jumped out of the car and disappeared in the crowd.

At ten minutes past midnight, Corporal Hans Lischke of the Wehrmacht regretfully interrupted the canasta game he had been playing with three of his comrades in the canteen of the Abwehr signal department compound in Berlin.

"I'll be back in fifteen minutes," he said.

"Do you think they'll call tonight?" asked his good friend, Sergeant Ernst Griefel.

Lischke shrugged. For three weeks London hadn't called. But then, they didn't establish contact regularly. There was only one Abwehr spy ring left in the British capital, and they radioed short messages only in cases of emergency. Five other networks had been dismantled and this one, the last, had to observe very tight security precautions.

Lischke entered the radio room, sat at his desk, plugged the heavy earphones into his radio set and pulled them over his ears. For the first five minutes there was just static in the air. He lit a *Soldaten* cigarette. In a few minutes the vigil would be over, and he could join his friends at the canasta game.

And then he heard the call sign. Very distant, but quite distinct. The Morse dots and dashes filled his ears. He immediately recognized the touch of London Lily, and his expert fingers deftly played the receiving signal on his transmitter. "Come on, Lily," he whispered to himself, "let's see what you have got for us tonight." he started scribbling the message on a pad of yellow paper.

Precisely at eight o'clock the next morning, Colonel Rudolf von Beck climbed the main staircase at Tirpitzufer 74, the Headquarters of the Abwehr in Berlin. He absentmindedly returned the salutes of the junior officers and NCOs whom he met on his way up. His orderly, a sturdy Bavarian by the name of Schneider, was waiting for him at the top of the stairs.

"The Admiral wants to see you, Herr Oberst," he said.

Von Beck went through the long corridor and into the outer office of the Abwehr chief. The Admiral's secretary ushered him into his boss's sanctuary. The windows were open and a cool invigorating wind penetrated the large room, rustling the sheaf of papers piled on the Admiral's desk.

Instead of greeting him, Canaris handed von Beck a thin blue form, crossed with two red stripes. "It arrived last night from London," the head of the Abwehr said.

Von Beck read the short message aloud:

IN SECRET MEETING HELD IN S.O.E. HEADQUARTERS IN BAKER STREET CHARTS AND DESIGNS OF ENIGMA MACHINE WERE DISCUSSED STOP DURING THE MEETING THE LOCATIONS OF TWENTY-SEVEN ENIGMA MACHINES THROUGHOUT FRANCE WERE MENTIONED STOP FOUR PEOPLE TOOK PART IN THE MEETING AMONG THEM THE DIRECTOR OF S.O.E. STOP END.

Von Beck looked speculatively at the small white-haired man who was leaning back in his upright wooden chair, gently patting the black Great Dane that lay by his side. "S.O.E. is in charge of all underground operations in France," von Beck said. "That report means that they want to get the Enigma."

"And I want you to protect it, Rudolf," Canaris said softly.

THE GIRL MUMBLED SOMETHING IN HER SLEEP AND ROLLED to the other side of the large bed. The woolen blanket slipped to the floor, revealing her delicate, sleek body. She was completely naked, except for a thin golden chain that encircled her waist. Her long raven-black hair spilled over her face and shoulders and made a dark splotch on the pillow.

Francis de Belvoir opened his eyes and lay immobile on his back for a few minutes. Morning had broken and a feeble light was filtering through the drawn curtains. He propped himself on his elbows and looked at the sleeping girl. Then he quietly slipped out of bed, came to the girl's side and gently pulled the blanket over her nude body. The tips of his fingers touched her smooth skin. The girl moved again and cuddled under the blanket. Belvoir bent over her and looked closely at her oval face. The girl was fast asleep; her breathing was regular and her miniature Eurasian features were peaceful. He didn't even remember her name: Was it Wendy, or Velda. Not that it really mattered. He had picked her from among the prostitutes hanging around the dark doorways of the animated Soho streets. It hadn't been a completely random choice, though. He needed a room in which to spend the night, and the best way was to spend it with a whore. He had chosen, however, a girl who was better dressed than the others, which let him rightly presume that she had a room of her own and wouldn't drag him to a hotel where his face and clothes might be remembered. He had also been right in assuming that she spoke English poorly; she wouldn't be able to give a precise description of him, if she were required to do so. And finally, as he admitted to himself, he had had an inclination for those petite, smooth-skinned Eurasian girls since his teen-age days, when they had initiated him in the art of love in the deluxe bordellos of Saigon and Macao. This one had also been quite good in bed, but he was too tense, too preoccupied. It had been very important to him to spend the night where nobody could trace him, so he could have complete freedom of movement during the crucial day that lay ahead. Tonight or tomorrow he would call one of his many friends in London and find a cozy hideaway for the next few days. He could even check into a hotel, under his real name. What really mattered was that as few of his usual connections as possible knew what he had done and whom he had met during his first day out of jail. Sooner or later Bodley's men might try to find out why he had insisted on that week of freedom before setting forth on his mission.

He tiptoed to the tiny bathroom, shaved and quickly dressed in the new, ready-made clothes he had bought the previous day: a three piece dark-gray suit, a white shirt and a conservative blue tie. He unpacked a new pair of black shoes and blue socks and stuffed his old clothes into a medium-sized pigskin valise which he had purchased in a department store. Inside lay the leather pouch which contained more than ninety-nine thousand pounds, in British and French currency. He examined himself critically in the mirror, He looked quite distinguishd, but then the sight of distinguished, well-dressed gentlemen sneaking furtively from Soho doorways early in the morning was certainly not an uncommon one. He left five one-pound notes on the table. He was tempted to add something more for the quite extraordinary services she had provided, but on second thought decided to refrain from doing so; he didn't want to be remembered because of an overgenerous tip. He gently closed the door behind him and ran down the stairs and into the busy Dean Street. It was a crisp, sunny morning, the sidewalks were crowded, and that suited his purposes perfectly. The weather, he said to himself, was a good omen.

De Belvoir turned into Carlisle Street, crossed Soho Square, and emerged through the short Sutton Row on Charing Cross Road. In Saint Giles Circus he descended to the Tottenham Court Road underground station and took the Central line to Liverpool Street. Then he changed trains and continued on the Circle line to Notting Hill Gate. He changed again to the Central line and got out at Marble Arch. In a small alley off Oxford Street he threw his old clothes in a garbage can and returned to the bustling commercial street. He walked along a distance of about two hundred yards, checking constantly in front and behind for any tails; he stopped a few times in front of the windows of several shops and examined the reflection of the street behind him. All seemed normal. He jumped on a double-decker London bus that brought him back to the corner of Wardour Street, barely a couple of hundred yards from the room where he had spent the night. It had taken him more than an hour to make sure he wasn't being followed. Now he could turn to his business.

Soho being the heart of London's theater district, he had no difficulty finding a shop for theatrical props and appliances. He spent more than an hour there, then visited two other shops until he found all the items he needed. Then he walked into a small printer's shop on Old Compton Street. The place looked shabby and neglected, and so did its owner, a fat balding man who wore baggy trousers and a dirty blue smock. His name, Dimitri Kakoyanis, was painted on an old peeling sign that hung over the shop's entrance. An antique phonograph diffused a plaintive Greek song.

Kakoyanis raised his eyes from his desk, where he had been setting some leaden type into a wooden framework, and looked suspiciously at the newcomer.

"What do you want?" he rasped. Such a welcome could discourage almost anybody, but Belvoir was not just anybody. He knew well that, behind his shabby facade, Kakoyanis was the best forger in England.

"A good friend sent me to you," he said.

"Who?" Kakoyanis asked warily.

Belvoir remembered the password well. "Alexander," he said. "He asked me to tell you that Maria is back."

The Greek nodded, but the suspicious glance didn't completely disappear from his small black eyes. "Let's go inside," he said.

First, he closed and locked the door of the shop; then he preceded Belvoir through a small back door into an inner room. He switched on two powerful lamps that flooded the room with light. This room was much bigger. An impressive array of small bottles, containing liquids of various colors, were neatly arranged on a large table. In several wooden trays lay pens, pencils, nibs and brushes. On a smaller table were stacked piles of virgin white paper of various kinds. A half-open drawer was filled to the top with ink pads. Close to the opposite wall stood an adjustable stool; the wall itself was covered with an immaculate white curtain. Facing it stood two big cameras, perched on wooden tripods. Belvoir noticed a large icon of the Holy Family hanging on the right wall and looking quite out of place in this forger's workshop. No doubt it served only for the purpose of concealing the wallsafe.

"Now, what do you need?" Kakoyanis asked.

Belvoir spoke very precisely. "I need several complete sets of papers and documents. French documents. For most of them I shall have to be photographed wearing a disguise and appropriate clothes. I brought everything with me, so that I could change here and have my pictures taken. You will fill in all the details on the documents according to my instructions, except the names. I shall write the names myself with your equipment. In some of the papers we shall leave blank spaces, and for each of them you will supply me with pen nibs of the corresponding caliber and with small bottles of ink of the identical quality. I shall fill in those spaces at a later stage according to the circumstances. I shall need all the documents today, even if you have to work late into the night. I shall stay with you the whole time, and you won't be allowed to leave the shop while you are working on the job."

Kakoyanis looked at him in dismay. "But that's impossible," he said. "I have other work to do. People might come to the shop. I shall have to go out for lunch—there is no food in the shop. And . . ."

He stopped in mid-sentence and stared avidly at the stack of ten-pound notes that materialized on the table. "That's to compensate you for keeping the shop closed all day and canceling all your other engagements," Belvoir said calmly. "We shall go out now, together, and we shall buy food and drink to keep us alive until tonight. Now, about the money. I shall pay you one thousand pounds for each set of documents. I shall give you another thousand for each set, in bills torn in half. That will be the price of your silence. In a few weeks I'll be back, and if you keep your mouth shut until then, I'll give you the matching halves of all those crisp new British banknotes."

Kakoyanis was completely taken aback. "That's good money," he admitted in a hoarse voice.

"I pay good money for a good job," Belvoir said, concluding the negotiations.

The work lasted until late evening. First Kakoyanis photographed Belvoir in various attire. For each set of pictures, Belvoir dressed in different clothes and applied an elaborate disguise. He went with Kakoyanis into his darkroom and watched him develop and print the photographs. When those were ready, he burned the negatives and all the extra prints. When Kakoyanis removed the icon and opened the safe where he kept his treasury of documents, Belvoir clung to him as a shadow, inspecting the various papers, the stamps, the inks, choosing the documents himself. He couldn't help admiring the Greek's resources. His safe hid a selection of almost every document in England and occupied Europe. Kakoyanis had agents and friends everywhere: His men paid top money for stolen papers of all kinds.

The forger himself soon discovered that he was working with a professional. He watched the meticulous work of Belvoir from the corner of his eye. When each set of documents was ready, Belvoir would inscribe the name, closely imitating Kakoyanis's handwriting, while taking utmost care that the Greek didn't catch even a fleeting glimpse of the name. Then he would pack the documents, the writing utensils, the clothes, the make-up and other materials he had used for his disguise in separate packages. He would wrap all those packages in a big bundle, in which he would slip a note he wrote on plain paper and sealed in a blank envelope.

In the evening, when several bundles had been stuffed into his bursting valise, Belvoir paid Kakoyanis his due, including the wad of bills torn in half. He complimented Kakoyanis for his work, left the shop and hailed a passing taxicab. He found a table in the buffet of Victoria Station, where the presence of a man carrying a traveling bag wouldn't look unnatural. He ordered a light supper, then dialed a number from the buffet's phone.

"Do you recognize my voice?" he asked cautiously when he got his connection.

"Say some more words," the voice on the other end of the line replied.

"It's been quite some time since the Duchess lost that string of pearls," Belvoir said.

His remark elicited a gasp of surprise. "You!"

"Yes, me," Belvoir laughed. "I need you, now, at Victoria Station. It will be worthwhile for you."

"With you it always is," the other voice said eagerly and the line went dead.

Half an hour later, a handsome man of about fifty, who looked very distinguished in his navy-blue blazer, cream-colored silk shirt and foulard scarf, materialized at Belvoir's table. In his lapel glistened a golden Imperial Airways pin.

"*Mon cher* Baron," he beamed, "it's been such a long time."

Belvoir nodded pleasantly. "You improve with age, Mortimer," he observed. "Those silver streaks at your temples make you look very respectable indeed. Why, somebody might even mistake you for an honest man."

The man called Mortimer smiled. "You don't look bad either, Baron."

"Let's skip the other preliminaries," the Baron said briskly. "This bag must be in Lisbon tomorrow. Are you on the flight?"

"No, as a matter of fact, I am not," Mortimer said and looked at his watch. "But I have a friend who can take it. Or, even better, I might take his place if it's really important."

"It is important," Belvoir said.

"Very well, then. I shall call him and substitute for him." For a moment, though, he hesitated. He cast a slightly nervous look at the pigskin bag. "Is there anything, I mean . . ."

"Nothing you should worry about," interrupted Belvoir. "No arms, no secret documents, no diamonds, no counterfeit money."

Mortimer smiled in relief. "I just wanted to be sure."

Belvoir nodded. From his pocket he took an envelope. A phone number was scribbled on the flap. "When you land, you'll call this number. It's in Cascais. The man who will answer speaks excellent English. You'll tell him that you have an urgent message from me. He'll come at once to see you. Give him the bag and tell him he must bring it to France, by the first train that goes via Spain. He must deliver each package to the address noted down in an envelope tucked under the wrapping paper. All the packages must reach their destinations in five days, no more."

Mortimer listened gravely. "What if your friend can't go to France on such short notice?"

"Don't worry," Belvoir said calmly. "He'll send somebody else. In any case, he won't do it alone. You just give him this envelope. Inside there are detailed instructions and enough money to cover his expenses and a few nights in the Cascais Casino." He handed Mortimer another envelope: "And that's my contribution to your champagne and caviar diet."

Mortimer expertly examined the thickness of the envelope with his fingers. He looked pleased. "It seems to me that I could also drop in to the Casino for a few minutes."

"Not before you deliver the bag," the Baron snapped.

After Mortimer left with the pigskin valise, Belvoir dialed the Savoy Hotel. He asked for the manager.

"This is the Baron de Belvoir," he said when he recognized the familiar voice. "I'd like a suite, for six nights."

"With pleasure, Monsieur le Baron," the manager of the Savoy said suavely. "We shall be delighted to see you again. Some chilled Veuve Clicquot at your bedside, as usual?"

"Of course," Belvoir said, "if it comes from your personal reserve, that is."

For the next six days he was going to act the role of the swashbuckling playboy, exactly as Bodley, MacAlister and their friends would expect him him to. Which, he had to admit, could be quite agreeable at times.

The black military Horch braked smoothly and parked behind a gray Mercedes in Hofjäger Allee, one of the main entrances of the Tiergarten, Berlin's famous park. It was barely six o'clock in the morning of March 26, and there was nobody in sight except the driver of the Mercedes, a fat sergeant, who was busy cleaning the windshield. "You'll wait for me here, Schneider," von Beck said to his orderly, who opened the car door for him. The cheerful Bavarian clicked his heels. *"Jawohl, Herr Oberst."*

Von Beck marched into the desolate Tiergarten. He immediately saw, farther along the path, the man who had summoned him here at this early hour: a small gray figure, peacefully strolling with a Great Dane. At some distance behind him moved two men in *feldgrau* uniforms, a bodyguard and the aide-de-camp, in charge of the security and the tranquility of their Admiral.

Canaris was wearing civilian clothes. He had the odd habit of going out every once in a while dressed as a civilian; his close aides had long ago given up guessing what pleasure he found in wearing old-fashioned double-breasted suits which hung loosely on his small, skinny frame. He was walking at a leisurely pace, his arms crossed, his head bent, seeming to muse in deep concentration. He answered von Beck's greeting with a perfunctory nod. Von Beck fell in step with him and kept quiet. The fine gravel of the path cracked softly under his boots.

After a few minutes Canaris took out of his pocket a thin sheet of blue paper, crossed with red.

"Another message from London Lily?" the young colonel asked with sudden interest.

Canaris nodded and handed it to von Beck. "It arrived last night."

SPECIAL S.O.E. AGENT WILL BE PARACHUTED IN FRANCE NIGHT MARCH 27 PROBABLY IN CONNECTION ENIGMA PROJECT STOP END.

"That means tonight," von Beck said and returned the telegram to his chief.

"I think you should go to Paris, Rudolf," Canaris said. "We have to stop this gentleman, whoever he may be. The Enigma must be protected at all costs."

"I'll leave tomorrow, Herr Admiral," von Beck replied.

They continued to stroll in silence, two men walking their dog in the Tiergarten, very far from the war and its horrors. Von Beck observed that the civilian attire seemed to soften the hard expression on Canaris's face and to lessen his aura of crushing authority. He felt more relaxed and dared venture a most impertinent remark.

"You didn't bring me here just to show me the telegram," he said, casting a quick glance at Canaris.

Canaris did not react at once, and von Beck thought that he might not have heard him, but then the Abwehr chief spoke.

"You are right," he said softly. "I brought you here for another reason. I wanted to talk to you without fearing that somebody might be eavesdropping or that Himmler had planted a microphone in my very office."

The Enigma

Michael Barak

A SIGNET BOOK
NEW AMERICAN LIBRARY
TIMES MIRROR

This is an authorized reprint of a hardcover edition published by
William Morrow and Company, Inc.

SIGNET TRADEMARK REG. U.S. PAT. OFF. AND FOREIGN COUNTRIES
REGISTERED TRADEMARK—MARCA REGISTRADA
HECHO EN CHICAGO, U.S.A.

SIGNET, SIGNET CLASSICS, MENTOR, PLUME AND MERIDIAN BOOKS
are published by The New American Library, Inc.,
1633 Broadway, New York, New York 10019.

FIRST SIGNET PRINTING, JANUARY, 1980

1 2 3 4 5 6 7 8 9

PRINTED IN THE UNITED STATES OF AMERICA

FOR JACQUES,

WHO DID NOT

LIVE TO READ IT

The Enigma

"It so happens," he went on, very slowly, very carefully, "that your forthcoming mission might come across another project that some of my friends and I have been planning for quite a long time."

Von Beck didn't dare utter a word. He understood that Canaris wanted to tell him something, and was groping for the right words.

"You remember our last visit to Hitler's headquarters?" Canaris said gravely. "The incident with the V-2 and all the excitement it created?"

"Of course I remember."

"You told me something about somebody then. You said 'the man is insane.'"

Von Beck nodded. "That man holds in his hands the fate of Germany."

Brusquely, Canaris stopped and turned to face him. His voice trembled with anger: "Not for long, Rudolf, I can tell you that, not for long. There is a group of officers who think like you and me, who love this country, and who want to put an end to this war and to this madness. Do you understand me? Things have gone far beyond what you could imagine."

All the blood drained from von Beck's face. A tremor ran through his body and his mouth went dry. Here he was, standing facing one of the leaders of the German Army, who was telling him that a group of officers were preparing to overthrow Hitler!

"Are you one of us, Rudolf?" Canaris asked bluntly.

Von Beck did not hesitate. "Yes, sir, wholeheartedly."

"Very well, then," Canaris said in his normal voice and resumed his stroll. "The time will come when I'll fill you in on the details of our plans. All I can tell you now is that we are not ready yet. It might take another three to four months, I don't know. Which brings me back to your mission."

Von Beck looked at him in puzzlement. Canaris took several papers out of his pocket and chose one of them, which he unfolded and gave to von Beck. "This is the list of the twenty-seven Enigma machines used by the Wehrmacht in France now. I guess the British intelligence service has gotten a copy of that list. Our people in London mentioned it in their message a week ago." He paused for a second, then added in a different tone: "That list mentions twenty-seven machines. As a matter of fact, there are twenty-eight."

The colonel frowned in surprise. "Because of private plans that I mentioned," Canaris went on, "I thought it necessary that a direct, unlisted means of communication be established between me and my people in Paris. That enables us to listen to all the secret radio exchanges between Hitler's supreme headquarters and the top local commanders of the Wehrmacht and the SS in France."

"Very clever, sir, if I may express my opinion."

Canaris ignored the remark. "Our Enigma is installed in our informal headquarters in Paris. Not in the Hotel Lutetia, where most of our offices are, but on the second floor of the Otto organization, in the square du Bois de Boulogne. You'll establish your command post in the Otto building. From there you'll supervise the protection of the Enigma machines. All twenty-eight of them."

Von Beck bowed formally: "Very well, sir."

He had turned and was walking away when he heard Canaris's voice calling him softly: "Rudy!" He noted that it was the first time that his chief had used that familiar abbreviation.

Canaris beckoned him back. "I admit that I envy you your trip to Paris." His voice suddenly sounded more human. "It is a marvelous city, the pride of the Western civilization. I was there many times, as a student, as a young officer. . . . But there is one particular visit I made to Paris that I'll never forget. A year ago I was taken blindfolded, in the utmost secrecy, to a convent in the heart of Paris. My blindfold was removed only after I was inside the place. Even today I don't know the name of the convent. I remember only its old stone walls and the medieval portrait of a priest hanging on one of them. Some nuns let me in and introduced me to a strange man with coal-black eyes. He was the chief of the British Intelligence Service in France. I asked him to convey a question to Churchill: What will be the Allied terms for the conclusion of a peace treaty with Germany, after we get rid of Hitler? I received the answer two weeks later. It was 'unconditional surrender.' "

He closed his eyes. "Maybe we shall have to pay that price," he murmured.

While he was walking to his car, it occurred to Rudolf

von Beck that Canaris had just entrusted him with a secret that could lead both of them straight to the scaffold.

That same morning, in his posh Savoy suite in London, Belvoir picked up his phone and called General Bodley.

At nightfall a black Halifax night-bomber crossed the channel at low altitude, heading for occupied France. Belvoir was the sole passenger.

BELVOIR SAT ALONE IN THE DARK FUSELAGE, WRAPPED IN A
rugged army blanket and smoking a long, thin cigar.
Through the multitude of cracks and fissures in the bat-
tered body of the aged war machine the wind shrieked and
howled, carrying with it the salty smell of the North Sea.
Belvoir shivered slightly. Here he was, on his most perilous
undertaking, and completely on his own. True, Bodley and
MacAlister, who had accompanied him to the air base,
had solemnly promised him the full assistance of the
French Resistance. They had also assured him that the
identity papers which they had issued for him were foolproof. But he didn't trust them. That's why he had secretly
prepared and sent to France false documents and elabor-
rate disguises. He would carry out his assignment, but he
would do it his way. He couldn't afford to trust anybody.
Now and then, when he closed his eyes, he would remember the same frighteningly intense scene in the back of his
mind: his father, lying in a pool of blood in that filthy
Paris bar, stabbed to death by his best friend after a dis-
pute over the spoils of some robbery. "Never trust those
bastards, Frankie," were the last words of his dying father
to the boy of sixteen he was then. "Never forget: *Chacun
pour soi*—Everybody for himself."

Those words remained a vivid part of his memory when
he started his own career in that tricky world of swindling
and larceny. And that was how he grew up—a loner, cold,
meticulous, calculating his coups to the smallest detail,
doubling his precautions, carefully picking his men. That
was the secret of his success. To all those around him he
offered the image of a lightheaded sybarite, a careless adventurer who embarked on crazy schemes and took unnec-

essary risks without thinking twice. In reality he was not
as reckless as he seemed; but undoubtedly his whole approach to life was affected by the predominant adventurous streak in his character that always enticed him to
attempt the impossible. He was highly admired by people
on both sides of the law. The only one who really saw
through him had been an American girl, a journalist, who
had doggedly stuck to him at the beginning of the war. He
believed she had just fallen in love with him, until that
night in a small pimps' bar in the rue Blanche, when she
had looked at him searchingly with her calm, wide-spaced
green eyes and had quietly said: "Be honest just once in
your life, Frankie. Stop acting, for Christ's sake! What are
you trying to show?"

Those words had suddenly struck a note deep inside
him, bringing back to the surface a long-suppressed
memory of his youth. It had happened the morning after
his father's death. He was a student then in the Collège
Saint-Eustache in Paris, a snobbish institution where the
flower of the blue-blooded aristocracy of the French Republic was being cultivated. His schoolmates were teen-
aged dukes and counts and barons, and he himself was
known as the young Baron de Belvoir. That morning,
however, he had been met with a wave of mocking laughter. On his desk somebody had spread the fresh edition of
the daily papers, where big, fat headlines told the real
story of his murdered father, describing him as a crook, a
criminal, an impostor. Then the priest who directed the
college, *Père* Dominique, had entered the schoolroom and
ordered him, in front of all the others, to leave the class
immediately. "Your presence here, Monsieur, dishonors
this institution," he had said bluntly. "You do not deserve
the title you bear nor the company of these gentlemen."
Tears had sprung into his eyes and he had gotten up and
walked to the door. But there he had turned to the silent
assembly and had shouted in a voice he didn't recognize:
"You'll pay for this one day! I'll show you who deserves
what!" He had run away, sobbing, never to set foot in that
school again, escaping to another world, the one in which
his father had lived.

Years later, in this smoke-filled Pigalle bar, with the
steady gaze of the American girl probing deeply into his
soul, he suddenly felt a deep sense of panic, as if he had
been stripped naked in public. He had tried to counter the

blow with a condescending smile and an indifferent shrug. "Oh, shit, Beverly," he said. "Cut it out." He had never seen her again.

But soon after that incident he had tried to really change, for the first and last time in his life. He had enrolled in the French Army and fought his way to Dunkerque. When he reached England, he joined the British Commandos. That was the first time he became part of a team, fighting with others, helping others, trusting others. That was the only time he ignored his father's last words: *Chacun pour soi.* But those words came back to him when he was badly wounded in the raid of Dieppe and left to die in a stinking alley by his comrades, who were too busy saving their own skins to bother carrying him to safety. He had dragged himself onto the sidewalk, his blood oozing from his perforated abdomen, and death had never been so close. But he had been miraculously rescued by a couple of old Frenchmen, who gave him shelter and attended to his wounds. When he recovered he swore that, for him, the war was over. That nightmarish day in Dieppe had left deep scars in his body and in his memory. From now on, he decided, he would fight only for himself. Which he had done, indeed, with cynicism and greed. He had returned to Paris, to his familiar milieu and his prewar way of life. Soon, he found very lucrative employment. The Germans used people like him—thieves, criminals, gangsters—to help them strip France of her treasures. He went to work for the Otto organization, an informal branch of the Abwehr that transferred to Germany the valuable property of individuals and of national museums and institutions: antique furniture, priceless paintings and statues, gold, precious stones, foreign currency. Some of the loot was sold in Switzerland, to finance the secret operations of the Abwehr. Most of the gold went to the Gestapo and was stacked in its cellars. Everybody in the Parisian underworld was fascinated by that gold treasure; nobody dared challenge the Gestapo. Those were two good reasons that made the temptation irresistible to Belvoir. He thoroughly prepared his coup, and one night he disappeared from Paris with all the Gestapo gold reserve, which he managed to bring to England. The furious Gestapo chief promptly put a handsome price on his head.

And now he was heading back, straight into the lion's den. Bodley had been right: The formidable challenge, the thrill of the most dangerous game of them all, was driving him to Paris again. And he knew he would never leave the city without the Enigma.

A red light suddenly blossomed in the dark fuselage. A tall young man in flying overalls came out of the cockpit and quickly opened the plane's hatch. He touched Belvoir's shoulder. "Get ready," he shouted, trying to make himself heard over the wailing wind. "It's any moment now. And good luck. How do you say it in French? *Merde!*"

The light switched from red to green. Belvoir grasped the ice-cold sides of the open hatch and jumped into the black abyss below.

In the damp pasture field that sloped gently toward the muddy banks of the Dordogne River, Gaston Aymard was nervously sucking his unlit pipe while glancing at the dark sky. Aymard was a tall, thick-set Gascon, still dressed in the clothes he wore on his farm near Bergerac: a peasant's peaked cap, a dirty sheepskin coat and knee-high rubber boots.

He rolled up his sleeve and glanced again at the luminous dial of his watch. It was almost midnight and the British plane should be very close now. Five days ago London had informed him by radio that an agent of the S.O.E. would be dropped in his region this night. The agent would carry papers in the name of Jean-Marie Langeais. Aymard's task was to provide him with civilian clothes and a train ticket and send him to Paris. He also had to brief him on how he should establish contact with the Resistance at the Gare de Lyon, one of the main railroad stations in Paris. Gaston had been worried and angered by that request. He was the chief of the underground network *"Espérance,"* that operated in the southwest of France, between Bergerac and Libourne. Until quite recently his city squads and his guerrillas in the *maquis* had accomplished many successful feats, culminating in the attack on the prison of Saint-Emilion, where fifty hostages were awaiting their execution by the SS. And then their luck had turned. For the last three months all the operations of his network had failed. Eight of his people had been killed in action, three during an unsuccessful attempt to ambush the car of a Luftwaffe general on his way to celebrate Christmas in Bordeaux; and five others during a raid on the armory of the Bergerac garrison. The dreaded *miliciens*—the French collaborationists with the Gestapo—and the Gestapo killers themselves had been expecting the freedom fighters and had hacked them to pieces. Six more members of the *"Espérance"* network had been arrested by the Gestapo: the brothers Bobet, who were the main suppliers of the guerrillas in the hills; the owner of the Hotel du Centre in Libourne and his wife, who used to report the conversations of high-ranking officers staying at their establishment; the treasurer of the network, Henri Monod, captured while transporting secret funds; and finally the radio operator himself, young Joseph Jacquinot, who was also Gaston's brother-in-law. All of them, except Jacquinot, had been tortured to death in the Gestapo headquarters. Jacquinot himself had been deported to a German concentration camp. And Gaston Aymard had reached the inevitable conclusion: His network had been infiltrated by a traitor.

He had done all that he could to unmask the Nazi agent, but in vain. After Jacquinot's arrest he had taken the radio transmitter to his own barn and had warned London that an enemy agent was slowly destroying the network from the inside. He had expected that the S.O.E. would order him to lay low for a while. Nevertheless, he had received instructions to take care of an agent who would be dropped that night. London had insisted, though, on very tight security measures. He had scrupulously complied. He didn't inform any of his men in advance of the night's assignment. Only in the late evening had he contacted the most trustworthy among them and led them to the field. At least he could be sure that the traitor—if he was in the group—wouldn't be able to alert the Germans. In his own rucksack he kept the clothes and documents for the agent. He had prepared them himself, and nobody else had seen them.

At 11:55 three of his men marched into the middle of the field and took positions in a triangular pattern. Each held a powerful flashlight fitted into an oblong tin sleeve shaped like a long cylinder. At exactly twelve o'clock they heard the low sound of the bomber's engines, which had been muffled during its dive over the Dordogne Valley. Aymard whistled softly. His men switched on their flashlights. Because of their metal sleeves, they were visible only from above as they marked the drop zone for the pilot. The Halifax slowed down, overflew the field and was soon far away. A lone figure, swaying under a black parachute quietly descended from the overcast sky. The man from London touched ground and rolled softly on the wet grass.

The Baron was back in France.

The men quickly converged on the London agent. He spoke excellent French, and was assailed with questions: but Aymard didn't let him utter more than a few words. "Leave our comrade alone," he ordered his men. "Bury the parachute by the river, and wait for me. Nobody leaves." He turned to the agent, who watched him quietly. "Come with me," he said, leading him to a small cluster of trees. Belvoir followed him, mildly puzzled by his brusque manners. Aymard knelt on the soft grass and fumbled with the leather straps of his rucksack. "Here are your papers," he whispered. "This is your train ticket to Paris. It is a return ticket. If you are asked what business you had in this region, you'll say that you came to visit your ailing godmother, Madame Louise Charpentier, in Libourne. She will confirm the story. Here is a letter from her, dated a week ago, that she sent to your Paris address, asking you to come. And here"—Aymard unbuttoned his heavy sheepskin coat and took out a worn-out black wallet—"are two thousand francs. That's more than enough for you to survive, until you establish contact with our people in Paris." He stuffed the money into the agent's hand. "Our people in Paris will recognize you by your red scarf," he added; he gave him the password by which he would be approached in Paris, as well as an alternative contact arrangement, in case something went wrong at the Gare de Lyon. Belvoir repeated and memorized the details. Finally Aymard got on his feet. "In the rucksack, here, you have a complete change of clothes. Put them on. Leave the clothes you are wearing now. I'll destroy them later. Then you'll walk straight ahead"—Aymard pointed to the west, in a direction roughly parallel to the river—'until you see the first houses of Saint-Emilion. There is a dirt road that goes north, starting at the river. You can't miss it. It by-passes Saint-Emilion and will lead you to the outskirts of Libourne. You'll have plenty of time to reach the railroad station. It's in the very center of the city. The train for Paris leaves at 1:55. Good luck."

Belvoir looked at him in surprise. "You want me to find my way alone?"

Aymard nodded, obviously embarrassed. "Yes," he said. "I can't explain now. *Adieu!*"

Belvoir was taken aback by the finality and the bitterness in the man's voice. "*Adieu*," he said, and started to undress. A few minutes later he was on his way. Aymard watched him gloomily until he disappeared in the darkness, then moved toward his men. "We'll stay here for another hour," he announced, "and then we'll go home."

Dawn was still hours away when three black Citroën cars stopped in a strident screeching of brakes in front of Gaston Aymard's farm. Aymard started from his bed. "*Les Boches!*" he groaned, grabbing his clothes from where they lay in a heap on a nearby chair and running through the kitchen to the back door. His young, pretty wife, Hélène, followed his swift movements with terror-stricken eyes. She was too shocked to follow, or to wish her hunted husband good luck.

But Gaston Aymard's luck had run out that night. As he opened the back door, several dazzling beams of light nailed him to his place. The farm had been surrounded even before the arrival of the Gestapo cars. The men carrying the portable projectors cautiously started to approach him. He recognized the black uniforms of the SS and the berets of the hated Milice. He was trapped. Slowly, reluctantly, he raised his hands over his head. When two men in long raincoats and brown fedora hats shoved him brutally into one of the waiting cars, he could hear the panicked screams of his wife.

The Citroëns sped along the empty road. In the car, where Aymard sat between two Gestapo men, nobody spoke. Aymard didn't have to look out of the window to know where they were going. For years he had dreaded the night when he would be taken to the Château de la Tournelle, the local headquarters of the Gestapo, where so many freedom-loving Frenchmen had met a grisly death.

The Château, all lights ablaze, was the center of feverish activity. Civil and military cars were coming and going, men were running in and out of the building. Wehrmacht couriers darted by on their powerful motorcycles. Aymard was kicked and pushed up the large staircase and into the hall. He looked around and saw the haggard, terrified faces of his comrades, the members of his organization. The Resistance in the Southwest had been dealt a terrible blow. The network *"Espérance"* had ceased to exist.

A familiar face suddenly appeared in front of him. "Hervé," Aymard started to say, and suddenly his voice died in his throat. Because Hervé Royan, his second in command, was free, and smiling, and wearing the uniform of the Milice. When he recovered from the initial shock, Aymard admitted bitterly to himself that he could stop guessing who the traitor was who had given them away.

His Gestapo captors pushed him through the crowd and down the narrow stairs to the cellar. He immediately reconized the damp underground room that some broken survivors had described to him, their voices quivering with horror. He knew the purpose of the bathtub in the corner; of the electric cord, plugged into a socket and ending in two naked, glistening pieces of wire; he guessed the use of the ugly-shaped steel instruments that lay on the large wooden table in the middle of the room. And he recognized the bloody corpse two *miliciens* indifferently dragged out of the torture chamber: It was all that remained of Justin Colombier, one of the men who had helped him meet the agent from London earlier that night.

Hervé Royan came into the room, accompanied by a stranger. He was tall, completely bald, and wore a black civilian suit over a black roll-neck pullover. His thin, bloodless mouth twitched nervously in a rhythmic spasm. When he came closer, Aymard noticed that the man was completely hairless; his watery blue eyes gazed coldly at him beneath bare eyelids, with the fixed cruel look of an octopus. The man had large hands and long, thin fingers that were constantly moving, stretching or digging into his white palms, like those of a piano player before a concert. Aymard couldn't take his eyes off him. He felt cold sweat popping out on his forehead.

Hervé Royan spoke very softly, with a mocking reproach in his voice: "It is all your fault, Gaston. We didn't want to disband the network. As far as we were concerned it could have continued to exist for quite a while. Without knowing it, you supplied us with most valuable information about the terrorists in other regions of France, and about your contacts with London. But you left us no choice. You see, if you had just told your comrades tonight who the agent from London was, where he was going, what password he would use—we wouldn't have touched the network. Not yet. But you kept the secrets for yourself. And we need those secrets more than we need your group terrorists. We need them now. So, instead of having all your friends killed one by one because of your stupidity—why not tell us everything and save everybody's skin?"

Aymard didn't say a word.

"I repeat my question," Royan said, his voice suddenly threatening. "Who was the man from London? Where did he go? What name does he use? Who are his contacts?"

He approached Aymard until his face, contorted with rage, was only inches away from the prisoner's. "Or would you like me to start killing our comrades?"

Aymard gathered all the saliva in his mouth and spat in Royan's face.

And then they were on him. Royan, the two Gestapo men, the two *miliciens* who were standing watch by the door—all five of them fell on him in an outburst of blind hatred. First they hit him with their bare fists until he collapsed; then they kicked him, savagely, in the face, in the stomach, in the groin. He screamed, unable to withstand the pain. And they hit again and again, as if possessed by demons, breaking his nose, turning his face into pieces of raw bleeding flesh, jumping on his chest and belly, kicking his genitals until they drove him to the verge of insanity. And yet, through all those moments of horror, Aymard's eyes stared, as if hypnotized, at the only person who didn't take part in the beating: the giant in black. The stranger stood there, motionless, his mouth and his fingers twitching, a bird of prey patiently waiting for its own turn.

Finally, the beating stopped. And then the man in black knelt close to Aymard. "Your friends say you are a very brave man, Monsieur Aymard," he said in perfect French, so that Aymard couldn't tell whether he was French or German. "They say it will be very difficult to make you talk. I told them not to worry. I'll make you talk. I have several means. You see, we'll start with the bathtub. We'll immerse you in it until you almost die of drowning. While you are still wet, I'll caress you with my electrical wires. Water makes them more efficient. Then I'll take those pliers and I shall pull out your nails, one by one. I might break your bones with an iron bar. And after, I'll use my favorite instrument: the acetylene torch. And please don't deceive me, Monsieur Aymard. Don't die before I finish. You see, I have another surprise in store for you."

He got up and smiled politely. "With what did I say we should start? Oh yes, the bathtub."

An hour later, Aymard was a living corpse. True, his heart still thumped irregularly in his chest; warm, salty blood still oozed from the open wounds in his face, and he still could see through the narrow slits in the tumefied tissue around his eyes. But he was a man in agony, a man who had been through hell and didn't have in him more than a feeble spark of life. His jaws and limbs were broken; ugly red stains marked the tips of his fingers and toes, where his nails had once been; charred bits and shreds of black, scorched skin and flesh hanging from his chest and limbs were the gruesome traces left by the acetylene torch. A sickening smell of burned flesh floated in the air. Even Royan and the *miliciens* had hastily left. The Gestapo men had retreated to the narrow corridor outside the horror chamber. Aymard was alone inside, alone with his torturer.

And still he wouldn't talk. That remnant of willpower that made him unconsciously cling to life gave him the force to keep his secret, to triumph over his foe. He had been through the seven circles of hell—and still he held on.

The torturer remained imperturbable. "I guess it's time for our little surprise, Monsieur Aymard," he said in his mellifluous voice. He went to the door and whispered something to the Gestapo men who waited outside. A few minutes later Aymard heard a heavy sound on the stone staircase, as if somebody was being dragged down by force. And then an inhuman scream echoed in the room and pervaded his agonized soul with terror. He recognized the voice—the voice of his wife, Hélène.

They dragged her into his field of vision—a half-mad, screaming, hysterical woman, twisting and writhing in horror at the sight of her mutilated husband. Her eyes rolled wildly, and unintelligible strings of words came out of her distorted mouth, while one of the Gestapo men pushed her head forward, holding her blond chignon tightly, in order to force her to look at him. The bald torturer approached her. With swift, violent movements he tore her dress and underwear and threw them on the floor. He examined her nude body coldly, then knelt over the terrified Aymard. "Your wife is my surprise," he said pleasantly. "And I'll tell you what I am going to do to her. First, as you saw, I stripped her of her clothes. Now, the boys will have some fun with her in front of you. And after"—he got up, and took from the table a big, sharp bayonet—"I am going to thrust that nice little weapon between her legs, deep into her vulva, and turn, and twist, and turn, until all her blood runs out. Would you like me to do that?"

"No," gasped Aymard in panic, "No, no, don't do that, I beg you, leave her alone, please . . ."

"But you believe I'll do it, don't you?" said the man in black kindly.

"Yes, I believe you," whispered Aymard.

"So, you'll talk, as I told you, right?"

And Aymard knew he would.

At 6:45 in the morning, a Gestapo man telephoned Paris.

When the night train from Bordeaux and Libourne reached the Gare de Lyon, the station was swarming with SS soldiers, Milice members and Gestapo agents. The train was surrounded, and nobody was allowed to alight; the station was completely sealed. The *miliciens* and the Gestapo men started a thorough search of the long train and checked each passenger aboard. They were looking for a dark-haired, gray-eyed young man, wearing an old blue serge suit, a heavy black coat and a red scarf, carrying papers in the name of Jean-Marie Langeais.

But nobody fitting that description was on the train.

II

THE SOLDIER

March 28, 1944

FRANCIS DE BELVOIR ALIGHTED FROM THE BORDEAUX TRAIN AT Tours, at 5:50 in the morning. He boarded the local that went to Orléans by way of the magnificent Loire Valley, resplendent with its green meadows and its picturesque *châteaux*, painted golden by the rays of the rising sun. From the Orléans station he walked to the *"Café du Rapide,"* which was open all night. He waited there until eight, slowly sipping a huge *café-crème* and munching some fresh *croissants*. When he heard the old-fashioned clock on the wall chime eight, he left fifteen francs on the zinc counter and strolled casually into the city. It didn't take him long to reach the gable-roofed house of Philippe Lonjac, discreetly located in the serene rue des Acacias. The door was opened by a fat, red-faced woman of about fifty. Her eyes lit up with pleasure. "Ah, Monsieur le Baron," she smiled happily. "What a pleasure! Come in, please. Philippe is not at home; he left early for the country."

"Of course," the Baron smiled in return. "And how is business these days?" Lonjac, an ex-con, was running a flourishing black market business, supplying his clients in Paris with tons of butter, meat, flour and cheeses from the farms of the Orléanais.

"We can't complain," said Madame Lonjac cheerfully. "Why don't you sit down? Your package arrived yesterday from Lisbon, and we were so glad you would be coming to visit us. Philippe will be sorry to have missed you. But let me first get you some real coffee, and your package, of course."

Belvoir smiled at the cheerful, plump woman as she hastened to her kitchen. Who would believe that this middle-

57

aged woman with the plain face of a peasant had carried out, all alone, one of the most lucrative coups of the year 1940? While the French and the British armies were still fighting the advancing Wehrmacht close to Lille, the Banque de France had dispatched to the surrounded city over ten million francs for its current expenses. The money had been loaded on two Glenn Martin planes, but the British gunners, unfamiliar with the new American aircraft, had shot them down in the very midst of the battlefield where German and Allied troops were engaged in fierce combat. Madeleine Lonjac lived at the time in Roubaix, close to the prison where her husband was serving a ten-year sentence. Without hesitating, she had donned peasant's clothes, hitched two Belgian horses to a cart full of hay and set out straight for the battlefield. She succeeded in crossing the French and German lines and was the first to reach the wreckage. When she crossed the front lines of the embattled armies again, under heavy fire, most of the money lay safely under the hay. The puzzled mayor of Lille only recovered 240,000 francs. Two weeks later, Philippe Lonjac was out of prison. In the atmosphere of chaos created by the French debacle, nobody asked any questions; but there could be no doubt that a part of the Banque de France special funds had bought the freedom of Madeleine's husband. Madeleine herself never talked about the affair; only seldom, in the presence of intimate friends, would she cheerfully admit that the considerable fortune of the Lonjacs had "come out of the blue," which was exactly the case.

The aroma of strong, fresh-ground coffee filled the room. Madeleine was back. "Here is your coffee, Monsieur le Baron," she said pleasantly and put a steaming cup on the Louis XVI table next to him, "and here is your package." Belvoir drank his coffee, locked himself in the bathroom, and set to work.

An hour later, his former clothes burned to ashes, the Baron left the house. He was blond now, wore a short beard and a bushy moustache, and was dressed in shabby farmer's clothes. His papers certified that he was Pierre Altmüller, a farmer from Saverne, in Alsace. He carried also a special *ausweis* from the authorities of the Reich, allowing him to travel to the Institute Pasteur in Paris to get some rare serum for the inoculation of his cattle.

He took the train east, changed at Troyes, Bar-le-Duc

and Châlons, and finally reached the Gare de l'Est, Paris's Eastern station, at 8:30 P.M. Except for routine checks by the German and French authorities, nobody bothered him.

While walking through the crowded hall of the station, Belvoir was pushed aside by a German officer who hurried toward a military Panhard waiting for him by the sidewalk. The German didn't even notice him, and Belvoir caught only a brief glimpse of his erect back.

He didn't know that this man had come to Paris with only one purpose: to hunt him down. Colonel von Beck had just alighted from the Berlin Express.

Rudolf von Beck leaned back in the Panhard seat and avidly looked out the window, savoring to the full his first encounter with the most beautiful city in the world. Paris lay before his eyes, unspoiled, untouched by the war that had destroyed most of Europe and hadn't spared even Berlin. The capital of France seemed to be on a different planet. The large boulevards were full of people coming out of the cafés and the cinemas. Spring was only a week old, but the delightful Parisian women had already discarded their winter coats and were daintily mincing along the sidewalks in their elegant thin dresses, their short skirts dancing gracefully around their legs. Many of them, probably complying with the commandments of this year's fashion, wore wide belts and a large variety of fancy hats—turbans, berets, wide-brimmed *chapeaux de mousquétaire*—that enhanced the delicate features of their faces. To the enchanted von Beck, even the thick wooden-soled shoes of the girls seemed most charming; only later was he to learn that they were mass-produced because of the lack of leather.

The car sped down the boulevard de Strasbourg, continued along the boulevard de Sébastopol and emerged on the cobbled quays on the right bank of the Seine. Von Beck looked with amused interest at the improvised "taxi-cabs" of Paris, in this period of gasoline shortage: They were mostly wooden crates fitted with a bench, covered with tarpaulin and towed by bicycles. He observed that even in these years of misfortune, the Parisian cabdrivers hadn't lost their Gallic sense of humor; on the back of their taxis were painted names like "By the grace of God," "Security-Rapidity," or even *Les temps modernes* . . .

He caught a brief glimpse of the dark twin towers of

Notre Dame and the needle-shaped dome of the Sainte-Chapelle, before the car darted along past the Louvre and the green gardens of the Tuileries, through the magnificent place de la Concorde and up the Champs Elysées. He was repelled though, at the sight of the big red-white-and-black flags of the Reich fluttering from the balconies of the most illustrious monuments of Paris. The huge swastika banner, gently swaying in the evening breeze between the majestic pillars of the Arc de Triomphe, suddenly seemed obscene to him.

Although he had never been here before, he was deeply in love with Paris and its culture. He was widely versed in French history and literature, spoke a quite correct French and deeply admired the great thinkers and philosophers of France. Often he would wonder how it happened that he, the son of a traditional conservative family of Prussian Junkers, had become such a liberal romantic at heart. He had been raised on the large estate of his family in Silesia, according to the basic principles of the Junker tradition: austerity in everyday life, attachment to the land, discipline, unconditional patriotism, following a military career. His grandfather, a distant relative of the king of Saxony had bravely fought in 1870 and was present at Bismarck's side when the German Empire was proclaimed at the Hall of Mirrors in Versailles. His father, the aging Graf Helmut von Beck, had lost an eye and a part of his left leg at the battle of the Somme in the First World War. Rudolf had been educated to follow that tradition: to command and to obey, to lead and to follow, to respect his superiors' authority and to impose his own. But behind the locked door of his teen-ager's room he had devoured the books of Karl May, Emilio Salgari, Edgar Rice Burroughs, Edgar Allan Poe. He had been fascinated by the romantic figures of Lord Byron, Lafayette, Bolivar—those brave men who had set out to fight for the freedom of oppressed nations at the far corners of the earth. He had hungrily read Jules Verne's books, and to his own surprise had found himself sympathizing with the freedom-loving French depicted by the writer, and resenting the heartless Germans. But most of all he had longed for the thrilling life some of his heroes had led; he had dreamed of becoming an adventurer, roaming around the world, traveling to faraway, exotic lands, living dangerous experiences and carrying on exciting love affairs with sensuous, mysterious women.

Could his dream come true? Once, only once, did he try to realize his long-cherished wish. A few days after his seventeenth birthday, using a boy-scout meeting in Kiel as his pretext, he packed his beloved books, his hunting knife and the antique pistol he had gotten as a birthday present and took the train for Hamburg. His only friend was with him—the eagereyed, black-haired Max, the one person on earth with whom he shared his romantic aspirations. Their plan was to board a boat going to the Far East. The exotic names of places like Hong Kong, Bali, Borneo, Kuala-Lumpur, the descriptions they had read of Buddhist temples, secret sects, gold treasures, unexplored jungles and strange customs stirred their imaginations and exercised upon them a fascinating, irresistible attraction. They were lucky: Not only did they find such a boat, the Panama-registered S.S. *Adventure*, but her captain, a soft-spoken, kind-eyed Swede, agreed to take them aboard as help. And then, during the last night before the ship sailed away, Rudolf backed down. He could not leave his ailing mother, he explained in an unsteady voice; he could not bring shame on his family; he would not shatter the hopes they had in him. "Why don't you admit the truth, that you just chickened out?" Max had asked in cold contempt. He had never seen him since, and he often wondered what had happened to his only friend. He was probably dead by now.

As for Rudolf, he returned home only a few hours later than he was expected. Nobody detected anything unusual in his behavior, no one perceived the deep pain that tortured him inwardly. He bitterly admitted to himself that Max had been right. He had lost his nerve. Max had done it; but for him, the adventurous life he longed for was just an impossible dream.

And that was how he kept it during the years to come. Nobody at home ever learned of this secret dream world he had conceived. Nobody suspected that the tall, blond, quiet Rudy could have become somebody completely different, had he been just a trifle more daring and had the circumstances allowed it. But the circumstances were what they were, and at the age of thirty-four he was a colonel in the German Abwehr, a former Panzer battalion commander who had fought with Rommel in Cyrenaica. Even his military career had followed the traditional pattern. He

had been wounded twice and decorated with the Iron
Cross. He suspected that his father, though, never forgave
him for not getting the oak leaves on his medal. But after
his second wound he had been retired from combat duty
and assigned to the General Staff of the Wehrmacht. He
believed, however, that he had been appointed to the personal staff of Canaris on the explicit recommendation of
his former commander, Erwin Rommel. During their long
tête-à-tête talks in Rommel's tent in the Lybian desert, the
field marshal had discovered his true feelings about the
Führer, and had sent him to the Abwehr in order to keep
him close to the inner circle of the anti-Nazi conspirators.

The car slowed and entered the round inner court of a
tall white mansion on the avenue Foch, very close to the
dark green mass of the Boulogne forest. "My orders were
to take you to your personal residence, Herr Oberst," the
driver said. "This building serves as quarters to several officers of the Commandant of Gross Paris. Your apartment will be on the top floor."

Von Beck nodded and got out of the car. He resented
the impassive, robot-like behavior of the bulky Schwab
driver. But it was of no importance. His orderly, the genial
Schneider, would be here tomorrow. He had stayed behind
to collect his personal belongings and then drive the Horch
all the way from Berlin.

They entered the elegant lobby of the building, leading
to a marble staircase. An old-fashioned elevator made of
polished brown wood panted all the way up to the fifth
floor. The apartment was splendid indeed, with its authentic Regence furniture and its marvelous view of the opu-
lent avenue Foch.

Von Beck absentmindedly dismissed the driver, lit a soldier's cigarette and leaned on the wrought-iron parapet of
his large balcony. Was the man from London somewhere
in this city briefly enjoying its peaceful beauty, like him
or perhaps already planning his moves? It suddenly occurred to the young colonel that his assignment was a kind of
paradox. On one hand, deep in his heart he wanted the Allied invasion to take place and to succeed—for it would
weaken Hitler's position and help overthrow him. On the
other hand, there was Junker blood in his veins; and he
knew that his genuine German patriotism and his sense of
duty would prevail. He would most certainly do anything

in his power to prevent the unknown British agent from getting the Enigma.

But who was he? And where?

The strident ring of the doorbell interrupted his musing. He crossed the brightly lit sitting room and the miniature hall and opened the door. In front of him stood a young Wehrmacht captain, clutching a briefcase in his left hand and visibly out of breath. At the sight of von Beck, he clicked his heels and saluted formally. "Captain Brandner, of the Abwehr Paris Department, at your orders, Herr Oberst."

Von Beck ignored the salute. "Come in, Brandner. What is so urgent?"

The captain followed him awkwardly to the sitting room. He was still a young boy in his early twenties. His lively brown eyes and rosy cheeks made him look more like a youngster masquerading in uniform than a genuine officer. "I have been assigned to your service, Herr Oberst, by General Hallstein, the head of the Abwehr Paris Department. I prepared a suite of offices in the Otto building for you, just around the corner in the Square du Bois de Boulogne. I have also organized a small team of officers and secretaries." He paused, then added eagerly: "We are ready for the operation."

Von Beck shrugged and turned away. He didn't like to have people imposed on him; he preferred to choose his own team. And yet, he had to admit that this time he couldn't afford any talent scouting. He had to content himself with the local people; moreover, this young captain and his friends certainly knew more about Paris than he did. He looked thoughtfully at the young officer. "You didn't come here just to welcome me and to give me my office address. Something made you hurry. What was it?"

The captain fumbled in his briefcase. "A joint report from the Gestapo and the SD. It just arrived, sir."

Von Beck scowled. He couldn't stand either the Gestapo or the *Sicherheitsdienst*, the army's security service, whom he considered a bunch of butchers and torturers. Since last year, the SD had been placed under the direct orders of the SS and enjoyed total freedom of action. The Army could just grind its teeth helplessly and bury its head deeper in the sand.

"What is it about?" he asked quickly, suddenly aware that Brandner was watching him very closely.

"A British agent, sir. He was parachuted last night near Bordeaux. According to the report, he was the only one who was dropped in France last night. He took a train for Paris. He might be our man."

"Let me see!" Suddenly excited, von Beck grabbed the report from Brandner's hands and feverishly turned the pages. "The bloody fools," he muttered angrily after a few minutes. "To seal the Gare de Lyon! If the man is a professional—and I am convinced he is—he would have spotted them immediately and quietly slipped away. They should have waited for him to establish contact and then gone after him. Who the hell do they think they are hunting?"

He angrily paced back and forth across the large room. Finally he returned to face Brandner.

"The first thing to do is to coordinate all the operations in this affair. We have to find a way to impose our authority on those dilettantes! I want you to convene a meeting at eight tomorrow morning. Have there the representatives of the Abwehr, the Paris police, the Commandment of Gross Paris. In my office. We have to establish an *ad hoc* committee that will meet regularly and decide on a common policy in the Enigma affair."

Brandner quickly jotted the orders on a writing pad. "Of course, you also want me to invite the representatives of the SS, the SD and the Gestapo," he said evenly.

Von Beck looked at him blankly. "Of course," he said.

March 29–April 4, 1944

IN THE CELLAR OF THE CHÂTEAU DE LA TOURNELLE, GASTON Aymard was dying. After he had revealed the cover-name and the disguise of the British agent to his torturers, they had left him on the stone floor, a miserable heap of scorched flesh and broken bones, barely breathing. In the late morning, however, Hervé Royan and his Gestapo cronies returned to the cellar. Royan entered the torture chamber and looked with disgust at the agonizing man at his feet, then sent one of his aides to bring a blanket and a bowl of hot soup. He fed the prisoner some spoonfuls of soup, then said to him in a tone of mild rebuke: "Your friend wasn't on the Bordeaux train, you know."

He had to repeat the sentence twice before Aymard's face showed some signs of understanding.

"But I told you the truth," he whispered.

"Oh, yes," said Royan. "I believe you did. But you didn't tell us the whole truth, and that might be very unfortunate. Especially for Hélène."

A flicker of panic crossed the bloodshot eyes of the prisoner.

"You don't want my friend to do to Hélène what he promised you?" Royan went on softly. "So you will have to tell me the rest of the story. I believe you gave the British agent instructions for an alternative contact, in case the meeting in the Gare de Lyon didn't take place. I want to know when and where that second contact will be established."

Aymard closed his eyes. "No . . ." he whispered, "no other contact . . . I don't know."

Royan said sharply, "Don't lie to me, Gaston, I have no time, and no more patience. I shall leave you now. But I

warn you that if I go out of here without knowledge—
Hélène will die. Because of you."

He got up and quickly strode to the door. He hadn't yet
covered half the distance when he heard the rasping voice
of the prisoner. "Wait! Hervé, wait! Don't go!" Royan
came back and stood over Aymard. "I am listening," he
said with a faint smile of satisfaction.

Aymard spoke with great effort. "A week later . . .
Café des Minettes . . . Pigalle . . . Afternoon, half past
four . . . Recognition sign is weekly magazine *Je suis partout* . . . Password, 'Voltaire' . . ."

"That's very nice, Gaston," Royan said in an almost
friendly tone. "They'll take care of you now. Hélène will
be fine, too."

The prisoner was moving his lips in a last effort. "I . . .
I . . ."

Royan bent over him: "What are you saying?"

"I . . . I don't want to live anymore . . ." Aymard said
painfully.

Royan got to his feet. "Well, that's exactly what I had
in mind."

He went up the stairs, scribbled a few words on a piece
of paper and handed it to one of his men. "Phone that
message to Paris," he ordered. "Gestapo headquarters." He
turned to the group of people who were scattered in the
hall, talking or smoking, their guns lying on their laps.
"Somebody should go down and finish Aymard. We don't
need him anymore. And his wife as well. We can't let her
walk out of here, after what she saw."

In the early afternoon of April 4, the Gestapo trap for
the London agent was set and ready. At half past three,
four Gestapo plainclothes agents separately entered the
Café des Minettes on the corner of the notorious Pigalle
square and the boulevard de Clichy. Two of them sat near
the entrances to the café. One went to the back and took
a position close to the doors marked *Toilettes* and
Téléphones. The fourth lingered by the counter, exchanging vulgar jokes with the few bored whores who were sipping their first afternoon Beaujolais.

In a black Hotchkiss car parked a few hundred yards
away, in the rue Duperré, Kurt Limmer, the Gestapo chief
for Gross Paris, waited for a call from his men. In adjacent streets several more cars were waiting, ready to be

alerted by radio. Limmer sat patiently in the back of his car, chewing a fat Dutch cigar. He was a massive, broad-shouldered German, with a big head, fat, fair-skinned —jowls and small, porcine eyes. He was quite pleased with himself. He hadn't bothered to inform von Beck about to-day's operation. Like all Gestapo men, he deeply distrust-ed the Abwehr and was highly suspicious of the loyalty of its officers to the Führer. Moreover, he was the one who had obtained the information and he wasn't about to let anybody else share the credit for the capture of the British Agent. His representative in the committee created by Colonel von Beck had strict orders not to volunteer any information during the meetings in the Otto building. Lim-mer was convinced that the Gestapo could handle the situ-ation by its own means, and alone.

By 4:00 P.M., a few more prostitutes and two well-dressed black-market dealers entered the café. Nobody bothered them. The Gestapo people could easily tell the difference between a terrorist and a crook.

At 4:15 two men approached the café separately, slowly walking on the northern sidewalk of the boulevard de Clichy. The first one, wearing a black coat and beret quickly examined the cars parked in the street and the people strolling along the shops or sitting on the shaded benches under the chestnut trees. All seemed perfectly nor-mal. Just a few strollers, two old couples, and the inevi-table whores, clustering on the corners. The man stepped quietly onto a porch opposite the entrance of the Café des Minettes. He slowly lit a cigarette to give his comrade the all-clear sign, then moved farther back into the deep shadow of the porch. His comrade crossed the boulevard. He was a young man in a pepper-and-salt suit and a gray hat, wearing rimless glasses a thin black moustache. In his right hand he carried, neatly folded, the collaborationist magazine *Je suis partout*.

He casually entered the café and threw an indifferent look around him, then chose a small table close to the door. Noticing that nobody paid him any particular atten-tion, he relaxed, lit a cigarette and ordered a coffee from the old waiter in a white apron who limped to his table. He didn't take off his hat.

One of the Gestapo men looked at his watch, left some coins on the table and went out. He sauntered to the southern part of the square and then into the rue Duperré.

He threw a quick look behind him, then bent to the window of the black Hotchkiss. "A man came in," he reported. "He carries the magazine. Gray hat, gray suit, black moustache. He is either the London agent or his contact."

Limmer looked at his watch. It was 4:25. "You get into the car, Marchais," he said to the agent, then tapped on the shoulder of the man sitting next to the driver. "You go in now. You'll wait there as long as he waits. If the other man doesn't show—we'll take this one." The Gestapo agent nodded, checked his gun, tucked it back into his belt and quickly walked to the café.

Half an hour later, the man in the pepper-and-salt suit was still alone at his table. He was obviously growing nervous. Now and again, he would look at his watch, open the magazine, pretend to read a few lines, close it again and push it aside. Every time the door of the café opened he would look up hopefully, but nobody approached his table.

At five o'clock he folded his magazine, left ten francs on the table and stood up. Stealthily, the Gestapo agents moved toward him. He was already by the door when he heard a voice behind him inquire softly, "Voltaire?"

He turned around quickly, too quickly. The man who was facing him flashed a small badge: "*Police allemande.* You are under arrest."

In panic, he hurled himself at the door. Another man stood there, his hand already drawing a gun. In desperation, the Frenchman quickly looked around him and noticed the two other agents moving to outflank him.

"Raise your hands, you are surrounded!" one of them hissed.

He hesitated a second, then suddenly dived to the left and flung himself on the large glass door, which shattered under his impact. He went through it and fell heavily on the sidewalk, among the splinters of glass. He tried to get on his feet. Two or three shots echoed almost simultaneously. In the café, a woman screamed. The man in the pepper-and-salt suit swayed and slowly dropped to the ground. Almost at once, three cars darted from different directions and braked by the café, blocking the escape routes. Limmer was the first to bend over the prostrate body. He spat out the butt of his cigar. "He is still alive," he said urgently to one of his men. "Quickly, an ambulance. This man must talk."

While the wail of the ambulance siren came closer and closer, somebody quietly stepped out of a porch on the opposite side of the boulevard. The friend of the wounded man, in the black coat and beret, had watched in horror the shooting and the collapse of his comrade. The total stillness of the body spread on the sidewalk made him assume that his friend was dead. Now he quickly walked away, turned the corner of the rue Lépic and started to climb the winding street that led to the crest of the Montmartre hill, dominated by the immaculate white domes of the Sacré Coeur church. He didn't notice that one of the prostitutes, who had been walking for hours back and forth on the sidewalk past his hiding place, quickly moved behind him. She kept at a reasonable distance, playfully swaying her bag, flashing provoking smiles at the passersby. Only once did the man in the black beret notice her, lagging behind, and quickly dismissed her from his mind. There could hardly be anything more natural and harmless than a *pute* in the streets of Pigalle.

The leggy, red-haired whore kept close to the man in the black beret until he entered a small restaurant, "La Provence." Passing slowly by its glass door, she managed to catch a glimpse of the man's legs disappearing up the narrow staircase behind the bar. She crossed the street and quickly hurried back. Ten minutes later she slipped into the entrance of a cheap brothel in the rue Blanche, a few hundred yards off Pigalle, and climbed the rotten wooden stairs to the third floor. She reached the second door on the left and knocked twice, paused, and knocked four more times in quick succession.

"Come in, Mado," said the Baron.

Dusk was settling down on Paris, and people coming home from work swarmed in the city streets. A noisy crowd had taken over the bar "Le Marseillais" in the rue Auber, a short distance from the massive Opera building. It was *l'heure de l'apéritif*—the time for the before-dinner drink—and the resourceful Parisians knew that "Le Marseillais" served the best *pastis* that could be obtained in those times of shortage. The owner himself, a huge red-faced Southerner, was busy at work behind the bar, simultaneously serving clients, exchanging salty jokes in the chanting accent of his native city, and shouting orders to his exhausted maids. "Denise, switch on the lights!

Thérèse, a bottle of Sancerre! Antoinette, a cognac to table three!"

Antoinette, oblivious to his shouts, was busy pushing her way through the crowd, trying to get to her employer. Finally she succeeded in reaching him. "*Patron*," she said, "telephone. In the booth behind, the man says it's urgent."

He glared at her. "Couldn't you tell them I was busy?"

She shrugged helplessly.

"Oh, *merde*!" The Marseillais, resigned, moved to the back of the bar while wiping his hands on a towel. He opened the door of the narrow phone booth and bumped into a blond bearded man who looked at him with a smile, an unlit cigar dangling from the corner of his mouth. "What . . ." he started angrily.

"You won't recognize the face, but you might recognize the voice," the stranger said.

"My God!" the Marseillais gasped. "The Baron! What are you doing here? You must be crazy!"

"I'll explain another time, Émile. I need two words with you, and it's urgent."

The bar owner beckoned him toward a side door marked "*Privè*." They entered a small room with a table, a few chairs, and a couch. "Here we shall not be disturbed," the big man said, still eyeing Belvoir with surprise. "*Bon Dieu*, I never would have recognized you in this disguise. When did you arrive in Paris?"

Belvoir ignored the question. "I need some information. You know most of the bars and restaurants run by people from your part of the country."

Émile nodded.

" 'La Provence,' at rue Lèpic. You know it?"

"Sure. It belongs to Roger Santini. He is from Toulon. A good man."

"I want to know if the man has any connections with the Resistance."

Émile frowned in thought. "That's a difficult question. I don't know, frankly. But . . . let me see . . . Pierrot, the *Toulonnais*, he must know. At this hour he usually drinks his anisette at the 'Royal Capucines.' "

The Baron sighed. "No, I saw Pierrot already. He is not sure."

The Marseillais sat heavily on his chair. "Let me think a moment . . . Who would know besides Pierrot?" Suddenly his eyes lit up. "Of course, I've got it. Laruche would know. Have you met him? The headwaiter at 'La Méditerranée.' I'll call him." He got up and moved swiftly to the door.

"Hey, don't say anything over the phone you could be sorry about," the Baron called after him.

"You can count on me," Émile smiled.

Barely two minutes later he was back. "You were right. The guy is involved with the Resistance. Up to his neck."

The Baron grinned with satisfaction. "Thank you, Émile. I'll remember that service."

"Anytime," the Marseillais said warmly. "Don't forget that I made my debut with your father, down on the Côte d'Azur. Take care, Baron."

In his office at the Gestapo headquarters at 9, rue des Saussaies, Kurt Limmer paced back and forth, biting his expensive cigar. He was sweating, and mopped his sticky forehead with a big blue handkerchief. Five minutes earlier, his assistant, Fritz Kaiser, had called to inform him that the wounded terrorist was out of danger, and had just been transferred to the cellars of the Gestapo for interrogation. "Put Berner to work on him," Limmer snapped fiercely. "He is the best man in that sort of matter. I need quick results!"

Berner was indeed the best man the Gestapo had in Paris. Born in Saxony, a onetime Abwehr spy, a former fighter in the Foreign Legion, he had earned his dubious glory by becoming the most savage, the most cruel torturer the Gestapo in France had ever counted in its ranks. Together with a group of sadists—German, French, Iranian and Italian—he was daily torturing and slaying French Resistance fighters. He had transformed his luxurious apartment at 180, rue da la Pompe in the aristocratic sixteenth *arrondissement* into a universe of death. Every one of his men was an expert in a specific method of torture: electroshocks, bathtub, beating, hanging by the wrists, woman torture. . . . He used to boast that his men had so refined the various ways of torture that they had upgraded it into a new form of art. More than two thirds of his wretched prisoners did not emerge alive from the immaculate bourgeois building at rue de la Pompe. But most of them talked before they died.

In emergency cases, the Gestapo would invite Berner to use its facilities in the cellars of the rue des Saussaies, close to Limmer's command post. And today's case was an emergency.

The telephone in Limmer's room buzzed discreetly. The Gestapo chief grabbed the receiver. "Yes?"

"This is Kaiser. Berner made the man talk. He gave us the address of the headquarters of his group. A restaurant in Montmartre."

"Wonderful," Limmer mumbled, "just wonderful." He looked at his watch. It was a quarter to nine. "In fifteen minutes we shall raid them. Four cars. Notify the SD also."

"Yes, sir."

Before returning the receiver to its cradle, Limmer added. "And congratulate Berner on my behalf. That was a quick job. By the way, how is the state of health of the terrorist?"

"That's very sad, sir," Kaiser replied. "He was killed while trying to escape."

"What a pity," sighed Limmer, bursting into a hoarse laugh in which his assistant joined him.

A thunderstorm had suddenly broken over Paris and the torrential rain drove the pedestrians away from the city streets. Soaked, Belvoir hurried up the tortuous rue Lépic. He tried his best to protect his head and face with a newspaper. The water could ruin his makeup, and unglue his false beard and moustache. He needed that disguise just for a few more hours. He had been seen wearing it in some Paris bars that night, and half a dozen people could give his description to the police. The time had come for Pierre Altmüller, the Alsatian Farmer, to disappear. Tomorrow he could open another of the packages that he had collected in Paris during the last few days. Maybe he should also start thinking about a new hideout. Mado was perfectly safe, and she was totally devoted to him since he had saved her from a gang that used to kidnap white whores and sell them to brothels and harems in the Middle East. But he shouldn't endanger the girl too much; and he shouldn't stay too long in one place.

He pushed open the door of the small restaurant. Because of the bad weather, "La Provence" was almost empty. He went straight to the balding, skeletal man in a brown suit who sat at the cashier's desk.

"You must be Santini," he said.

The man nodded.

Belvoir spread the soaked magazine before him, showing him the title: *Je suis partout*. Then he asked: "Does the name 'Voltaire' mean anything to you?"

Santini looked at him suspiciously. "I don't know what you mean."

"You certainly do," the Baron said sharply. "and if not, your friends upstairs will." He didn't wait for an answer, but quickly walked past him and climbed the stairs. The corridor on the first floor was dark, but he heard voices behind a door on his right. He pushed it open. The room was dimly lit, the curtains drawn. Five people were sitting around a long wooden table. There were four men and a middle-aged woman. They stopped talking as he came in. One of them, a young man with a fierce look in his dark eyes, was already on his feet. "Who are you?" he asked angrily. "What are you doing here?"

Before Belvoir could answer, he felt a slight pressure on his back. He was too familiar with the barrel of a gun prodding his vertebrae not to raise his hands docilely and walk in. Santini pushed him into the room and closed the door behind him. "He just arrived," he said, his voice heavy with anxiety. "He showed me the magazine and gave me the password. I tried to stop him, but he ran up here. He knew you were meeting upstairs."

"Give me your gun, Santini," the fierce-looking young man said. "Check the street to make sure he was alone. I'll carry on." After the Toulonnais had closed the door behind him, he turned to Belvoir, steadily pointing the gun at him. "Who are you?" he asked again.

Belvoir spoke sparingly. "I was parachuted from London a week ago. I missed my first contact at the Gare de Lyon, because I believed it to be too dangerous. Today I couldn't come to the Café des Minettes, but a friend of mine followed one of your men to this place, so here I am."

The people around the table exchanged glances. The young leader of the group looked at Belvoir in contempt. "And I say that you are a liar and an agent provocateur. If what you say is correct, then you've been sowing death everywhere in your path. Our network in the Southwest is destroyed; the Gare de Lyon was full of Gestapo agents and SS troops when you were supposed to make your contact; one of our men was wounded and captured by the

Gestapo today, while waiting for you at the Café des Minettes. No, Monsieur, I believe you are not the man you pretend to be, and I think you have put yourself·in a very risky situation indeed."

The woman intervened. "There is something else. The man who came from London was dark-haired and . . ."

". . . and he had to wear a black coat and a red scarf," Belvoir completed her phrase. "Yes, Now let me show you something." He quickly removed his false beard and moustache, then looked around him, dipped his fingers in a half-full glass of cognac that was on the table, and rubbed his left sideburn. Some of the blond dye dissolved and revealed the natural dark-brown color of his hair.

The people around the table were stunned by his quick transformation. Still, they were not convinced. "I need proof," said the young man suspiciously. "Solid proof. Everything you showed us could be done also by a Gestapo agent who took the place of our man in Libourne."

Belvoir leaned across the table. "I have come here to carry out an important assignment. I need your help, and I need it as quickly as possible. You don't trust me and you want proof. Very well. I'll give you some information that is known only to the head of the S.O.E. in London. I'll give you my true name. I am the Baron Francis de Belvoir."

Nobody reacted to the name. They continued to observe him sulkily. Belvoir exploded, "You do maintain a radio contact with London, don't you? So call them, give them my name and you'll get your confirmation!" He turned to the door. "I will be back here in twenty-four hours." Then he pointed mockingly at the gun in the young man's hand. "And put that thing away. It might go off and you could hurt yourself."

Nobody tried to stop him. He walked out of the room and slammed the door behind him.

He was halfway down the stairs when he heard a rapid series of alarming sounds. First, the unmistakable screeching of several cars' brakes, then running footsteps on the sidewalk, the brutal banging of the door, and shouts, in German and in French. He knelt quickly, took off his shoes and ran up the stairs, past the first and the second floors, until he reached the top floor of the house. He looked quickly around for an escape route. Above his head, a small skylight in the low ceiling gave access to the roof. He opened a door at random and dragged a chair out of the empty room. He jumped on it and tried to open the skylight. It was jammed. He cursed silently and tried again.

On the stairs below he heard heavy steps, then more shouts, orders in German, and immediately after, bursts of submachine-gun fire. These were the Germans again. Somebody—most probably the wounded prisoner—had talked and revealed to the Gestapo the secret hideout of his comrades.

The steps, the shouts and the firing were getting nearer. Somebody bellowed in French, "The roof! Check the roof!" In desperation, he hit the glass of the skylight with his bare fist, and while the splinters of glass were raining on his head and shoulders he caught the jagged lid of the skylight with his bleeding hand and pushed with all his force. This time the rusty framework gave way. He caught the sides of the opening and heaved himself up and into the rainy Parisian night. He climbed on the gabled roof, slipping and falling on the wet tiles, struggling to get as far as he could from the gaping skylight. He reached the crest of the gable and slid to the other side. The roof was too steep and too slippery, and he suddenly lost contact and was flung into the air. Only his instinct saved him, at the last fraction of a second before he fell to the stone pavement fifty feet below. His left hand, slipping on the treacherous tiles, encountered the iron drainpipe and locked around it. The steady grip of his hand on the providential anchor braked the momentum of his falling body and he hung in the air, clutching the rusty pipe that could give at any moment. He brought his whole body against the wall and with his last ounce of energy heaved himself until his right hand also reached and gripped the drainpipe. He began to move his hands, one after the other, his whole weight hanging on one arm at a time, but advancing, inch by inch, to the far left corner of the roof. With each movement an agonizing pain pierced his hands, which had been deeply cut by the shattered glass of the skylight. Panting, biting his lips, he moved on until he noticed below him the protruding shape of a balcony six feet below. He let go the drainpipe and landed on his stockinged feet. He ran around the corner of the building on the long L-shaped balcony. He was now on the back side of the house. Barely a few feet away, and a little below him, was the flat roof of the neighboring building. He quickly climbed onto the thin iron railing of the balustrade and crouched. Above his head, on his right, he heard shouts, and somebody fired at him. The sound of bullets whistled in his ears and he felt a throb of pain in his left thigh. He swayed, but succeeded in regaining his balance, then pulled his whole body tight and jumped.

As he landed on the roof below he knew he had won. Ahead of him stretched the roofs of Montmartre in a long succession—flat and gabled, close to each other, almost touching over the tangle of the narrow, twisting streets of the hill. It was his territory now, a familiar, concrete jungle where he had made so many spectacular escapes. He moved confidently into the darkness while the sound of shooting became more sparse and more distant.

Two hours later, his hands and thigh bleeding profusely, he reached the rue Blanche and surreptitiously sneaked into Mado's brothel room.

April 4, 10:00 P.M.–April 5, dawn

THE BLACK HOTCHKISS SLOWED WHEN IT REACHED THE place du Palais Royal, and turned into the rue de Rivoli, past the 130-year-old arcades that stretched as far as the place de la Concorde. It stopped in front of the brightly lit entrance to the Hotel Meurice, headquarters of the High Commandment of Gross Paris. Kurt Limmer, a grim expression set on his face, hurried past the helmeted Wehrmacht guards and up the blue-carpeted staircase to the first floor. A dandyish lieutenant ushered him to a big office, lavishly furnished. A tall, gray-haired officer got up from behind a massive oak desk. He wore general's pips on his epaulets and the Iron Cross on his neck. Behind him, a huge map of Paris and its suburbs covered the wall. The man was General-leutnant Horst Wulff, Commanding General of Gross Paris.

He didn't ask his visitor to sit down, Instead, he slowly said in a cold, sharp voice: "I asked you to come here to explain your intolerable behavior this afternoon and tonight."

A gray pallor settled on Limmer's face, and his eyes flashed in anger. "Did you say 'intolerable'?" he muttered.

"You heard me perfectly well," the general said.

"I could add a few more adjectives to describe your conduct," said a new voice behind him. Limmer started and turned back. At the other end of the room, his clenched fists leaning on the long conference table, Colonel von Beck looked at him spitefully. "I could call it stupid, amateurish, incompetent, and criminal."

"Criminal? Do you call the protection of German rule against terrorists criminal?" Limmer slowly paced toward the young colonel, pointing his index finger at him in a threatening gesture. "I would watch my tongue if I were you. I would think twice before daring to insult a high Gestapo official doing his duty. Let me give you some free advice, my young friend. If I were you, I would refrain from describing Gestapo actions as criminal!"

"I said criminal and I mean it," Von Beck glared back furiously at the fuming Gestapo chief. "I consider it a crime to endanger the security of the Reich, and that's exactly what you have been doing. An enemy agent is in Paris, trying to get hold of Germany's most precious secret, and instead of helping to uncover him, you hunt and butcher people all over Paris. That's sabotage and that's what I wrote in my report."

"What report?" Limmer inquired, his voice slightly less belligerent.

The commander of Gross Paris took a sheaf of papers from his desk. "A report to the chief of the Abwehr, with copies to the O.K.W. and to your own boss, Himmler. And if you would like to know, Limmer, I approved and countersigned every single page in this report."

For the first time, Limmer's self-confidence wavered. "Just a moment," he said. "You have no power over me. I don't depend on you. My orders . . ."

"Your orders were to cooperate in the Enigma affair," von Beck cut him off brutally. "Instead, you kept your information for yourself, and blew the most valuable lead we had on the British agent."

"And what would you have done if you were in my place?" Limmer asked angrily.

"I would have tailed the man who came today to the Café des Minettes. I would have set a trap in the restaurant in Montmartre. The British agent would have come sooner or later. He was there minutes before you raided the place. Instead of shooting your way in, you could have captured him by now."

"Now, wait a moment," Limmer said, on the defensive. "Don't send your report yet. Let us try to cooperate."

The phone on General Wulff's desk rang twice. He picked up the receiver. "It's for you," he said dryly and handed it to Limmer. The Gestapo chief grabbed the phone.

"Limmer."

He listened for a few moments; then a slow, sardonic smile spread on his face. He slammed the phone. "You

can send your report," he said with contempt. Some of his
old bluntness had crept into his voice. "Because while you
sit, doing nothing in your handsome offices, I get results!
One of the terrorists captured tonight gave us the name of
the British agent. He is a Frenchman whom we know well.
He calls himself Francis de Belvoir!"

He opened the door. "One day, we'll settle our ac-
counts, Herr Oberst," he spat venomously and was gone.

Von Beck didn't even look at him. He was already by
Wulff's desk, reaching for the telephone. "Brandner? Von
Beck here. I want you to call immediately all the branches
of the French administration: police, *Milice, Affaires
intérieures*, tax offices. Check with them if they have any
knowledge or a record on a man called Francis de Belvoir.
The Gestapo pretend they know him. Call me back at the
Otto building. I am on my way."

He hung up, saluted, and ran out of Wulff's office to his
waiting car. All the way up to the Champs Elysées and down
the avenue Foch, he tried to evaluate the first piece of information he had got about the enemy agent. He was a
Frenchman, then, and a nobleman. But was this his true
name? And could he be found, among forty million
Frenchmen? Did Laimmer really know this Belvoir, or was
he again trying to mislead him?

Still lost in his thoughts, he was slowly climbing the
staircase to his own office when Brandner ran down to
meet him. The young captain was disheveled, his cheeks
were flushed and his eyes shone with emotion. "I talked to
the police," he reported, stammering with excitement.
"They say the man has a criminal record! They are sending over his file!"

Half an hour later, von Beck shut himself in his office,
unbuttoned his tunic, and sat behind his desk. On the
green blotter in front of him, under the bright light cast by
a powerful reading lamp, lay a voluminous file. On its
blue cover was written in big red characters: "Francis de
Belvoir, alias Le Baron."

The hours slowly ticked away, but von Beck didn't
move from his desk. He was deeply immersed in the fascinating story unrolling before him, spellbound by the life of
Francis de Belvoir. Even though it was written in dry, official police language, the story of Francis de Belvoir read
like an adventure story. The documents in the file depicted

young Belvoir's flight from Paris after his father's death, his departure for the Far East aboard a cargo ship, his adolescence in the ill-famed districts of Saigon, Macao and Hong Kong. They told the story of Belvoir's first successful coups: the sacking of the house of the French *Gouverneur* in Saigon, after the seduction of his daughter; his flight to Bangkok and Rangoon with a convoy of Buddhist priests; the theft of a small chest of precious stones from a Shinto temple in Mandalay, for which he was hunted all the way to India by the revenge-thirsty monks. In India, at the age of twenty-two, he had worked his way into a British general's residence and had sold him a nonexistent mansion on the French Riviera. Using a disguise for the first time, he had escaped aboard a sailing ship to the Middle East. In Beirut he had fallen madly in love with a married Italian woman and had eloped with her to Cairo, where their love affair had ended as suddenly as it had begun. He had worked his way through Ethiopia, the Congo, Algeria, encountering countless dangers, swindling rich European businessmen, stealing valuables, using elaborate disguises. For a year, 1935, he had lived in Tangier, where he had made a fortune running a small navy of contraband vessels along the Mediterranean coast. In that same year he had been briefly married to a White Russian émigrée, whom he introduced everywhere as a princess. And in January 1936, at the age of twenty-six, he had returned to Europe. He landed illegally in Marseille and, until the war started, carried out numerous reckless adventures in Paris, London, and Rome that made him famous. He soon became a legendary figure in the Parisian underworld. But the stunning, the unique feature in that extraordinary life story was the fact that Belvoir had never been caught. The police in half a dozen countries had issued warrants for his arrest; charges were pending against him in most of the capitals of Europe: but his meticulous planning, the complicities he bought or acquired by seduction and his talent for disguise had always saved him at the eleventh hour.

For a long moment, von Beck sank into a strange reverie. Contemplating the photographs of the handsome gray-eyed young man who was about his own age, he couldn't help feeling admiration and jealousy. This man, whom he intended to hunt and ruthlessly destroy, had actually lived the kind of life that he, Rudy von Beck, had so much longed for when he was a young boy. He had become a real adventurer, he had roamed the world, risked his life, overcome deadly perils, lived passionate love affairs. Von Beck sighed. Belvoir had accomplished what for him would always be just a romantic, unattainable dream.

He went on scanning the documents in the file. A brilliant report, entitled "Modus Operandi of Francis de Belvoir" succinctly described the working methods of the Baron. It disclosed in detail his systems of gathering intelligence, his habit of introducing his agents into the close entourage of the people he wanted to rob or swindle; his inclination to engage in risky, challenging games with the other side. Von Beck read slowly, trying to penetrate the cunning mind of his opponent, to guess his intentions and his future moves. He made some surprising discoveries: Belvoir had never mixed in affairs of drugs and weapons. He had never killed, and never carried a gun.

Two documents concluded the file. One of them, recently drawn up by the French police, was a long list of Belvoir's contacts, his accomplices in the underworld, the addresses of his usual hideouts. The other was a report on the Gestapo gold affair. Belvoir was accused of the theft of half a ton of gold from "the Gestapo reserves." Limmer hadn't lied, then. The Gestapo had its own account to settle with the Baron, and von Beck guessed exactly what they had reserved for him. And then he knew that he had to beat Limmer and his butchers in the hunt for the Baron.

He closed the file with a sigh. He had noted on a small pad several names and addresses. He picked up the phone. "Rouse all our people, Brandner," he said urgently when he heard the sleepy voice of his assistant. "We have work to do tonight."

In the Préfecture de Police, located close to the Palais de Justice in the Île de la Cité, the exhausted chief archivist locked the archives section and went out. It was about midnight and he was too tired to go to sleep. First the Gestapo, then the Abwehr had driven him mad with their urgent requests for the Belvoir files. Well, he guessed he had the right to a last pint of beer before the midnight curfew. He crossed the street and entered the Café du Palais de Justice, where a cop could still get some real, tap-drawn beer. He leaned on the counter, got his drink, and wearily looked around him. On his right, he saw an old acquaintance whose file had often passed through his hands: Jeannot Leroux, a petty crook, who had been arrested and released on bail only half an hour ago. The ruffian was dressed in a leather jacket, baggy black trousers and an "apache cap." Jeannot saw him too, and smiled at him. "Shall I buy you a drink, *chef*?" he asked.

"With pleasure," the archivist said and moved closer to Jeannot. In their particular world of cops and robbers, there was nothing more usual than an off-duty cop and an off-duty robber having a drink together like good old friends. They engaged in small talk about the present hard times.

"Well," the archivist said casually, "I hear that your friend the Baron is back in Paris."

Jeannot looked at him in disbelief. "Come on," he said. "*Le Baron* in Paris? Nonsense. He is not that crazy. He should know that half of the French police and the Gestapo are after him."

"You can add the Abwehr to the list," grinned the archivist, pleased that for once he was able to amaze somebody. He told Jeannot about the surprising request of Colonel von Beck.

Jeannot uttered the appropriate exclamations, then adroitly changed the subject and launched into expert speculations about tomorrow's horse race in Vincennes. After a few minutes, he excused himself. "I must go to the men's room," he mumbled. "I'll be back in a moment." The archivist nodded absently.

Jeannot hurried to the basement of the vast café and slipped into the public phone booth. He dropped a token into the slot, dialed a number, and whispered urgently into the mouthpiece.

It was past four in the morning when a gentle but persistent tapping on the door awoke the Baron. His sleep that night was lighter than usual, because of the sharp pains he suffered from his wounds. "Don't move!" he whispered to Mado, who had propped herself on her elbows beside him. He slipped out of bed and with silent, catlike movements, approached the door. He listened, immobile, for a long moment, then motioned to Mado.

"Who is it?" she asked.

"Mado, is the Baron there?" whispered a voice. "It's me, Lagache."

The Baron sighed in relief. He knew the man well.

"Are you alone?" the girl asked.

"Yes. Open up."

The Baron opened a crack in the door, and recognized the dark, mousy face of his friend. He quickly stepped aside and let in the short, skinny man. Lagache smiled, but his big eyes remained worried. "So you are in Paris," he whispered in disbelief. Then his quick eyes noticed Belvoir's bandaged hands. "You have been wounded?"

"It's nothing," the Baron replied. "Superficial scratches. Now, what brings you here?"

"Baron, get away from here," whispered Lagache nervously. "The Gestapo and the Abwehr are after you. You are hot." In a few confused phrases he told the Baron about the urgent requests for his file by Limmer and von Beck. The Baron listened in silence. "Shortly after midnight they started a manhunt all over town. The police have joined the search. They are raiding all your friends' places," Lagache continued. "We are a little ahead of them, five of us, checking all your hideouts to find you. Dress and get out of here."

"Where can I go?" Belvoir asked quickly, but in a calm voice.

"Louison's place. They just left and they won't come back. He'll take care of you."

The Baron nodded. In a few minutes he was packed and ready. He stuffed in his bag all the items that could even distantly hint at his sojourn in Mado's place, including the blood-soaked gauze the redhead had used to treat his wounds.

He kissed Mado's cheeks twice, the French way, and discreetly left a thick wad of francs on the bedside table. With Lagache moving stealthily ahead, he sneaked through the dark corridor.

Half an hour later, Mado was startled again by a heavy pounding on the door.

"Open the door," a voice shouted with a heavy German accent. "Gestapo!"

April 5, 1944–April 20, 1944

SLOWLY, PAINFULLY, BELVOIR AWOKE AND GULPED FRANTI-cally for air. He felt as if he were emerging from a bottomless black abyss. His aching body was wet with sweat, and he had a sticky, bitter taste in his mouth. He opened his eyes. The room was pitch dark and it took him a few moments to realize where he was. He was fully dressed and his jacket was tucked under his pillow. He waited patiently for some minutes until his eyes partially became accustomed to the darkness. He got up from his narrow bed, found his shoes on the floor, and felt his way to the door. He opened it carefully, went through a dimly lit corridor and reached a narrow staircase. He climbed the stairs slowly. Coming from above, he heard sounds of laughter and music; the sharp odor of liquor and of cigarette smoke wafted in the air. At the top of the stairs there was a heavy wooden door. He pulled it back a few inches and looked.

The famous transvestite cabaret "Chez Louison" was crowded. From his place at the back of the big restaurant, Belvoir had a good view of the public—mostly men in tuxedoes and starched shirts, plus a few women in long evening dresses. Many high-ranking German officers were scattered among the civilians, thoroughly enjoying themselves. The place was as sumptuous as ever. The walls were covered with thick crimson velvet, the reddish copper railing of the rosewood-paneled bar was burnished to perfection, the crystal chandeliers hanging from the ceiling blazed with light which was reflected in the big gilt-framed mural mirrors. Waiters in tailcoats and bow ties hurried among the tables with food-laden silver salvers and buckets of ice from which protruded the gilded seals of prewar champagne. A hidden orchestra was playing soft music.

Gradually, almost imperceptibly at first, the light in the chandeliers dimmed and went out. The waiters lit long thin candles placed in silver candlesticks on the tables. The music became louder, more rhythmic, and several projectors cast a multicolored rhapsody of light on a small stage at the far end of the room. The show was starting. A group of transvestites, dressed in costumes of feathers, sequins and spangles, got on stage. They looked like women in every respect, flashing long lithe legs, provocatively moving their ample bosoms. Some of them were astoundingly beautiful and drew cries of admiration from the audience. They executed a languorous, sexy dance, which was enthusiastically applauded. A new group of five transvestites ascended to the stage and began a burlesque act rich with innuendos and vulgar allusions. The audience bellowed with laughter. The show was well under way.

Belvoir sneaked out the door and leaned back against the wall. He caught a passing waiter by the sleeve and murmured: "Get Louison." There was something in his voice that made the waiter dart off and disappear behind the stage. A minute later Louison was beside him, still dressed in a black body-stocking that clung to his sleek figure. His face was covered with heavy makeup, which enhanced his effeminate, graceful looks. Blue and black shadows, artfully applied, accentuated the almond shape of his big green eyes. The blood-red lipstick glistening on his pouting full mouth evoked an inviting, sinful sensuality.

Louison moved close to the Baron with a tempting smile, but his voice wasn't nearly as seductive. "You must be crazy," he hissed and deftly maneuvered Belvoir to a more secluded corner. "They'll spot you and that will be my funeral as well."

Belvoir tried to calm him. "Take it easy, Louison. Nobody would believe that I might walk into a crowded cabaret tonight."

"Don't stretch your luck too far, Baron," Louison warned him. "Come."

He moved along the dark red walls in the direction of the bar until he reached a discreet door, also covered with velvet, that would have been almost unnoticeable, if it weren't for its small gold-colored handle. Louison dragged his friend in and locked the door behind him. They were in a small corridor decorated with blue wallpaper and framed sketches of nude masculine bodies. Louison looked more relaxed now.

"Look, Louison," Belvoir asked all of a sudden, "what time is it?"

"It's almost eleven." The transvestite smiled. "You slept deeply the whole day."

"Did you manage to reach Bruno?"

"Yes. He is waiting for you in my office. This way—you'll be safe there." Louison pushed the Baron through an immaculate white door at the end of the corridor, and started to close it behind him.

"You are not coming in?"

Louison smiled cunningly, mimicked a curtsy and blew him a kiss. "The less I know, the better for me, *mon chéri.*"

The Baron turned around. He was in the most extraordinary office he had ever seen in his life. Three colors reigned over the room, its furnishings and its tapestry: white, pink and baby blue. The ankle-deep wall-to-wall carpet was pink, and so were the delicate lace curtains, framed by heavy taffeta draperies. The walls were covered with blue silk, patterned with roses and lilies whose contours were embroidered in thin golden thread. The Louis XVI desk and the cozy armchair behind it were painted in a soft, creamy white. The upholstery of the armchair matched the tapestry. Even the old-fashioned telephone was covered with pink enamel, except the nacre mouthpiece and the gold-rimmed dial, under which lay the numbers and letters, each one artfully decorated with miniature paintings of roses and orchids.

Facing the desk was a huge round bed, covered with enormous rugs of pure-white fur. From a golden ring embedded in the ceiling was suspended a diaphanous baldachin of the finest voile. On the wall behind the bed hung a large, suggestive painting of two nude young men, eyes burning with desire, stretching their long, delicate hands until their fingers touched.

Opposite the door, between the two windows, stood an enormous dressing table, crowned by a big round mirror. It was covered with a multitude of bottles, cans and cream jars. Porcelain vases filled with bunches of fresh pink roses were scattered all over the room. A heavy smell of sweet perfume floated in the air.

The Baron's attention was drawn to the man standing in the middle of the room. He was very tall, broad-shouldered and barrel-chested, with enormous muscular hands and a heavy-jowled, swarthy face. His hair was cropped short, and his low forehead and broken boxer's nose made him look quite stupid at first sight. But at first sight only, for a closer look at the man's small dark eyes quickly reversed the judgment: they had a sly, scheming expression and were definitely not the eyes of a fool. He was in his middle forties, dressed in a double-breasted blue suit which seemed on the point of bursting at the seams, but then in wartime Paris it was very difficult to find any garment that could suit such dimensions.

"Bruno!" the Baron exclaimed with joy, and the two men warmly embraced. The giant happily patted Belvoir's shoulders with his hairy paws. "It is good to see you, and it is time, too," he sighed. "I was starting to feel like a sissy myself in this queer's place. Well, all that counts is that you are alive, in one piece, and that the *boches* haven't laid their hands on you yet."

"They never will," the Baron said gravely. "But you know that the English got all our gold. They even put me in prison, for the first time in my life."

Bruno shrugged. "Better them than the Germans," he smiled and added cheerfully: "And forget about the gold. The fun of stealing it was the best part of the whole affair. They still can't understand how we did it."

The Baron looked thoughtfully at his friend. In his youth, after a disastrous boxing career, Bruno Morel had gradually slid into the life of a typical Parisian *apache* in the crime-infested quarters behind the place de la République. One night he got mixed in a shady murder, about which he refused to talk, even fifteen years later. He escaped to Marseille with all the French police on his trail, and succeeded in reaching the Foreign Legion recruitment office shortly before his pursuers. The Foreign Legion, under the Third Republic, was a quasi-official sanctuary for criminals on the run. Morel joined the Legion and for ten years fought in the name of France in the blackest places in the Empire: Madagascar, Central Africa, Indochina, the Sahara. Shortly before the World War he got in trouble again, deserted and was promptly apprehended by the

French police in the "Bal Tabarin" cabaret in Paris. He had seemed a very likely candidate for the guillotine until the Baron organized his escape from the very Palais de Justice. He didn't do it for altruistic reasons; he needed Bruno's formidable muscle for an operation he had been planning for a long time. The coup never took place, but a strange friendship sprang up between the two rogues. Bruno Morel, who became one of the pillars of the Paris underworld, used to boast that he was loyal only to money; but all those around him knew of his genuine devotion to the Baron. Nobody knew, however, that Bruno was the only man whom the Baron trusted, and that he had been his secret partner in the notorious theft of the Gestapo gold treasure.

The Baron sat behind Louison's desk and reached in his pocket for a cheroot. "Let me fill you in, Bruno," he said to his companion, who suspiciously eyed the thin-legged taboret in front of the dressing table before resting his bulk on its brocade cushion. The Baron described his release from Dartmoor prison and admitted that he had been sent to Paris on a mission by the British intelligence service. He refrained, however, from disclosing the specific goal of his assignment. Bruno listened in silence. "Where do I come in?" he finally asked.

"First of all, you have to find a safe house. I need a quiet, secluded place for at least a couple of weeks to plan my next steps and to make all the necessary preparations. As long as the Germans are looking for me, I should stay away from my usual hangouts. It was very clever to hide in a place they had already searched, but the other side might get the same idea. I also need some rest. My leg hurts. It isn't serious—it is only a flesh wound—but I am handicapped in my movements."

Bruno nodded in approval. "I can easily arrange what you ask by tomorrow morning."

"You must also get in touch with a network of the Resistance." the Baron continued. "All my contacts in Paris are gone. I need the Resistance to help me carry out my assignment. The underground group originally designated to give me aid has been completely destroyed, and somebody else should take its place and contact London for instructions.

"And another thing," he said slowly, his chin thrust forward and his eyes becoming narrow slits dully glowing with a steel-gray glint. "I want to know everything about this Colonel von Beck, of the Abwehr. Ever heard of him?"

"Never before," Bruno said.

"But you still work with the Otto organization?"

"Yes."

"And the Abwehr is still on the second floor, right? Well, I guess you can gather a lot of information there. Put the word through the grapevine. I'll pay a lot for any information about this man."

"The Gestapo is also after you," Bruno reminded him.

"I don't care about the Gestapo," Belvoir said angrily. "They are a gang of stupid butchers. They'll never get me. But this von Beck is something else. He might be really dangerous."

Bruno got up. "Fine. What's this all about? Your assignment, I mean."

The Baron didn't answer.

Bruno smiled and left the room.

Bruno Morel was his usual efficient self. At 7:45 the following morning, his black Citroën came to a halt at the back entrance of Louison's nightclub, at the serene rue des Abbesses. The Baron quickly entered the car, which moved unobtrusively toward the Porte de la Villette, one of the main gates of Paris.

Fifteen minutes later, at exactly eight o'clock, Rudolf von Beck opened the meeting of his committee, on the second floor of the Otto building. Gathered around the rectangular table in the medium-sized room that von Beck had chosen for his command post, were the representatives of the various security branches operating in Paris. The Commandment of Gross Paris, the French police and the collaborationist Milice had sent, as usual, top-ranking representatives. The Gestapo, the SD and the SS were again represented by low-graded officers. That was their own way of hinting to von Beck that they didn't think highly of his committee and accepted his authority only *pro forma*.

One by one, the officers reported on their search for Belvoir during the last thirty-six hours. "The fact is he has disappeared," declared the representative of the Commandment of Gross Paris, Lieutenant-colonel Strauss. "He was not in his usual hideouts, and his friends don't know anything about him."

"Any leads on your side?" von Beck asked the assistant prefect of the Parisian police.

The fat, balding Divisionnaire Louis Jobert shook his head. "We momentarily suspected a Pigalle prostitute, Mado Bonnier, of sheltering him, but we found no proof that she had ever seen him. Neither did the Gestapo agents who questioned her the same night."

"Questioned?" interrupted von Beck mockingly, but his eyes burned with sudden rage. "You call that questioning! The poor girl was half dead by the time the Gestapo finished with her. She was lucky that the police wanted her for interrogation and asked me to intervene and save her from the rue des Saussaies. Had I been half an hour late she would have been cut to pieces."

The Gestapo delegate, Helmut Muller, didn't look at von Beck. "What we do know is that, until the shooting at rue Lépic, Belvoir was wearing a disguise," he said impassively. "A blond beard and a moustache. One of our informers tells us he saw a man corresponding to that description a few hours before the shooting at a café on boulevard des Capucines."

"Which café?" von Beck quickly asked.

"I don't remember the name," the lean, dark-faced Gestapo agent shot back, and held von Beck's angry gaze with cold, arrogant eyes.

"In any case, I am sure he won't wear the same disguise anymore and won't visit the same café again," Divisionnaire Jobert intervened.

Von Beck nodded. "Nevertheless," he said slowly, "tonight I'd like to launch another raid on all of Belvoir's hiding places that we have on our lists. The chances of finding him are very slim, I know, but he just might think that his old hideouts are safe now, once we have checked them and found nothing."

Most of the participants nodded in agreement. "However," von Beck added, "our main concern now should be to conceive a foolproof system for the protection of the Enigma machine."

"You believe he still intends to go along with his project?" SD Captain Franz Kunzle asked with overt skepticism. "Even though he is now on the run, and completely alone?"

Von Beck smiled coldly. "The man is a loner and a gambler," he said. "I have no doubt that he will try to get the Enigma." He nodded a Brandner, who circled the table, distributing to each participant a copy of the list that specified the twenty-seven emplacements of the top-secret enciphering machine.

"But how can we guess where he is going to hit?" insisted Captain Kunzle, puzzled.

Von Beck slowly lighted a French "Gauloises" cigarette and deeply inhaled the acrid smoke. "If I read his file correctly, gentlemen—and I think I did,"— he paused for a second—"the Baron de Belvoir will let us know himself."

A warm sun was shining out of a limpid April sky when, two weeks later, Bruno Morel's Citroën left the main road to Meaux, spent half an hour wandering on small country roads, and finally emerged on the shady driveway of a coquettish white villa in the luxuriant Marne Valley. The villa was a discreet lovers' nest, appropriately named *"Le Rendez-vous des Amoureux."* Like quite a few other similar pretty houses hidden in the abundant vegetation on shores of the Marne River, it had lived through many sinful weekends of middle-aged Parisian businessmen, with their obliging secretaries, on a stolen leave from an aging wife. The inhabitants of the neighboring villages were clever enough never to ask questions and never to remember names, which were phony anyway. They knew that they could go on demanding and obtaining exorbitant prices for their produce, high wages for their maintenance services and fat tips for their discretion only as long as they kept their mouths shut.

Bruno climbed the two steps leading to the villa's entrance and knocked on the heavy rustic door. Nobody answered. He knocked again, with no results. He bent his head to the door and listened. The house was silent.

Suddenly, a twig snapped with a dry crackle in the bushes on his left. Quickly, Bruno flung himself on the ground, rolled twice on the gravel, and was back on his feet, crouching low, his outstretched right hand steadily pointing in the direction of the noise. A heavy German Mauser had miraculously materialized in his grip.

The Baron emerged from the bushes, a shadow of a grin on his tanned face, and paused to light a cheroot. "That was quick," he observed casually. "Your reflexes are as good as ever, *mon cher Bruno.*"

The big man got up slowly, tucked the gun in his belt and dusted his knees. "What was that supposed to be?" He frowned. "Playing at cops and robbers? Why aren't you in the house?"

"I had to make sure you were alone," the Baron said in all seriousness. "How could I know that there was nobody lurking in the back seat of the car, pointing a gun at you?"

Bruno grunted, and took out of the car a heavy bag, full of groceries. He followed the Baron up the steps and into the large, gaily decorated sitting room. "I still think you should get yourself a gun," he said. "You are defenseless here. The Germans aren't playing games."

"I've never carried a gun and never will," Belvoir answered belligerently. "Neither did my father."

"He didn't and you know very well what happened to him," said Bruno viciously.

"But you did and you know very well what happened to you," snapped the Baron. "You lost your head once, and if I hadn't been hanging around, you would have lost it again, that time for good."

Bruno took no offense. He raised his hands, palms up, in mocking despair. "*Ça va, ça va,*" he mumbled, and started piling on the massive oak table huge quantities of food—a black, crusty loaf of bread, a smoked ham, some French sausage, a box of cheese, several cans of tinned food and half a dozen bottles of wine. The Baron opened the bottle of Sancerre, sniffed it, tasted it and, duly satisfied, filled two glasses with the pale liquid. Bruno emptied his glass with one gulp, wiped his mouth and stared gravely at the Baron. "Bad news first," he said. "I got in touch with the Gaullist Resistance. They are in permanent contact with London. The other underground organization, the Communists, receive their orders from Moscow."

"Yes, I know," said Belvoir.

"Well, the underground radioed London about you. The answer was"—he drew a deep breath—"the operation has been called off."

"What!" Belvoir was on his feet.

"You heard me. You should abandon all preparations and get ready to leave. Your instructions are to report at a certain address in Paris—I have it here—and the network will organize your escape."

"Who signed the London message?" Belvoir asked quickly.

"They said it was the head of the S.O.E. himself."

"MacAlister," the Baron murmured. Then, in a sudden

flurry of rage, he smashed his fist on the table. "The bastards!" he said furiously. "They want me back, don't they? Even if I die somewhere along the way! Well, it's too late now. I am not going to die for them."

"What the hell are you talking about?" Bruno asked, puzzled.

The Baron looked at him steadily, his eyes flashing angry sparkles. "In the two weeks that I have been hiding here, I have done some thinking. There is a traitor, somewhere in the S.O.E., probably very close to the top. I was betrayed even before I arrived here. Look! Everywhere I went, the Germans were waiting for me. The men who met me when I was parachuted in were arrested the same night. The Gare de Lyon was swarming with Gestapo when I was supposed to arrive. The Café des Minettes had been turned into a trap for me. 'La Provence' was raided while I was still there. And this von Beck. What is he doing here, if not chasing me? He is Abwehr, German Intelligence service. Why did he come to Paris, if not to hunt me down? And how did the Abwehr learn about me? No, Bruno, I have no doubt that somebody high up in London is feeding them information about me. And I am not going to pay with my head for their games."

Bruno had been listening intently, his forehead furrowed.

"That's one more reason for you to do what you are asked and go back," he said finally.

"Is it?" sneered Belvoir. "So you think that I have just to report at that Resistance address and let them send me back to London? Well, I guarantee you that the same son-ofabitch in London who informed the Germans how I was coming to France will let them know how I am leaving. I'll never reach London alive, you can be sure of that."

Bruno sighed. "So what are you going to do?"

"I'll get to London by my own means," Belvoir said firmly and straightened up. "But I won't go back there empty-handed. First I'll carry out the bloody operation, as I promised."

Bruno didn't argue. "You know what that means. You'll be completely on your own. Nobody will help you do it."

"Oh, yes, somebody will." Belvoir smiled suddenly. "I know somebody who will do a fantastic job for money, and he is well placed to do it. You! I'll pay you fifty thousand pounds."

Bruno whistled softly. "For that sum I'd sell my own mother," he admitted.

"My job will be worse than that," said Belvoir grimly. He was lost in thought for a moment, then said briskly: "Well, we've wasted enough time already. Let's go to work."

Precisely, without wasting words, Belvoir described the Enigma mission to his friend, careful not to omit any relevant detail. When he finished, he left the room and was back in two minutes holding a sheaf of papers. "Here is the list of the Enigma machines in service in France," he remarked. Bruno thoroughly studied the list. "Most of them are outside of Paris, in fortified army camps," he observed gloomily.

"Naturally," admitted the Baron. With his right hand he swept the heap of groceries and delicacies to the far end of the table; then he spread in front of him some charts and drawings. "These are the sketches of the Enigma."

Bruno glanced at them casually at first, then suddenly started with dismay. "Just a moment," he said, pointing at one of the drawings. "I have seen a machine like that!"

"What?" Belvoir looked at him with disbelief. "Oh, come on, Bruno, you have never seen it, and neither have I. I told you, this is the most guarded . . ."

"If I say that I saw one, then I saw one," the big man cut him off sharply. "It might be top secret, but I saw it."

"Where?" the Baron asked, his voice still heavy with irony.

"Where could I? In the Otto building, of course. On the second floor, where the Abwehr offices are. A few months ago, I had to get a signature for a shipment to Germany, and I went up to the clearing office, which is also on the second floor, on the other side of the landing. The guard who always stands watch at the entrance to the Abwehr section wasn't there, and the door of the communications room was open. It never was before, so I peeped in. I saw a guy operating the machine. First it looked like a typewriter to me, and then I noticed the difference. I was fascinated."

"That can't be," Belvoir said slowly, but this time there was no trace of mockery in his voice. "That sounds impossible. Why, this machine should have been listed here! I have twenty-seven emplacements here and no mention of the Otto building. Now listen: This list was updated in February. Did you see the machine before or after?"

"Definitely before," Bruno said firmly. "I remember very well—it was about a couple of weeks after you escaped."

The Baron leaned back in his chair and closed his eyes. "It all seems to be quite improbable," he said slowly. "And yet . . . if what you say is true, then it leads to one and only one conclusion: There is an unlisted Enigma machine in Paris, for the private use of the Abwehr."

Bruno shrugged. "What difference does it make?"

"Yes, indeed," Belvoir admitted. "Maybe you're right. Nevertheless . . ." He fell silent, got up, lit another cigar and looked thoughtfully at the grayish smoke that spiraled toward the ceiling. After a while, he returned to the table. "We'll have to check that matter at the Otto building, anyway, before deciding on any further moves," he summed up and moved eagerly to another subject. "Now, what about von Beck?"

"Oh, I forgot about that one," smiled Bruno. "That was my good news for you. I learned quite a lot about him."

From the inner pocket of his jacket he produced three glossy pictures, the size of postcards, and arranged them neatly in front of the Baron. "This is your man."

The photographs obviously had been taken with a hidden camera. They were slightly blurred, but on the whole quite adequate. Two of them showed, from quite a short distance, a tall, handsome officer in Wehrmacht uniform, holding a thin black-leather briefcase under his arm. His profile wore a purposeful expression. The third picture showed the same officer *en face*, from a considerably longer range. He was bareheaded, his blond hair disheveled, and he was showing a pretty young woman out of the distinguished-looking mansion, while his left hand, holding his officer's cap, was in the middle of a swing, as if he was on the point of putting it on his head.

"What do you think?" Bruno asked proudly. "I took them myself, from the interior of the car. Those two were taken when he was entering the Otto building. And that one"—he pointed at the photograph with the girl—"shows him coming out of his house, on the avenue Foch. What do you say, Baron? A handsome man, isn't he?—and quite gallant, too. That girl there had spent the night with him."

"Who is she?" the Baron asked quickly.

Bruno dismissed her with a wave of his hand. "Oh, nobody of importance. A German secretary in the Hotel Meurice. It was a one-night stand, quite trivial."

The Baron examined the photographs thoroughly. "That's good. Now, what do you know about him?"

Bruno's report was concise and succinct. "Rudolf von Beck. Colonel in the Abwehr, Iron Cross. About your age, came to Paris approximately at the same time as you. His office is in the Otto building. Twice a week, sometimes even more frequently, at eight sharp, there is a morning meeting in his office. In the meetings participate . ."— he took a bit of paper from his pocket and read: "Divisionnaire Louis Jobert, Préfecture de Police; Armand Moreau, Milice; Helmut Muller, Gestapo; Captain Franz Kunzle, SD; an SS officer, whom we didn't identify; and Lieutenant-colonel Heinrich Strauss, Commandment of Gross Paris. The meetings are convened by his chief of staff, a Captain Brandner. He has an orderly named Schneider."

The Baron studied the names on the small bit of paper, then lighted a match and burned it to ashes. "Next time, learn those names by heart," he snapped. "If somebody found that list in your possession, you'd earn yourself a one-way ticket to the Gestapo cellars."

"All right, all right," said Bruno, irritated. "Do you want to hear the rest?"

"Go on."

"There are two subjects to the meetings," Bruno went on. "The first one is the protection of a certain machine, which I understood must be the Enigma. The second is you!"

"What are your sources?" asked the Baron coldly.

"I spoke to several people who work in the Otto building. A German telephone operator has taken a fancy to one of our guys there, Sébastien Dupuis. Maybe you know him. He used to work with the Corsicans' gang."

The Baron nodded.

"She told him a few things about the meetings up there. Then, there is the cleaning woman who tidies up von Beck's office after the meetings. She told the Germans that she doesn't know how to read, but she reads well enough to notice your name scribbled again and again on all those scraps of paper. Von Beck's orderly, Schneider, shacks up with one of the whores of Suzy la Belge on his evenings off, punctual as a Swiss clock. He never speaks about his boss's work, but is quite eloquent about his private life."

"Tell me about his private life."

"Von Beck has never been married, is very devoted to his job, likes girls, occasionally brings one to the apartment. Speaks good French, admires French culture, and is fond of classical music. He regularly attends the concerts of the Orchestre symphonique de Paris, in the salle Gaveau; and twice a week—the current spectacle in the Opéra. Schneider speaks of him as though he were God himself; he claims that von Beck is the most intelligent colonel in the Abwehr."

"I don't doubt it," said the Baron slowly. "The best brain in the Abwehr, sent especially to Paris to get me. Isn't that flattering, *mon cher* Bruno?"

Bruno nodded. "It seems that he knows your file by heart. The telephone operator overheard him once, on a long-distance call to Berlin. He said to the other party on the phone that he knows you and your methods better than you do."

To the surprise of Bruno Morel, the Baron suddenly smiled. "That's good news," he observed cheerfully. "Now, let's have some lunch."

The two men ate in silence. The Baron hardly nibbled at his food. He was lost in thought, and his half-closed eyes had a distant, faraway look. Finally, he came back to life.

"First of all, I want you to get me a job in the Otto building. I shall be disguised, of course."

"That will be no problem," Bruno remarked. "They are always glad to have Frenchmen robbing their country for them."

Belvoir looked at him with mild surprise. "Getting patriotic, Bruno?"

The giant smiled uneasily. He opened his mouth as if to say something, but changed his mind and remained quiet.

"I want you also to put me in touch with the Communists."

"The Communists? Are you crazy?"

"We need them," said Belvoir calmly. "I can't work anymore with the Gaullist underground. I can't work with anybody who gets his orders from London. But the Reds will help me, I assure you. Can you arrange a meeting?"

Bruno shrugged skeptically. "I can try."

"That's fine. And the third thing: I need a girl. A very beautiful girl. One who will do exactly what I tell her."

"Well," Bruno smiled broadly, "that's the easiest thing

for me to do. I can get you the best *poule de luxe* in Paris."

"No," said Belvoir. "Not that kind—not a prostitute. I need a good girl. With class and brains. Not our kind, Bruno."

"And you want her to obey you to the word?" Bruno looked annoyed. "That will be very difficult."

"But you'll find one, won't you?" the ironic smile flashed on Belvoir's lips. "Don't do it for the money. Do it for France."

Bruno threw him an angry look, then burst into laughter, Only one who knew Bruno Morel intimately, as the Baron did, could detect that his laughter had an edge and was slightly forced.

III

THE
GIRL

April 21–April 22, 1944

As soon as he opened his eyes, at dawn on April 21, Bruno Morel knew how to find a girl for the Baron.

He had slept very little the previous night, in his apartment on Quai Montebello. For hours he rolled his massive bulk on the large bed, weighing and dismissing various schemes. Finally he fell into an agitated sleep, and somehow found the solution.

He arose, donned a loose Moroccan *jellaba*, a memento from his Foreign Legion past, and with quick, precise gestures ground a handful of coffee beans, struck a match to light the gas stove and put the kettle on the fire. He moved into the bathroom, showered quickly with ice-cold water, and deftly sharpened his old-fashioned razor on a rough leather strap hanging by the sink. He shaved quickly, splashed his face with cold water, and dressed in a freshly pressed pinstriped suit, a white shirt, a flashy red tie and black shoes shined to perfection. On the stove, the coffee was ready now. He did not add any sugar or cream. He drew open the heavy velvet curtains and sipped the bitter liquid while his eyes absently contemplated the black shape of Notre Dame de Paris facing his windows from the other side of the river. It was still winter, and a heavy rain was falling on Paris again, its large drops whipping the muddy surface of the Seine into small foaming crests. He gulped his coffee, lit a strong cigarette, and plucked a beige raincoat from the cupboard. He took his Mauser from under the pillow, checked it and stuck it in his belt, then sneaked quietly down the steps. He decided not to take his car, which was parked in the inner court of the elegant apartment house. Cars were scarce in Paris because of the acute fuel shortage; he intended to move as discreetly as possible around town this morning, and didn't want his black Citroën to be noticed close to the places he was going to visit. He hailed one of the rare Paris *taxis à gazogène*, wartime monstrosities whose engines were powered by wood, burned in boilers soldered to their trunks. "Rue Mouffetard," he said to the driver, heading for the first of five addresses he was going to visit on this dreary April morning—those of the best document forgers in Paris.

His first visit, to a decrepit apartment house in the famous Paris market street behind the massive dome-roofed Pantheon, didn't yield any results. Nor did his second, to a discreet back shop in the rue Saint-Paul, off the place de la Bastille. But the initial reaction of the third man he spoke to, in a shabby billiard room on the Grands Boulevards, was just ambiguous enough to make Bruno feel he was on the right path, after all.

"A beautiful girl? What do you mean by that?" said the thin, cadaverous man, without looking at him, and carefully aimed his cue at the white ivory ball lying impossibly close to the ledge. But Bruno noticed the split-second hesitation, and knew the cunning mind of his interlocutor well enough to understand that he was trying to gain time, and to find out what possible profit there might be for him.

"I mean what I said," snapped Bruno coldly. "Do you remember having forged any identity papers for some very beautiful girl? I need a quick answer, Rital—I have no time to waste."

Dédé le Rital—"the Italian"—closed a pale, watery eye, licked his discolored lips with his sharp tongue and drove his cue forward. The ivory ball darted on the green carpet just a few inches before Bruno quickly stretched out his hand over it. "Play no games with me, Rital," Bruno said.

The Italian slowly straightened up. "I don't remember," he said candidly, but his sly eyes closely watched Bruno's face. "With all the business I handle, how do you want me to remember a pretty face?"

Bruno suddenly grabbed the Italian's stained necktie and pulled it viciously. Dédé choked and his face grew purple. He didn't try to pry loose, though, just gasped for air. Bruno slowly loosened his grip and let the Italian go. His strained voice showed he was dangerously close to losing his temper. "Listen to me, you bastard. I know you've been making a lot of money lately. Before the war only the scum would come to you for papers, and most of them regretted it. But now, with all those Jews and Communists and Gaullists and anti-Nazis running for their lives, nobody cares for your reputation and they are only too happy to pay you five times the usual price for a piece of paper with a different name on it. But I know you. I know how you would have spoken if you didn't have what I'm seeking." Bruno looked around quickly and, satisfied that the billiard room was completely deserted, drew out his gun with his right hand, while his left hand came out of his pocket holding a thick wad of banknotes. "You can choose between the two. I shall not hesitate to blow your brains out, tonight or any other night, and check the records you hide in your sister's house." A glint of surprise flashed in the Italian's pale eyes. "Or you can just cooperate," Bruno went on, throwing the money on the billiard table, "and go on sucking other people's blood."

The Italian stared speculatively at Bruno, then he nodded: "I remember now. I have exactly what you want. A beauty!" His pale lips curled in a concupiscent smile. "She came to me about a year ago. I have met quite a number of pretty girls in my life, but this one was really something special. Let's go, I'll show you her picture."

Bruno calmly pocketed his gun. The Italian grabbed the money from the table and hurried after him.

Half an hour later, Bruno came out of a filthy doorway in the busy rue du Faubourg Montmartre. He carefully folded a piece of paper and put it in his breast pocket. The paper carried a name and an address.

The girl turned the corner and hurried along the paved sidewalk of the rue Surcouf, in the aristocratic Seventh Arrondissement of Paris. The narrow street was dark, and the clatter of her wooden soles on the pavement was the only sound that echoed in its emptiness, although it was early in the evening. Moving fast, and nervously glancing behind her, the girl reached a large porch, buzzed the heavy wooden door and let herself in. From their observation post in the front seat of Bruno's Citroën that was parked on the opposite side of the street, the big man and the Baron watched her disappear into the building. They sat immobile for five more minutes, then the Baron glanced at his watch and said: "Let's go, now."

They surreptitiously entered the building and climbed the

staircase to the second floor. Bruno looked at the Baron, who nodded, and knocked sharply. A small, gray-haired woman wearing a black woolen shawl, opened the door. "Messieurs?" she said in a clear, confident voice, but a frightened look crept into her eyes, and her hand, clutching the doorknob, trembled slightly.

Bruno nodded; his voice had the flat ring of authority characteristic of cops all over the world. "Madame Lemaire? We would like to have a word with your niece."

The old woman grew pale and her voice wavered. "She . . . she is not in," she mumbled. "I don't know when she'll be back." She started to close the door, but Bruno's right foot caught it before it clicked shut. "She is there all right, and she'll see us now." Without waiting for an answer, the two men entered the small vestibule.

The old woman swayed and her left hand instinctively clutched her throat. "Are you from the police?" she asked, terror-stricken.

Bruno ignored the question and walked past the woman into the dining room. The table was laid for two. The Baron observed the impeccable white tablecloth and napkins, the Sèvres china and the silver cutlery. At that moment a door opened on the other side of the room, and the girl appeared on the doorstep. She seemed petrified.

The Baron almost gasped with admiration. She possessed a sensual, pulsating, almost savage beauty that stirred in him a pang of raw physical pain and made his whole body tighten in involuntary response. For a short moment he looked, fascinated, at that perfect body, at her round shoulders, her proud, full breasts, her thin waist and shapely legs. She had long, raven-black hair, an oval face, full red lips and two big blue eyes that were looking at them in unspoken fear.

"You don't have to be afraid," the Baron said quickly, hardly recognizing his hoarse voice. "We are not the Gestapo. We are on the other side. We want to talk to you." He looked back at the old woman, immobile in the doorway, and added "alone."

"Come in," she said in a low voice that could be very musical but now was choked with terror and emotion. She moved back and the two men followed her into her room. Bruno closed the door. The room was small, and quite austere for a young girl: a single bed, a cupboard, a small dressing table with an old, cracked mirror. The only discordant mark of affluence were the leather-bound books lying in a heap on the night table. Belvoir picked up one of them. It was a rare edition of the poems of François Villon.

He turned to the girl, and only now noticed the simplicity of her blue woolen dress. He noted mentally the difference between her room and the dining room. "We know exactly who you are," he said coldly. "Your papers are in the name of Michèle Lemaire, but that is not your true name. Your family name is Levine, and you are hiding here because you are Jewish and you're afraid that the Gestapo will get you."

The girl didn't move. Bruno noticed her nails digging into the palms of her hands. She bit her lower lip, trying to fight back the tears that flooded her eyes, and suddenly burst into a low, wailing sob. "I am sorry," the Baron said quickly. He looked at the desperate girl, bitterly crying and said again, foolishly: "I am sorry." Bruno threw him a surprised look.

The Baron drew a long breath. "Please listen to me," he said. "Can you listen?"

She nodded, but the tears continued to course down her cheeks.

"I am sorry, but we have no choice," the Baron went on and his voice became firm and cold again. "We need you. We need your help. You'll have to do exactly what we tell you, if you don't want us to inform the Gestapo about you. Do you understand? It's your cooperation—or your death in the Gestapo cellars."

He told the shocked girl what he wanted from her. Michèle's eyes widened with horror. For a long moment she looked at him, speechless. Finally, she managed to speak. "You are sending me to my death," she said in a small, desperate voice.

"Nonsense," the Baron lied. "Nothing will happen to you. Tomorrow or the day after, we shall see you again, and give you more detailed instructions."

He turned back and walked out of the room and the apartment. Bruno stopped for a moment in the vestibule. The old woman hadn't changed her position. "And don't try to escape or to hide your niece, Madame Lemaire," he said viciously, "if you care for her life. There's no place in France where I wouldn't find her."

Out on the landing, when the door closed behind their backs, the Baron suddenly burst into a string of curses. Trembling with anger, he struck the wall with his clenched fist.

Bruno looked at him again in amazement, but didn't say a word.

They drove in silence all the way to the Marne Valley.

Michèle didn't sleep that night.

For hours she sat immobile by her window, occasionally shivering in her thin nightgown, staring lifelessly into the black moonless night that had quietly settled over Paris. She remembered vaguely a biblical story her grandfather had told her once, about the daughter of Jephthah, an ancient Hebrew hero, who had been destined to be sacrificed to Jehovah. She felt like that helpless maiden whose father had told her she was going to die. Jephthah's daughter had asked to be spared for two months so she could bewail her fate with her friends. But Michèle had no friends, her time was much shorter, and her eyes had dried. She couldn't escape the cruel fate that had struck her people and her family: first her grandparents in Vienna, then her mother and younger brother, after them her father. And now it was her turn.

Her past seemed to her now as something pertaining to somebody else, in another age, in a faraway country. Everything seemed so unreal: her happy childhood; the big white house in the exclusive suburb of Neuilly; her parents, the beautiful Vienna-born opera singer Nelly Levine, and the world-renowned professor of medicine in the Université de Paris. She had studied in the best schools and colleges in Paris and Geneva; at the age of sixteen her teachers already predicted a brilliant acting career for her, because of her beauty and her talent for drama. During the last summer before the war, when she was spending a vacation in Antibes, on the Riviera, she had accepted, just for laughs, an invitation to take part in a beauty contest. The next morning, her pictures were all over the papers, which announced the election of "stunning Michèle Levine" as *Miss Côte d'Azur*. And then came the receptions, the parties, the offers of acting parts in the movies and the theater. It was a glorious summer. The world was beckoning, she was beautiful, clever, she had a future and she was madly in love with one of the most brilliant graduates of the Polytechnique, and the only son of one of the oldest aristocratic families in France, the handsome Dominique de Boissy. They shared the same passions for horses, travel, theater, literature; they were so startlingly handsome, she with her dark smooth skin, her bright eyes and long black hair, he with the blond head of a Roman god, his muscular body and his enthralling smile. They had been born for each other and no force on earth could come between them. Michèle remembered that evening when her mother came from Paris to talk to her. Lively Nelly Levine, always so easygoing and cheerful, had been deeply embarrassed and ill at ease that night, stammering, groping for words, unable to communicate with her daughter. She had come to warn her, she said, to ask her to think twice before she got more deeply involved with Dominique. "Don't go too far in your relations with him," she had said quite miserably.

"But Mother," Michèle had flared, "we are going to get married."

"Are you sure?" Nelly Levine had asked with a curious, sad smile. "His family is very conservative, very strict, you know. They are devout Catholics. We are Jewish. They might not accept you."

"Who cares?" Michèle had countered with youthful candor and confidence. "We love each other and that's all that counts!"

And they had loved each other, totally. Dominique was the first man she ever slept with. And even now, five years later, she shuddered under the flow of memories, so vivid, so present in her mind and body. She could almost feel again the touch of his lips, the warmth of his skin, his tender caresses, his fierce passion.

They had returned to Paris together. And on the next day the war had started, cruelly smashing her life and her dreams. First, like the faraway rolling thunder heralding the storm, news had come from Vienna that her aging grandparents had been deported to a concentration camp. They never heard of them again. Then the Germans marched into Paris, and quickly, painfully, she learned what being Jewish meant. Their telephone was disconnected, as the Jews had no more right to possess one. In the middle of the night, a group of policemen brutally broke into their house and took away her parents' valuable collection of Picasso and Matisse paintings. Her father lost his job in the University; Nelly Levine was banned from the Grand Opéra. One April afternoon, Michèle came home to find her mother, crying, sewing on her clothes big yellow patches in the form of a star and stamped with the word *"Juif."* For Michèle, who had never been self-conscious about her race and religion, the shock of being officially defined a leper and a pariah was terrible. But the worst was yet to come. She remembered the morning when she went to see her fiancé, and the majordomo of his parents' house in Auteuil, the always-smiling, affable Honoré had looked at her yellow star and had coldly informed her that "Monsieur had no longer any wish to associate with persons belonging to the Jewish race." She was furious and revolted. She didn't believe, not for a second, that her Dominique had anything to do with the servant's outrageous behavior. She had waited for him in the street, and there, under the blossoming trees of an enchanting Paris spring he had told her bluntly that he had accepted his parents' advice and didn't wish to see her anymore. She never remembered how she walked all the way home, went up to her mother's bathroom and found her vial of sleeping pills. She just recalled emerging from a thick, stifling mist, and becoming violently sick. Her mother told her later that she had been unconscious for a couple of days; if not for her father's frantic efforts, she would never have awakened.

She bitterly reflected now that death at that moment, when her suffering had resulted merely from a broken heart, would have been the best solution for her. For the real horror struck only later. In the summer, when she had gone with her father to buy some food from the farms of Normandy, the Germans rounded up the Jews of Paris. When they came back, her mother and brother were gone forever—first to the dreary concentration camp of Drancy, later to the death camps in Germany. Their house had been seized and their furniture shipped to Berlin. They hid for a few weeks in the apartments of non-Jewish friends. One morning, at the beginning of September 1942, her father had awakened her, excited, to tell her that he had discovered the means for them to escape to South America. A Paris physician, Doctor Petiot, who had his clinic in the rue Le Sueur, could arrange their trip. It would cost a fortune, her father had added, all the money and valuables they had managed to save, but they would be lucky to escape from this living hell. Professor Levine had been eager and enthusiastic that morning. He had managed a smile for the first time since the deportation of his wife and son. Michèle always remembered his shining eyes, his light kiss, his quick stride when he went to Doctor Petiot's clinic, carrying all his money and jewelry in a small cloth bag.

He never came back. After a few days, worried friends started to inquire about his disappearance. She told them about Doctor Petiot. One of them called at the physician's clinic, but Petiot's answers were evasive and bizarre. He had never met a Professor Levine, he said, and had never arranged any trip to South America. Puzzled, as a last resort her father's friend had called a police officer whom he knew well. The same night, a detachment of the Paris Police raided the clinic. What they found was beyond the limits of horror. Pieces of corpses—heads, limbs and decapitated trunks—were discovered in the cellar. Charred bones, ashes of cremated human flesh and parched bits of skin were found in the big furnace that served to heat the whole building. A sickening stench hung over the place. The horrified policemen discovered the diabolical business Doctor Petiot had been running in his clinic on the rue Le Sueur. Together with his accomplices, a barber and a beautician, he used to strangle the wretched victims who came to his office with all their possessions, believing they were about to set out on a trip to South America. The devilish trio then cut the corpses to pieces and fed them to the furnace.

In an adjoining room Doctor Petiot had stored the victims' belongings, neatly sorted. The police found 13 pairs of trousers, 110 shirts, 120 skirts and 28 suits. One of those suits had been worn by Professor Levine on the day of his disappearance.

For a few moments after her father's friend had told her the gruesome truth, Michèle stood completely still, her eyes wide with horror. Then she let out a wild, inhuman scream and ran away. Somebody tried to stop her, but she struggled and kicked and bit savagely until she shook him off and escaped.

For weeks she wandered the streets of Paris, half mad, sleeping in doorways, fed like a stray dog by merciful strangers. One cold night, a woman tripped over her as she lay half conscious, shivering in her rags, in a back alley off the rue de la Huchette. She wouldn't have recognized her, were it not for her burning, deep-blue eyes. "Michèle!" she gasped, horrified as if she had seen a ghost. The woman was Louise Lemaire, the widow of a former colleague of Michèle's father in the Paris Faculty of Medicine. She took her home and cared for her like a baby. Very slowly, very painfully, her mind started to clear and she came back to life. After six months in Madame Lemaire's apartment, Michèle was able to walk and talk again. Madame Lemaire's only son, Jacques, a student in the Sorbonne, was involved with the Paris Resistance. He sent Michèle to Dédé le Rital, who provided her with false papers in the name of Michèle Le-

maire. Madame Lemaire introduced her as her niece from
Lyon, who had come to live with her in Paris. With
Michèle's return to normalcy, she also regained some of her
old pride. She stubbornly refused to move into one of the
nicely furnished rooms in the apartment in the rue Surcouf,
and insisted on living in the tiny maid's room. She was rapidly recovering when another disaster struck her benefactors:
Young Jacques Lemaire was killed by the SS at a roadblock,
while driving a carload of arms for the Resistance. Louise
Lemaire accepted his death stoically. She embraced Michèle
and said quietly: "You are all I have left in this world."

Now, while she was sitting by her window and watching
morning slowly dawn over Paris, Michèle heard the soft steps
of Louise, restlessly pacing in the big dining room. She
couldn't bear the strain any longer. She opened the door.
"Louise," she called. The small woman, her face drawn with
fear and worry, stepped in. "I must talk to you," Michèle
said. She told her in a sobbing desperate voice about the
blackmail threat of the two strangers.

But instead of pitying her for her plight, Louise Lemaire
had an astonishing reaction. She put both her hands on
Michèle's shoulders and looked closely, unwaveringly at her
face. "You have lost all your family by the hands of the Na-
zis," she murmured. "I have lost my only son. Maybe it's
time for us to learn to hit back. I don't know what those two
men want, and who they are. But I understand that they are
fighting the Germans, in their own way. And you should do
what they tell you, Michèle. For two women like us, the only
thing left in this cursed life might well be the sweet taste of
revenge."

Michèle closed her eyes, and the tears streamed down her
tormented, lovely face.

The phone call that Rudolf von Beck received at his apartment the next evening after 11:00 P.M. was most unusual. A
certain Colonel Stahl, who introduced himself as Deputy
Chief of Staff of O.B. West, the Germany Army Western
Command, summoned him immediately to the Duchesse
restaurant, on the Quai des Grands Augustins. He specified
that he was speaking on behalf of the Supreme Commander,
General Karl Heinrich von Stülpnagel. Von Beck was
puzzled. He couldn't think of any plausible reason that could
explain such a call at such an odd hour. He had never met
the general before, and wondered why he had chosen an ex-

clusive gourmet restaurant on the Left Bank for their first meeting. He didn't question Colonel Stahl, though. General von Stülpnagel was the highest-ranking German officer in France, and his summons had to be obeyed.

Driving his Horch himself—Schneider was off that evening—von Beck sped up the avenue Foch, around the dark Arc de Triomphe and down the Champs Elysées. He crossed the Seine by the pont de la Concorde, and reached the 200-year-old corner building which housed the world-famous restaurant. The sidewalk was deserted. Von Beck had drawn to a halt, wondering where Stülpnagel's car was, when two officers suddenly materialized beside his own vehicle. "Oberst von Beck?" A lean officer with a grave expression on his aquiline features bent over to the car's window. "I am Stahl. Will you come with me, please? Steiner, here, will take care of your car."

Von Beck followed him through a discreet side door and up a thickly carpeted narrow staircase. At the top of the stairs stood another officer, a captain. Von Beck gasped at the sight of the captain's face: the right side was fair-skinned and smooth, the left terribly charred and disfigured by a dreadful black scar. A bright eye, miraculously intact, shone with intense vitality, like a blue fire, in the midst of the dead tissue. Von Beck's sharp eyes didn't miss the small insignia of Rommel's desert rats and the oak leaves on the captain's Iron Cross, which explained quite eloquently the nature of the repulsive scar. He had seen quite a few of those in the Lybian Desert. The captain must have been half burned to death in the turret of his tank.

Von Beck sighed and followed the officer down a softly lit corridor. At the fifth door on their left the captain knocked, turned the handle and announced quietly: "Oberst von Beck."

Sitting at the head of a cleared dinner table, his back turned to the large window overlooking the silvery waters of the Seine, General von Stülpnagel looked up and nodded slightly. Von Beck clicked his heels and was about to report, when he suddenly realized that they weren't alone. On the plush-covered sofa on his right sat a man he knew well, his own former commander, Field Marshal Erwin Rommel. And next to the Field Marshall, a glass of cognac in his right hand, looking at him with an amused smile, stood Admiral Wilhelm Canaris.

"You see, my dear Rudy," he said casually, as if pursuing

a friendly chat started hours ago, "the unique advantage of 'La Duchesse' is not in its exquisite dishes, as you might think, but in those private dining rooms on the first floor. They call them 'the love chambers.' This was a very discreet place for a wealthy French bourgeois to take a young lady to lunch or dinner and seduce her after the dessert on that convenient sofa. It is also a most suitable place for three people like us"—he gestured at Stülpnagel and Rommel—"to meet quietly and discuss our private matters without any interference." He turned to his fellow officers. "We can talk freely. Rudy is one of us."

He poured a generous portion of Courvoisier into a bell-shaped cognac glass and handed it to Von Beck. "I took the liberty to ask my good friend Stülpnagel to summon you here, for the sake of discretion, as you can certainly understand. I don't want the whole of the Paris garrison to know that I am here."

"Well," Stülpnagel said briskly and got up, "now that your young friend is here, we'll leave you to your business."

Rommel looked at his watch. "That's right. And I should be back on the Channel coast by dawn. Good night, Canaris." He patted von Beck's shoulder, but his alert gray eyes watched him intently.

"Everything is agreed, then," Canaris said. Stülpnagel nodded and followed Rommel out of the room. Canaris moved to the window, and for a long moment watched the river and the dark shape of the Louvre on the opposite bank. "This was an important meeting, Rudy," he said. "It holds great hopes and great dangers for Germany. Are you with me?"

"Yes, sir," von Beck replied. "I remember our talk in the Tiergarten."

Canaris nodded. "We might soon have to use our private Enigma machine." He paused. "And that's what I wanted to talk to you about." His voice suddenly became colder and demanding. "What is going on, Rudy? You are here more than a month already. No results."

The palms of von Beck's hands became damp with sweat. He tried to sound assured and confident. "We know that the agent is here, Herr Admiral. We know his name and we expect him to hit soon. We are quite ready for him."

"I got a curious report from London yesterday." Canaris turned, to better observe von Beck's reaction. "It says that the

S.O.E. has ordered Belvoir back, and that his operation has been called off. What do you think?"

Von Beck frowned. "I don't believe it," he said slowly. "I think he is going through with his plans. He is making his preparations right now."

"What makes you so sure?" Canaris's voice was sharp and he watched von Beck intently.

"I have read his file," von Beck replied. "I have learned his methods. He studies the habits and the behavior of his rivals thoroughly before striking. Right now, he is studying me."

"How do you know?" Canaris asked skeptically.

"Lately I am being watched. Quite a few secretaries and telephone operators in the Otto building are being approached, very casually, by different people, and subtly questioned about me. As a matter of fact, at this very moment a fat Paris whore is interrogating my orderly. I don't doubt that she reports to Belvoir. He is going to strike all right."

Canaris's face became grave. "And knowing his methods, having studied his field, you think you know how he's going to proceed."

Rudolf von Beck nodded. "Yes, sir. I know how."

Canaris shrugged, then said in an old, weary voice, "Beware, Rudy. In this game of wits that is ours, you can never know who will outwit whom."

He locked eyes with von Beck to make sure that his words had made their impact, then quickly walked out of the room.

The love chamber at "La Duchesse" was not the only love nest to be used that night for a secret meeting. In "Le Rendezvous des Amoureux," the secluded villa in the Marne Valley, the Baron was conferring with the leaders of the Communist Resistance and doing his very best to make them his allies.

It was not an easy task, and from the start he was compelled to take unprecedented risks. He had asked that the meeting be held either in a Communist safehouse or on neutral ground. The Communists had flatly refused, and agreed to meet him only in his hiding place. He understood their motives perfectly. By discovering his hideout they wanted to gain an advantage over him, and to obtain a lever for forcing him into concessions. He had no other choice but to agree. Which meant that on the next morning he had to move to a new hideout and use the villa only for further meetings with the Communists.

They arrived at the house in three different cars, each using an independent itinerary. The three drivers, strong silent men, inspected the villa with drawn guns in their hands. When they were satisfied that the house was clean they took positions around it, and their leaders alighted from the cars and came in.

There were five—four men and one woman—all of them cold, taut, aloof and overtly hostile. They introduced themselves by perfunctory handshakes and Christian names which they used as noms de guerre. The first to enter was "Yvette"—a tall, thin, slightly stooped woman with an ascetic face and sparse salt-and-pepper hair drawn back in a tight bun. She wore an austere black dress and a gray knitted shawl. She seemed weak and vulnerable but her firm handshake and her cold, hard stare betrayed the tough, powerful character that lurked behind her deceptively frail looks. She was followed by a short, chubby, red-faced man dressed in blue work overalls, a sweater and a black beret. His dark eyes, set in a puffy, rubicund face, were surrounded by a web of laughter wrinkles and he introduced himself as "Maurice" with the colorful accent of Marseille. He was about forty-five, and looked like a typical Provençal whom one would expect to see nursing his *pastis* and playing *pétanque* by the seashore. For a moment Belvoir wondered what such an easy-going, genial Southerner could be doing at the head of the most powerful and most disciplined underground organization in France.

He didn't wonder, though, about the two young men who followed Maurice into the villa. Both were in their early twenties. The first of them, "Henri," was tall and muscular, his open-necked blue shirt and nondescript cheap jacket enhancing his large, powerful frame. His brown eyes were sharp and intelligent, and his wide mouth had a stern expression. He had a deep voice, very used to authority. The other young man, "Raymond," was hatchet-faced, slim, with sallow skin and a firmly set mouth. He was well dressed in a brown suit of good quality, a clean white shirt and a beige tie, but there was something vaguely disconcerting about him. At a second look, Belvoir concluded that this impression emanated from his eyes—deep-set, narrow-spaced, with the look of a fanatic. Or a killer.

The last to enter was an abnormally thin man of average height, whose pallid waxen face was covered with liver spots. He was undoubtedly a sick man, and even though it was late April he wore a thick coat and a woolen scarf. But the tight-lipped mouth, the aggressive chin, the large, penetrating eyes behind the rimless spectacles, were those of a leader. "My name is Jacques," he said quietly.

The five Communists sat woodenly around the heavy oak table in the living room. All of them refused the drinks Bruno offered them. "We came to listen, not to celebrate," said the woman, Yvette. Belvoir nodded and stood up. "I asked to meet you," he said quietly, "because you and your organization are the only ones in France who can carry out a crucial operation on which the outcome of the war might depend."

Ignoring the ironical smiles by which his opening statement was received, Belvoir went on. He spoke for a long time. He told the whole story of his mission, from its start. He emphasized strongly the importance of the Allied invasion of France. He knew well how desperately Russia needed the opening of a second front in Europe, and assumed that this argument might influence the Communists. He explained the importance of the Enigma machine in the communications system of the German army, then circulated the charts of the Enigma among his five guests. Finally he told his audience what he wanted them to do: to join him in the raid on one of the German military installations in France, in order to get the Enigma machine and ship it to England. There was only one piece of information which he didn't disclose: Bruno Morel's discovery of the twenty-eighth Enigma.

After he finished his long explanation, the Communists started asking questions. The main speakers were Henri and Raymond, the young leader. But the perceptive Baron immediately realized that the real decision-makers were the two people who preferred to keep silent—Yvette and Jacques, the sick man. After a few questions asked by the fat Marseillais, Maurice, the Baron understood the reason for his presence. Behind his placid and indolent appearance lay the scheming, brilliant mind of a top-notch operations officer.

Finally, the man called Jacques spoke. He took off his glasses and carefully wiped them. "May we be left alone for a while? We'd like to ponder your proposal and consult among ourselves."

The Baron and Bruno left the room. The meeting was surprisingly short. About ten minutes later, Jacques came out of the house and walked painfully toward the two men, who were smoking in the driveway. "We shall take part in the operation," he announced evenly. "Not because we trust you. We don't. We are very reluctant to associate with people of your kind. But this is war, and we can't be choosy." He added bluntly: "I hope we aren't making a mistake."

The Baron ignored the implied insult. "I am pleased to hear your decision, Jacques."

"One last point," Jacques added. "How are we going to choose which of the twenty-seven German command posts we are going to attack, in order to get the machine?"

"Leave that to me," Belvoir said. "I have a plan for infiltrating the German command in Paris. Give me a few weeks, and I hope to pinpoint the objective which will be the easiest for us to take."

"How do you intend to do that?" Jacques asked coldly.

Belvoir told him.

The Communist leader nodded. "Very well. It sounds like a good plan. But let me warn you: Don't try to double-cross us. Don't try to betray us. We have people everywhere. We'll get rid of you at the first wrong step you make."

The Baron nodded calmly. "I know. I also know that you wouldn't have come to this meeting without making some preliminary inquiries about me, and you wouldn't have agreed to go along, if you didn't believe that I told you the truth. I promise you that we shall continue to the end in the same spirit."

Without another word spoken, Jacques shook the Baron's and Bruno's hands and walked to his car. His four comrades followed him, taking leave of their hosts with cold, formal handshakes. Their bodyguards were already in the drivers' seats and the cars' engines were softly purring. In less than a minute, the courtyard was deserted.

The moment they were alone, Bruno exploded. "My God, this time you went too far!"

The Baron looked at him, faintly amused. "What do you mean?"

"Damn it, don't you see what they intend to do? They'll use you to obtain the information about the machine, then they'll get hold of it by themselves and they'll pass it to the Russians."

The Baron nodded. "You're right," he said. "That's exactly what they intend to do."

Bruno almost choked in anger and indignation. "But you are delivering the Enigma into their hands."

Belvoir smiled.

"Don't worry. They'll never see the damn thing, *mon cher* Bruno."

May 4–May 15, 1944

THE LIGHTS SPARKLING IN THE PRICELESS CRYSTAL CHANDE-
liers slowly died, leaving in the dark the colorful Second Empire fresco that covered the ceiling of the Grand Opéra de
Paris. The chatter in the neo-Baroque theater faded away as
the concealed spotlights cast half a circle of yellowish illumination on the dark-red folds of the heavy velvet curtain and
the orchestra struck the bold and proud concords of the over-
ture to *Carmen*. Rudolf von Beck closed his eyes and leaned
back in his gilt-framed armchair, savoring to the full the vig-
orous music of Georges Bizet and quickly sinking into a feeling of sheer elation. He was a passionate music lover. For
nothing in the world would he miss a concert while he was in
Berlin; and even the Enigma assignment could not prevent
him from regularly attending the performances of the *Orchestre symphonique de Paris*, in the salle Gaveou. But his real
passion was the opera, which triggered a deep emotional response in the romantic chords that vibrated in his soul. The
commander of Gross Paris, Generalleutnant Horst Wulff, with
whom he had struck up a growing friendship, had enthusiastically offered him his reserved box in the Opéra. Every Monday and Friday, punctual as a Swiss clock, von Beck would
climb the Royal staircase of the magnificent theater, imbibe
the sumptuous decor designed nearly one hundred years ago
by the great Charles Garnier, and then totally relax as the
magic of the music washed over him. Sitting in the semi-
darkness of his box, mostly resting his cheeks on his open
palms while his elbows dug into the soft padded parapet overlooking the huge scene, he would plunge into the dramatic
stories of the love and death of flamboyant characters in picturesque costumes.

His pleasure tonight was interrupted by the opening of a

door, the rustling of clothes and a low murmur in the box on his left. He threw a quick, annoyed glance over his shoulder with the intention of hushing the latecomers, but he was struck speechless. On the other side of the partition, the darkness adding to her appearance a touch of unreality, stood the most beautiful woman he had ever seen.

The name of Carmen instinctively flashed through his mind. That's the way he visualized the heroine of the savage drama on which the curtain was rising. That lithe body, the heavy black hair, the dark smooth skin, the sensual mouth were those of a stunning, bewitching woman who could easily provoke the outburst of jealousy and raw passions depicted in Bizet's opera. Suddenly, the imaginary story on the stage became very real, very much alive in his eyes. Yes, if the young gypsy girl of the play had that mesmerizing appeal, he could understand why her rejected lover became an insane killer— and killed her, in despair.

She looked at him. He smiled awkwardly at the bright blue eyes, and felt a fierce surge of desire for that mysterious, beguiling woman.

At that very moment, at the other end of Paris, Francis de Belvoir was staring at the barrel of a Schmeisser submachine gun, steadily pointed at his chest. The deadly weapon was in the hands of a tall young man in black SS uniform who was guarding the entrance of the main building in the Otto compound. Standing beside him, an SS sergeant flipped open the special Otto pass that Belvoir handed him and attentively compared the photograph fastened on the document with the face of the man in front of him. "What is your name?" the sergeant asked in French, with a strong German accent.

"Étienne Duclos."

"Étienne Duclos . . . *Ja.*" The sergeant was satisfied with his check. The document was authentic and the photograph was good. It represented accurately the features of the Frenchman: the low forehead, the wire-rimmed glasses, the drooping black moustache and even the rather dumb expression on his face.

"You are new here?" The sergeant asked his last routine question.

The Baron nodded and calmly pocketed the pass that the German returned to him. The document had been issued that very morning by the Otto personnel department, after Bruno Morel had vouched for him. The photograph had been taken in the back of Kakoyanis's shop in London, and sent to Paris with the same disguise—spectacles and false moustache—that Belvoir was wearing now. Even for a photograph he couldn't rely on a Parisian forger or photographer. He knew from previous experience that the local forgers cracked quickly when questioned by the Gestapo.

He lit a cigarette and walked unhurriedly into the large hall of the building at 23, square du Bois de Boulogne. It was a massive, unimaginative edifice six stories high, with an off-white facade and rows of rectangular windows. In spite of the late hour the headquarters of the Otto organization were swarming with people. Three big trucks were parked outside, and about twenty Germans and Frenchmen in civilian clothes were carrying today's haul—heavy crates, statues and paintings—through the lobby and down to the cellar. The Otto people had raided two small museums in the suburbs of Paris. After robbing the property of Jews and anti-Nazis all over France, the Otto organization had started to seize the art treasures in the national museums, despite the protests of the Vichy authorities. The loot was sorted and packed in the cellar at the headquarters and dispatched daily to the Gare du Nord, where the huge warehouses and railroad facilities of the *Compagnie des Chemins de Fer du Nord* had been requisitioned for the exclusive use of the Otto organization. In other centers scattered throughout Paris the Otto people stored antique furniture, china, furs, silver cutlery, and even wines, drugs, perfumes and jewelry. Special trains were regularly leaving the Gare du Nord, carrying the goods to Berlin. Often, Air Marshal Göring was waiting in person for the trains at the Berlin central station, to inspect the works of art, which he considered his own treasure and kept in several requisitioned castles in the Third Reich.

Belvoir contemplated in silence the Frenchmen carrying the immortal masterpieces to the storage room. He knew a few of them—thugs, thieves and petty criminals. Otto Brandl himself—the man after whom the organization was named—very rarely came to the compound and preferred to manage the huge enterprise from his offices at the former Paris residence of Prince George of Greece, at rue Adolphe-Yvon. Belvoir had met Otto only once. An old Abwehr fox, Otto was a man in his late forties, very elegant, refined, with abundant silver hair and a double chin. He was a frequent guest in the best cabarets of Paris and a connoisseur of art, good food and rare wines. A ladies' man, very polite and very discreet, he would, however, metamorphose into a violent, cruel brute when his authority was questioned. Then his real character would emerge: that of a tremendously powerful, vicious man, driven by a consuming ambition. This violent streak in him was widely known, though very seldom revealed. The ruffians who worked for him admired his gift for management and business, but mostly feared his violence.

Bruno Morel approached and stood close to the Baron.

"I see that nothing has changed," Belvoir said. "Otto is as prosperous as ever."

"What do you know," Morel said dryly. "Would you believe that more than five hundred people work for Otto today? And that two thirds of them are French?" He fell silent for a moment, then murmured: "Come. Now that the lobby is crowded, we can go up unnoticed. I'll tell you the rest later."

The large staircase was deserted, as were the Otto offices on the first floor. Bruno pushed the Baron into one of them and briefed him rapidly. "It's nine o'clock now. There is nobody left in the Otto offices. At night they work only on the ground floor and in the cellar."

"And what about the Abwehr?" Belvoir asked impatiently.

"I'm coming to that. As a general rule, they are not there at this hour. Except in the communications room, where they work in shifts, around the clock. And the Enigma is there."

Belvoir looked at him skeptically. "Or what you believe is the Enigma."

"That's what we are going to check now, aren't we?" Bruno said, mildly irritated.

"How? You say there are always people inside?"

"There are, yes. But there is a way to look inside the room without being seen. The communications room has two doors. One opens onto the corridor. We can't even get near it. The second one connects the room with von Beck's office. We are going to sneak into von Beck's outer office, cross to his own room, open the connecting door and peep inside the communications room. The technicians won't see us—they are facing the opposite wall. A few of them wear earphones, and the clatter of the instruments inside is such that they won't hear us opening the door. We need just a few seconds, right?"

"How are we going to get into von Beck's office?"

Bruno produced two flat keys out of his pocket. "Duplicates of the cleaning woman's. I made them myself. One opens the outer office; the second, the communicating door into von Beck's room."

"What about guards? Is there no guard at the Abwehr section?"

"There is," Bruno said. "He leaves his post only once during the night. That's why I brought you here now. At nine-fifteen, regularly, he goes down and over to the Brasserie Dauphine, around the corner, to have a beer and a sandwich. It's not allowed, but he does it anyway. He is absent for about ten minutes. That's all the time we have to get in, look at your bloody machine and come back."

"Ten minutes is more than enough," the Baron observed.

"Fine. We'll wait here until we hear him going down, then we'll climb to the second floor."

They fell silent. A few minutes later they heard quick footsteps coming down the stairs and fading away. "Now," Bruno whispered urgently. They moved swiftly, quiet as shadows. The second-floor landing was deserted. They advanced stealthily into the dark corridor. The muffled rattle coming from the communications room echoed in the stillness of the empty corridor. With quick, precise movements Bruno inserted the key into the lock of the second door on their right and turned it. The door opened and they let themselves in, plunging into complete darkness. They waited a few seconds to get their eyes used to the darkness. With astonishing suppleness for a man of his heavy build, Bruno moved noiselessly to the second door and opened it. Now they were in von Beck's office. The Baron couldn't help looking around him. Here he was in the very command post of the man who had come from Berlin to hunt and destroy him. The pale moonlight filtering through the window shutters dimly outlined the contours of a modest desk, two telephones, a long conference table surrounded by simple wooden chairs. Belvoir could visualize the morning meetings of officers and civilians around that table, conceiving new ways and means to hunt and get him, to prevent him from accomplishing his mission, to bring him to his death. And looking at the empty armchair behind the desk, he felt now, more than ever, that his mission had turned into a duel, an old-fashioned deadly combat between him and that cunning German, who was relaxing at that very moment to the sounds and sights of *Carmen*.

Bruno dragged him impatiently by the sleeve, putting an

abrupt end to his brooding. "Come over here," he hissed. "The quicker the better."

The connecting door to the communications room stood out as a dark rectangle on the white wall on the other side of the conference table. It was heavily padded with some spongy insulating material, covered with soft leather. There was no lock on that door. Belvoir whispered to Bruno: "There must be another door behind that one." He grasped the handle and slowly, smoothly, pressed it down and pulled it back, opening a crack of about a quarter of an inch. The clatter of the wireless devices could be heard very clearly now, but no light came from the other side of the door. The Baron was right. Von Beck's office was connected with the communications room by two doors, both of them padded, separated from each other by barely five inches. Belvoir opened the first door wide and clung to the second one, the last. He breathed deeply and very gently turned the handle.

Bright light and heavy sound burst through the hairline crack formed by the opening of the door. Belvoir steadily continued to pull the door, all his muscles tight, a film of sweat forming on his forehead. Any wrong move now could result in the failure of his mission and maybe in his own death.

With the corner of his eye he noticed the sharp angle of an object standing close to the door. He pulled the door another inch back and pressed his face against the narrow aperture. The view into the communications room was partly blocked by a big filing cabinet of light gray metal. He sighed in relief; the cabinet concealed most of the door and its handle from the eyes of the people in the room. It left a wide enough field of vision, though, for him to view the large room.

He saw three German soldiers, sitting at the opposite wall, their backs to him, bent over their instruments. He guessed that a fourth one was sitting farther to the right, concealed by the filing cabinet. The three soldiers he saw were all wearing earphones and were busy transcribing incoming messages or operating conventional Morse transmitters with their right hands. Farther to the left, a few Telex machines were ticking messages on unwinding rolls of yellow paper. That was not what he was looking for. Now he knew he had to see the fourth man.

"Well?" whispered Bruno's voice in his ear. Belvoir hushed him by impatiently waving his hand. Then he turned back. "Kneel down by the door, and hold it," he murmured urgently. Bruno didn't ask any questions. He crouched on the threshold, his powerful right arm immobilizing the open door. Belvoir gripped the door's upper edge and carefully heaved himself up until he stood on his friend's back. Now he could look into the right side of the room, beyond the cabinet. And he saw it.

Sitting by a single table, behind the Morse operators, was an older soldier, a lieutenant. His head was bald and he wore thick-lensed rimless spectacles. He was bent forward over his desk, like a scholar deeply immersed in his studies. In front of him stood a curious contraption, made of wood and metal. Connecting wires hung in loose loops from the lower part of the machine; a longer wire was plugged into an electric socket on the closest wall, on the right. Belvoir noticed the long, delicate fingers of the officer; they were gently dancing on the keyboard of the machine. An oblong sheet of paper covered with letters was slowly coming out of the device, while three indented disks were steadily revolving on its left side.

"I'll be damned," Belvoir gasped inwardly. "The twenty-eighth Enigma!"

When the last, tragic notes of *Carmen* died away and the red curtain slowly descended on the macabre finale of the opera, von Beck hurried out of his box and into the gallery. He had to see the girl who had moved him so deeply. During the performance he had behaved quite foolishly, staring at her over the thin partition of the box much more than watching the spectacle. She had pretended to ignore him, but he was sure that she had perceived his stubborn, burning gaze moving hungrily over her face and body. During the intermission he had vainly waited for her outside, but she stayed in the box with her chaperone, an old, rather haggard woman.

Pacing now in the gallery, he heard the enthusiastic applause of the public saluting the end of the performance. In quick succession the doors of the neighboring boxes opened and people moved slowly, contentedly, toward the exits. Finally, the two women came out of their box. Von Beck glanced nervously at the girl. Her classic white dress, cut from a soft, clinging fabric, enhanced the statuesque lines of her body. She was as beautiful under the bright light of the gallery chandeliers as she had been mysterious and enthralling in the semi-darkness of the theater. She walked quickly out with the old woman. He waited by the staircase. She had to pass close to him on her way down.

"Excusez-moi," she murmured softly, and he moved aside to let her pass. For a moment, the bright blue eyes met his. There was no message for him in that casual glance, and yet he could swear that it conveyed something utterly miserable and desperate, which left him perplexed. He didn't try to follow the girl down the crowded staircase. Only his eyes accompanied her slender figure until she disappeared by one of the side doors. He walked away slowly, lost in thought. He knew he would give anything to see the girl again.

During the weekend he tried to dismiss her from his mind. He was a grown man and a senior officer, he kept repeating to himself, past the age of the consuming romantic involvements befitting a light-headed adolescent. Nevertheless, he was in a state of intense emotion when he returned to his box at the Opéra on Monday, for the performance of *Madame Butterfly*. And the girl was there again.

This time, he openly smiled at her and bowed politely when she left her box. She was startled at first, but finally she smiled back timidly. The old woman beside her smiled too. The following Friday, the two women didn't turn up; but three days later the girl attended *La Bohème* alone.

The performance was painful torture for him. He watched the spectacle, but he didn't see and didn't hear anything. He knew he was going to make his move that night, and he feared the result. For he didn't believe in fairy tales and in coincidences. Three times in a row this strikingly beautiful girl, whom he had never seen before, had appeared in the box next to his, on the same nights as he. The box had been mostly unoccupied during the major part of the season; in those hard times very few Parisians could afford to rent an opera box. Who paid for the girl's box? The old lady? Or was she a kept woman? Never had she come accompanied by a man. Tonight she was alone. Wasn't it too obvious an invitation? Wasn't somebody serving her to him on a silver platter? For a short while he made up his mind not to address her at all, to stop coming to the Opera, and to bury her in the depths of his mind as a memory of somebody he could have loved. But the temptation burned inside him like a live flame. He decided finally that he would talk to her at the end of the opera. And when he walked down the stairs after her, he curiously hoped that she would reject him flatly.

But she didn't. It was raining outside, a heavy spring

shower, She stopped by the main doors, looking confused. He coughed discreetly. His heart was thumping like a sledgehammer in his chest. She looked at him, puzzled.

"Excuse me, *mademoiselle*," he said in French. "We happen to be neighbors twice a week." He tried to smile. "Our boxes are adjacent. I took the liberty to address you, because I guess that in this rain it will be quite difficult for you to get home. May I offer you a lift? My car is waiting outside."

She hesitated. He grinned boyishly. "Please say yes. The rain will spoil your hairdo and your beautiful dress. And I shall be most proud to escort such an attractive lady."

She smiled demurely. "Thank you." She had a low, melodious voice. "You are very kind."

The practical Schneider was waiting by the entrance with a big black umbrella. Von Beck gallantly escorted the girl to the waiting Horch and opened the door for her. "Where can I drop you?" he asked politely.

"Rue Surcouf," she said. She looked at him, and for a moment her eyes had the same hurt, sad look he had noticed the first time he saw her.

"Allow me to introduce myself," he said formally. "My name is Rudolf von Beck."

"I am Michèle," she said slowly. "Michèle Lemaire."

From behind the lace curtains of Louise Lemaire's apartment, the Baron watched her alight from von Beck's car and quickly cross the street. A few moments later he heard her footsteps on the staircase, and her key turned in the door's lock. She went through the hall and into the dining room. "Louise?" she called in a voice trembling with distress. And then she saw him.

"You" she hissed spitefully.

"I asked Madame Lemaire to go to bed earlier tonight," he said softly. "I wanted to see you alone."

She walked past him to her room and he followed her. "You wanted to make sure that your puppet has performed well." Her voice was a blend of pain and contained rage. "You should be proud of yourself. Everything went according to your plan. He approached me, took me home, and invited me to dinner. At this time tomorrow he will certainly be sleeping with me, lying naked on top of me, touching me all over. That is what you wish, isn't it?"

He didn't answer.

"Do you understand what you are forcing me to do?" she

cried bitterly. Sobs of hopelessness and despair shook her whole body. "You want me to sleep, like the cheapest whore, with a man I don't love. With a man I loathe, for he is a German officer, one of those who have murdered my whole family. And I must obey you, and excite him, make him caress me, and let him thrust into me and spurt his cursed seed into my body! Oh my God, I want to die!" She buried her face in her hands and cried bitterly.

A deathly pallor settled on the Baron's face. He sat on the bed beside her. "Let me talk to you," he said in an uncertain voice. "Let me tell you why I asked you to do it."

"You didn't ask me," she retorted, choking with tears. "You blackmailed me into doing it!"

Her face was desperate, and her eyes had a miserable look, like those of a beaten dog.

"I had no choice," he said hurriedly. He realized he was quickly losing ground. He felt real pain for this girl and was suddenly swept by an overwhelming sense of guilt. He didn't know how to talk to her, but he wanted to win her confidence, to convince her, to justify himself for what he was doing to her. Tonight, while waiting for Michèle to come back from the opera, he had spent an hour with Louise Lemaire. She told him the story of Michèle's misfortune, and described to him the grisly deaths of her beloved. The ghastly narrative had shaken him to the very depths of his soul. For the first time in his life he had come across a horrible human tragedy, and he didn't know how to deal with it. That girl was utterly different from the rogues and the prostitutes he so deftly maneuvered, either threatening them into submission or tempting them with money. She was a fine girl, broken by a devilish fate—and now he was breaking her again. For the first time ever, he couldn't remain aloof and detached, dispassionately scheming his moves, using people as pawns in his cunning game. At this moment, facing this unusual girl who was plunged into unfathomable desperation, he felt disgusted with himself. And all of a sudden it became clear to him that the only way to treat her was by being truthful.

"Do you know who I am?" he asked.

She looked at him in mild surprise. "No . . . somebody from the Resistance, I think."

He locked his eyes with hers. "I am a thief, a swindler and an impostor," he said slowly. "I am wanted by the Gestapo not because I am a freedom fighter, but because I stole their gold. I am now on an assignment for the British Intelligence—not for love of France, but for money. However, I have been betrayed. The Resistance wouldn't help me. I am using criminals and whores for my operation. I am paying them for that. I have no moral right to ask you for your help. I can't evoke your love for your country, your hatred for the Germans, your desire for revenge. But I have no choice. I can't use a whore for my operation. I need a girl of your class, of your beauty. You wouldn't do it for money, and you wouldn't do it for patriotism—not in association with me, anyway. So I had to use blackmail. You may not believe me, but I despise myself for it."

Her eyes were wide open with astonishment. "I can't believe it," she murmured.

He drew a deep breath. "That's the truth, though."

"You said you were a thief?" she asked curiously.

"Yes, and many other things." He changed the subject. "Now let me tell you about the operation."

She raised her hand. "Later." Her voice was unsteady, tinted with shyness. "I would like, I mean . . . tell me more about yourself."

It was his turn to frown in surprise. "Are you sure that is what you want to hear?"

She nodded.

He started way back, in his youth. At first he was tense, restless, fidgeting and searching for words, but slowly he calmed down, and his story flowed easily. He described his parents, his adolescence, the death of his father, his flight, his adventures, his coups. Never before had he exposed himself so fully, never had he dared to remove the protective shield of silence and secrecy that had become an integral part of his character. But that night, in the small, dark room of a forlorn Jewish girl, he spoke for hours, not concealing anything. His narrative was rarely interrupted by a question from Michèle. It was almost dawn when he finished. An awkward silence settled in the room, and he got up to leave. She sat on her bed, motionless and outwardly calm.

"For a moment, you took me far away from here," she murmured finally. "You made me forget that nightmare. It was like being hurled far away, to a different planet, to an imaginary world." Her voice was sad and dreamy. He looked at her, embarrassed.

"You must see him tonight, you know."

She didn't say a word.

On a sudden impulse, he reached over and caressed her face with the tips of his fingers. "It will soon be over," he said soothingly. "Everything will be all right. Please, believe me." Spontaneously, she pressed his hand to her face, and he felt her tears burning against his skin.

He opened the door.

"Wait," Michèle called after him. He stopped, his hand on the doorknob.

"Tell me," she asked rather oddly, "did you ever kill anybody?"

He shook his head. "Never."

He had the fleeting impression of a faint smile touching her lips. "Maybe you are not so bad, after all," she whispered.

They had an excellent *diner au champagne* at Maxim's, danced to the violins of the gypsy orchestra, and finally he invited her to his flat on the Avenue Foch, "to admire the beautiful sight of the Bois de Boulogne." She accepted with what seemed to him a too-eager submission. When von Beck put his glass on the small wrought-iron table on his balcony and pulled her toward him, Michèle shivered slightly but didn't object. He kissed her passionately, and she returned his kiss. His head turned with excitement and desire. He took her in and with trembling fingers undressed her, then threw her on his large bed and hurled himself on her in an uncontrollable outburst of lust.

But late that night, while she was sleeping restlessly in his bed, he tiptoed to the sitting room, searched her handbag and carefully checked her papers. Then he dialed Brandner's number and gave him detailed instructions. An hour later, Brandner called back. Von Beck listened intently. "Exactly as I thought," he mumbled and hung up.

The next morning he walked briskly into his office, where his *ad hoc* committee held its regular meeting. He looked excited and almost happy. "I told you that we'd hear from the Baron again," he said triumphantly. "Well, he did exactly as I expected and established contact."

He told his stunned audience about the girl. "She was too willing, and her papers are phony," he explained. "Brandner checked them last night with the central records of the Préfecture de Police. I anticipated that. You see, this is one of the Baron's classical moves—to introduce his agent into my bedroom. Very clever indeed, but once we know that, we can play the game. I have my plan ready."

Von Beck concluded the meeting with a smile. But deep inside he felt like crying.

IV

THE
ENIGMA

May 23–May 2, 1944

THE BULKY, STONY-FACED DRUM MAJOR, STEEL HELMET tightly strapped to his square jaw, *feldgrau* uniform freshly pressed, buttons and belt buckle polished to perfection, high boots shining like black mirrors, thrust his baton forward and up, toward the radiant blue sky. The three drummers behind him hit their flat drums with their sleek white sticks. The military brass band struck up the opening notes of the Prussian march *"Preussen glorie,"* and in ranks of three followed the drum major in their daily parade around the Arc de Triomphe and down the Champs Elysées. Behind the band, led by a captain riding a chestnut stallion, the two hundred and fifty men of the First Sicherungsregiment of the Paris Garrison hit the macadam of the avenue in an impeccable goose step. It was exactly twelve o'clock, and the thumping of the nailed boots on their most beloved avenue reminded the Parisians that they were living through another day of humiliation and defeat.

As if by an unspoken, secret order, the usually crowded avenue emptied at the approach of the gray mass topped by combat helmets and tightly grasped rifles. Only a few passersby remained on the sidewalks, glaring with sullen hostility at the German soldiers. The Baron, contemplating the parade, was leaning on a tree at the corner of the Champs Elysées and the avenue Montaigne. He heard a familiar voice hiss: "The bastards!" He turned in surprise. Bruno Morel stood behind him, head bent forward, fists clenched in frustration, hatred oozing from every pore in his huge body. Belvoir was on the point of offering a sardonic remark, but then he remembered Bruno's angry reaction when he mocked his patriotism a few weeks ago, and kept quiet. The former legionnaire said in a muffled voice, without looking at him: "You

131

must think I am growing sentimental. Remember Renée, my little *danseuse* from the Folies Bergère? She had a brother, François, a kid of eighteen. The Gestapo picked him up at random in the street and held him hostage for a month in the Fresnes prison. A German soldier had been killed by the underground near Notre Dame, and the Germans avenged him by murdering twenty hostages. They took François this morning to one of the Gestapo death chambers, in the cellar of the Air Ministry, and shot him like a dog. Goddamn pigs! A kid of eighteen who had never hurt anybody!"

The Baron put his hand compassionately on his friend's shoulder. Bruno raised his eyes. His voice was suddenly weary and old. "There is a war going on, Baron. We can't get away from it. We tried for a while to play it the easy way, like before the war. But then this war suddenly hits you too, and it hurts. I just want to tell you this: I'll help you steal their bloody Enigma, even if you don't pay me a penny. Now I have my own account to settle with the *boches*."

Belvoir nodded, trying to conceal the slight shudder that ran through his body. "Let's go," he said gently. Bruno threw a last glance at the marching soldiers, spat on the pavement and turned away.

They stopped before an elegant antique dealer's shop on the rue de la Boétie. In the display window an exquisite Rococo desk stood next to an Empire dressing table and a cabinet covered with fitting patterns of brass and tortoiseshell, which were the hallmark of the famous seventeenth-century designer André-Charles Boulle. Bruno had regained his calm. "Aren't they gorgeous?" he said. "Antique furniture, each piece sold with a certificate attesting its age and authenticity. Authenticity my foot! The oldest piece of furniture in this shop is the cash register. Everything, absolutely everything is fake!"

"Yes," chuckled Belvoir, "but you'll never prove it."

"The guy has class, that's certain," Bruno agreed and opened the door. A delightful middle-aged Parisian woman, neatly dressed and combed and looking very respectable, flashed an enchanting smile. "Messieurs?" she chirped. "What can I do for you? Are you interested in something special? We just received an adorable dining room set and . . ."

"Stop the circus, *mignonne*," Bruno interposed bluntly. "Keep that nonsense for some real suckers. We want to see Eugène."

"Eugène? I don't know . . . I mean, whom do I have the

honor to . . ." The bewildered saleswoman nervously read-justed her chignon, striving to regain her shaken dignity. Bruno and the Baron walked past her into the big workshop in the back, where a slim, wiry old man with a mop of rebel-lious white hair was carefully applying a last layer of reddish-brown paint to a round tea table. "Ah, Bruno!" he muttered without even turning back. "Don't be too hard on Yvonne, the poor girl is doing her best. I'll be with you in a moment, as soon as I finish this beautiful, unequaled eighteenth-century piece." He stepped back, to better contem-plate his work. "Isn't that divine?" he asked.

"Better than the original, I am sure," cracked the Baron.

Eugène turned and examined him. The Baron was wearing the moustache and glasses of his current disguise. The old man looked him over suspiciously, then a sly expression crept into his eyes. "If I didn't have a very good ear and if I didn't know you were coming today, *mon cher* Baron, I would never have recognized you. You are almost as genuine as my furniture." He laughed happily at his own joke.

"Let's not waste time, Eugène," the Baron said. From in-side his shirt he extracted a few papers covered with charts and designs. "Here is the design of the . . . piece I want you to duplicate for me." He spread the papers on the floor, and the three men knelt around them. Eugène adjusted a pince-nez on the tip of his nose and peered closely at the blueprints. "What is that?" he asked, puzzled. "I've never seen anything like it."

The Baron ignored the question. "Here you have the exact measurements," he said briskly. "For the box you should use some oak, of ordinary quality, and paint it deep brown." He pointed to a chest in the corner of the workshop. "Exactly like that." He went on: "The keyboard might be taken from a German Knaur typewriter. But you should pry the keys loose and mount them on tiny aluminum cylinders, about three millimeters in diameter. Wires, plugs and sockets must be German made, of the standard type used by the Wehrmacht. The three rotors on the top are made of steel." He went on, systematically pointing out to the old craftsman the various components of the device and describing in detail their sizes and positions.

"You don't take notes?" Bruno asked.

"No, it's not necessary," grinned the crook. He tapped his forehead with his pointed index finger. "It's all recorded here."

When the Baron completed his instructions, Eugène asked cautiously: "When do you want it ready?"

"Let's see," Belvoir said slowly. "You need today and to-morrow to get the material; three or four days for building the machine, one more day for the paint to dry. Shall we say Thursday? May 30?"

The old man nodded. "Fine. But it will cost you double. That's not my usual line of work."

"Fine," the Baron said.

"Fifty thousand francs," the old man said quietly, "plus the cost of the materials."

"I'll leave you twenty thousand now, the rest on delivery."

The Baron turned to leave. "Just a moment," Eugène said. "In the design, here, there is a small plaque on the left side of the box. What should I put on it?"

"Stamp it with one-inch Gothic letters," the Baron said. "Black on gray, standard Wehrmacht type. It should read 'Enigma.' "

The strident ring of the telephone woke von Beck and Michèle. After their second night together she had moved to his apartment, on his insistence, and had openly become his mistress. Thus had begun the strangest period of his life, when short spells of sexual ecstasy reaching the verge of insanity alternated with hours of unbearable torment and pain. He knew he was madly in love with her, he couldn't help it, and he was living through his long days obsessed by the image of that perfect nude body lying on his large bed and waiting for him. But it was not only Michèle's body that drove him crazy. He was dismayed to discover in her a deeply sensitive, highly intelligent human being. When they lay beside each other after having satisfied their sexual desire, they would talk for hours, sometimes until dawn. Reluctant at first, he slowly opened to Michèle the most private, the most intimate compartments of his soul, telling her of his dreams as a youth, exposing his romantic inclinations, making her penetrate into his secret world. He found in her a warmth, an understanding, he hadn't suspected before. They realized that they shared the same tastes for music, literature, drama. Sometimes he would feel a deep spiritual communion between them that seemed to be real and genuine.

And yet, he couldn't shake away even for a moment the cruel awareness that Michèle, the only girl he had ever loved, was a spy, an enemy. Sometimes he would call her Carmen.

She thought that he had nicknamed her so in memory of the night they first met. The true reason was that he viewed her, in his romantic imagination, as a modern reincarnation of Bizet's Carmen: the bewitching woman, loved by the soldier, but loving somebody else—the bullfighter, the adventurer. That was why the soldier slew her at the end. And he was the soldier! He was haunted by the idea of her death by his own hands. He was torn between a never-quenched sexual desire and an overwhelming feeling of duty, of a mission he had to accomplish. The raw, unbearable suffering that resulted turned his existence into living hell, drew his skin pale and his eyes haggard, and drove him to the very limits of madness.

He jumped out of bed at the first ring of the telephone, not forgetting for one second that it was he who had asked for it. He uttered a string of curses. "What time is it?" he groaned, irritated, and without waiting for the sleepy girl to answer, took the receiver. "Von Beck," he said angrily. He listened for a moment. "All right, I'll be there. He hung up. Michèle looked at him, surprised. "It's only half past six," she said.

"I am sorry." He started to dress quickly. "I must go to the office for a few minutes; it's just around the corner. I'll be back in no time, and we'll have breakfast together." He kissed Michèle casually on her exposed neck, and for a second smelled the perfrume of her skin. She smiled sleepily and curled back under the covers.

But as soon as he slammed the door shut, she jumped out of bed. Oblivious of her nudity, she ran to the sitting room. On the table lay his black leather briefcase. She opened it quickly and leafed through the files inside. She was quite fluent in German, thanks to her Austrian mother. A perfunctory glance sufficed for her to determine the importance of the documents.

The third file was the right one. "87th Panzer Division—Enigma protection," read the inscription on the cover. She scrutinized the documents inside. There was a copy of an urgent order of movement for the Panzer division from its present position in Nancy to Boulogne in the Pas-de-Calais. The division was to travel on June 2, aboard fourteen special trains. The headquarters of the division was scheduled to depart on a night train that would leave Nancy on June 1, at 10:00 P.M., and travel for eight hours via Bar-le-Duc, Reims, Laon, Saint-Quentin and Amiens. The four wagons in the middle of the train were reserved for communications. The

Enigma was to be transported, under armed guard, in the second communications wagon. Precise details followed about the speed of the train, the stops it would make, the numbers of soldiers aboard. Feverishly, Michèle fumbled in her bag and took out a miniature camera. Her hands were trembling, but she managed nevertheless to photograph the main documents in the file. Her work completed, she stuffed the file back into Rudy's briefcase and snapped the locks. Still naked, she ran to the kitchen, put the kettle on the fire, grilled some toast and fried a couple of eggs.

When Rudy von Beck returned to his apartment, he was delighted to find breakfast waiting. And then he felt a throb of burning pain when he noticed that the thin thread he had slipped under one of the locks of his briefcase the previous evening was missing.

His beloved spy had swallowed the bait.

The brass bells of Saint-Augustin were musically chiming four o'clock in the afternoon when Michèle came out of the Métro station at La Madeleine. She walked past the classical church, built in the style of an ancient Greek temple, and hurried purposefully on the eastern sidewalk of the fashionable rue Tronchet. She didn't spare a glance for the exquisite boutiques displaying the new summer fashions, nor did she pay any attention to the hungry stares of the men in the street and their elaborate attempts to catch her eye. She stopped in front of a glass door with its big copper knob artfully sculped in the shape of a nude woman's body. A discreet inscription in golden italics was engraved in the greenish glass: "Amédée—*Salon de Beauté*—by appointment only." She entered. A stout blonde woman, nearly forty, wearing a green gown of raw silk, came to meet her. She smiled at Michèle, revealing two rows of perfect teeth and hinting, in her own way, that not very long ago she had been a most attractive woman. "Madame?" she asked sweetly.

"Lemaire, Michèle Lemaire."

The blonde hostess consulted a small leather-bound register she held in her left hand. "Ah, *oui*, Mademoiselle Lemaire. Body massage and hairdo. I suggest we start with the massage. Will you please come this way?"

Michèle followed her through a succession of spacious rooms, decorated with expensive furniture, rugs and paintings. In most of the rooms well-groomed women waited for their turn or relaxed after a session with the masseur or the beautician. The last room was empty. The blonde woman pushed aside a gold thread curtain, revealing a small door. She unlocked it and handed the key to Michèle. "Take care," she murmured, her face suddenly grave and concerned.

Michèle opened the door and stepped into an inner court paved in stone. A miserable tree was striving to survive in the eternal shadow cast upon the yard by the big black-walled buildings surrounding it. Michèle crossed the open space and turned the cheap tin knob of a decrepit door in the opposite wall. She reached the service staircase through a narrow, dark corridor and climbed to the second floor. The door on the right was unlocked. She crossed a tiny kitchen and entered an enormous living room, strewn with deep, comfortable sofas and armchairs. The curtains were drawn and the room was in semidarkness, except for the soft light spreading from a single lamp standing on a corner table and covered with a bell-shaped brown velvet shade.

From the opposite corner, the darkest in the room, the Baron stepped forward. "Are you all right?" he asked quickly.

She nodded.

"Nobody saw you coming?"

"The woman in the beauty parlor, of course."

"She is all right." He tried to smile. "She is indebted to me. She wasn't always the most fashionable beautician in Paris, you understand?"

There was a sort of cold tension in the air. The closeness which had sprung up between them that night in her room, ages ago, seemed to have disappeared. Michèle opened her bag and took out the small camera he had given her. "The film is inside," she said evenly. "I think I've got what you needed. An Enigma machine will be transported on a special train on the night of the first of June."

"The first of June. Perfect." A detached look came into his eyes, and his mind drifted far away. After a few minutes he looked at her. "In a moment you'll go back, the same way you came here. Have your hair done. I'll go out by the other exit on rue Vignon. Now, you'll return to von Beck's apartment. On the second of June—remember that—you'll leave his house immediately after he goes out. You'll come straight to the beauty parlor. Amédée will take care of you. Your mission will be over. You'll never see von Beck again."

"And Louise?" she asked in a low voice.

"You'll see Louise after the war. It will be safer for her not to know about you now."

She nodded docilely. There was something lifeless, robot-like in her gestures. He came closer to her. Her eyes were dull, devoid of any expression. He stroked her face gently. "Is it so hard?" he asked with compassion.

For a second she stood still, deadly quiet; and all of a sudden a deep sob, strident and painful like an animal's savage wail, burst from her chest. She buried her face in her hands, crying, her whole body shivering. He pulled her gently to him, trying to soothe her, confused by that outburst of overwhelming grief. She clung to him desperately, sheltering her head in his shoulder, an image of utter dejection and pain.

He led her to a sofa and sat beside her, stroking her hair, foolishly whispering in her ear: "It will be all right, you'll see, in three days it will all be over." He tried to get up but she clung to him. "Hold me," she murmured, "don't leave me alone, please, don't leave me alone."

He held her tightly and tenderly patted her tear-streaked face. Long minutes passed and her sobs subsided. His lips brushed against her cheek. She raised her face eagerly. He kissed her again, gently, on her soft, trembling lips. Her eyes were closed, and she returned his kiss with a surge of passion. The fire touched his mouth and spread throughout his body. Her breath came quickly, her lips moved all over his face, her demanding hands clawed his back and neck, pulling him to her. He felt he was losing control over himself; a wave of rising desire swept his taut body. They fell against each other, panting, embracing in a torrid trance, sinking into total oblivion. They removed their clothes in a frenzy; their bodies merged in a whirlpool of ectasy and together reached an exploding climax that left them spent and exhausted.

Long after, while she was nestled against him in blissful elation, she murmured: "You were surprised. You didn't want that to happen."

"No," he confessed. "I tried to restrain myself. I didn't think I had the right after . . ."

". . . after what you did to me," she finished his phrase, and added with disarming frankness: "But *I* had the right. Just for once, I had the right to be a human being, and not a puppet executing orders."

"And I happened to be here," he said too quickly, immediately regretting it. "I am sorry," he blurted.

She bit her lip and the hurt look was back in her eyes.

"You are cruel," she said. "I wanted you. Very much. I don't know why. Maybe . . . because you are the only human being who can take me away, even briefly, from the nightmare that is my life. The other night in my apartment, you made me believe for a moment that a different world could exist, where the worst danger for a girl like me was to be robbed or seduced by a rogue of your kind. Don't you see? You made me escape, you made me smile and forget that horrible madness that surrounds me."

He kissed her gently. "I was attracted by you the moment I saw you. But I didn't dare to hope that you'd ever let me come close to you. You are an extraordinary woman Michèle."

For the first time, golden sparkles of laughter danced in her deep blue eyes. Then, abruptly, her face clouded and she returned to reality. "You know," she looked away. "Von Beck is not one of those Nazi killers. He is a good man." She shivered. "Too good. I am afraid to stay there too long."

He looked at her sharply. "What do you mean?"

"Francis, he is good to me," she whispered in quiet desperation. "He cares about me. Last night I suddenly realized that I was waiting for him. I am afraid. I don't want that to happen. I don't want to need him! Do you understand? I don't want to see him ever again."

He felt a throb of unexpected jealousy. "You never will," he said forcefully. "In three days it will all be over." He hugged her closely, warmly, surprising himself with the sudden promise that so spontaneously came from the depths of his heart: "Whatever happens, wherever you are, I shall come for you, after this is over."

May 31, 1944

In the early morning of May 31, two meetings were held. The first one took place at the *"Rendez-vous des Amoureux,"* the villa on the bank of the Marne River that now served the Baron exclusively for his negotiations with the Communists. Fifteen underground fighters, most of them commanders of *maquis* units all over the country, came by different routes to the decisive gathering on the eve of the Enigma operation. Among them, the Baron recognized three of the participants in his first meeting with the Communists: the head of operations, Maurice, and the two young leaders, the hawk-faced, fanatic Raymond, and the tall, authoritative Henri. On entering, Henri shook his hand firmly and said: "I am going to be in charge of the raid. I hope we'll get along well."

Now they sprawled over the living room, some on sofas and chairs, others on the polished wooden floor. Most wore crumpled, old-fashioned clothes, a few came in rough peasant attire. All carried pistols and revolvers, which they didn't try to conceal, once inside the house. Belvoir was sure that in the cars that brought them were stacked rifles, hand grenades and submachine guns. Those people knew they had no chance to survive if captured, and they were determined to fight to their death. They were of varied stock and build, but they had something in common: the indomitable, resolute look of brave men risking their lives daily, living in constant danger and dedicated to a noble cause.

Belvoir unrolled a big map of France and hung it on the wall facing the assembly. Henri opened the meeting: "Comrades, we are gathered here to prepare one of the most important operations of the war. Tomorrow night, as I told you in our earlier briefing, we are going to attack a heavily guarded German train. We have to capture a machine—the Enigma—which will be aboard this train, and later blow the train to pieces. That machine is crucial for the Allied effort to win the war. Each of you will come to this operation with twenty of his best men. We shall be, therefore, about three hundred."

"That's a lot," a short, black-eyed man protested with the clipped accent of Auvergne. "Why do we need so many people? Two months ago, I attacked the Clermont-Ferrand train at Chamalières, and succeeded in getting hold of one and a half billion francs! It solved all our budgetary problems for the next year. And do you know how many people I had with me? Seven!"

Henri threw him a murderous look. "We all know you are a big hero, François, but the small difference is that you attacked a civilian train and the money was guarded by regular policemen. Here we have to take over a German military train, transporting the headquarters of a tank division. I agree that most of the people on that train will be clerks and not fighters, but I can promise you that we are in for quite a bit of fighting this time." He swept the audience with his chilly gaze. "Any other free advice?" he asked aggressively. Nobody spoke.

"Fine," Henri said. "Three hundred fighters it will be, then. Now, let's get down to business."

The Baron circulated among the men a translation of the documents photographed by Michèle three days ago. While they were reading, Henri sketched on an old piece of blackboard a schematic drawing of the train, indicating with an arrow the position of the car carrying the Enigma. The Baron got up and approached the map of France. "We have to choose the place where we shall set our ambush," he said. "Now, here is the itinerary of the train." His hand followed the sinuous line of the railroad from Nancy, in the Northeast region of France, north along the Rhine, southwest to Bar-le-Duc on the Marne River, then northwest, bypassing Paris by Reims, Laon and Saint-Quentin, and joining the Somme Valley in Amiens, to depart from it again in Abbeville to take a course parallel to the Channel coast and up to Boulogne.

"Let's eliminate first all the regions where we can't do it," Maurice said. The rubicund Marseillais walked to the map, and his voice suddenly rang with a new note of authority. "I think we'll all agree that we can't do it between Nancy and Bar-le-Duc. First, because this portion of the railroad runs too close to the heavy concentrations of troops along the German border. Second, because it will be too early in the evening, and the guards on the train will still be alert and vigilant. For quite a similar reason we can't do it during the last leg of the journey." His chubby finger pointed at the narrow strip of coastland stretching between Amiens and the English Channel. "The Pas-de-Calais, as we all know, is swarming with German units perpetually on the alert, because of the danger of an Allied landing. If we attack the train there, reinforcements will be on the spot within minutes, Anyway, the train will reach that part of France at dawn, and I'd absolutely rule out any assault in daylight."

"So, that leaves us with the central portion, between Bar-le-Duc and Amiens," remarked Henri.

"Not quite," frowned Maurice. "I wouldn't attack the train in the vicinity of Reims. That part of the railroad is very busy and there is a lot of military traffic, especially at night."

"The same is true about Amiens," intervened a young, thin Breton with penetrating black eyes.

Maurice nodded. "Which leaves us with three possible points where we can intercept the train: in the Marne Valley, between Bar-le-Duc and Vitry-le-François; in the northern plain, a few kilometers before Laon; and at the stretch where the railroad approaches the bank of the Somme River, between Saint-Quentin and Amiens."

"What do you suggest?" Henri asked eagerly.

Maurice smiled. "I have my own idea, but first I'd like to hear from you, comrades, where you think our advantage will be the greatest. You have to take into account the presence of armed forces in the area, the characteristics of the terrain and our own capacity to bring three hundred people there in twenty-four hours and to ensure access to escape routes after the raid."

Henri turned to his comrades and smiled. "Let's hear the people's voice," he said. The discussion began.

While the *maquisards* were eagerly debating in the Baron's villa, a second meeting was underway in Rudolf von Beck's office in the Otto building. The two meetings were strikingly similar. The main subject discussed by von Beck's committee was identical to the topic debated at exactly the same time by the Baron and his guests: the forthcoming attack on the train carrying the Enigma. In von Beck's office, as in the Baron's living room, a rough sketch on a blackboard represented the headquarters train of the 87th Panzer Division; a map of France hung on the wall, and a young lieutenant from the Western Command of the Wehrmacht was drawing on it with China ink the track of the Nancy-Boulogne railroad journey across Northern France. A few other staff officers of O.B. West (the Western high command) were present at today's meeting, as well as a paratroop colonel, his clothes still rumpled from the all-night trip from Normandy.

Von Beck opened the meeting by distributing to the participants copies of the documents related to the transport of the 87th Panzer Division and its Enigma machine. He explained the situation briskly. "As most of you know, we have been expecting for these last weeks an attempt by a British agent to seize an Enigma machine and to smuggle it to England. The British agent will certainly be assisted by French terrorists in his endeavor. I don't think I should dwell on the importance of that machine, and on the disastrous consequences in the event of its capture by the British. It is clear that they are trying desperately to get their hands on it in view of the approaching invasion of France."

He cleared his throat. "The British agent tried to obtain information about the Enigma machines in France, by infiltrating one of his accomplices to my immediate vicinity."

Helmut Muller, the Gestapo representative, smirked, and von Beck fixed him with a fierce glare before continuing. "I was fully aware of that scheme, and the day before yesterday I conveniently absented myself from my house to let the infiltrator search my files and find the documents you hold in your hands now."

One of the officers gasped in surprise. A few others looked at von Beck in astonishment. Only the permanent members of the committee kept their outward calm. They were familiar with the devious stratagem of their chairman.

Von Beck smiled at the military. "The documents you hold in your hands are false," he revealed. "They were faked on my orders for one and only one purpose: to lure the British agent, a thug named Belvoir, and all his accomplices into a deadly trap."

He let the excited murmur in the room subside, and went on: "The only true element in those documents is the fact that a special train will leave Nancy tomorrow night at ten and will travel to Boulogne following the itinerary you have in your hands. But the Enigma will not be on that train. Instead, the train will transport five hundred highly trained SS troops, ready to crush any attack. Standartenführer Liszt, who will be in charge of the train, will give you the details."

The *Standartenführer*, whose rank in the SS corresponded to that of colonel in the Wehrmacht, was a thick-set Schwab with a protruding chin and a powerful stare. He approached the sketch of the train, picking up on his way a long, polished white stick that had been leaning against the wall. He pointed it at the blackboard: "As you see, the train will consist of ten cars. The four cars in the middle, which are supposed to carry the Enigma and its escort, will be completely empty. We believe the French terrorists and the British agents will ambush the train and concentrate their attack on those four wagons; so we shall keep them unmanned, in order to avoid unnecessary casualties. They should serve only as bait and as the objective of the attack, nothing else. My five hundred men will be traveling in the six other cars. One group of ten soldiers, armed with MG-34 machine guns, hand grenades and Schmeisser submachine guns will travel on the locomotive and the tender. Two similar detachments will cover the rear of the train.

"The bulk of my troops," he continued, "will be divided in two. A part of them will occupy the passengers' compartments, and will be equipped with machine guns and grenades. As soon as the terrorist attack starts, they will open murderous fire from all the windows, on both sides of the train. The other men—about three hundred, divided by groups of fifty in each wagon—will jump out of the train the moment it is stopped, and engage the terrorists in close combat. They will carry Schmeissers and MG's, of course, as well as twenty small eighty-millimeter mortars. As you see, gentlemen," he smiled cruelly, "the train will be a machine of death." He walked back to his place.

"This is only a part of the plan, though," von Beck remarked quickly. "I don't doubt the ability of Liszt and his men to repel any attack on the train and inflict heavy casualties on the other side. But I want more: I want to annihilate completely the terrorists who will attack the train. I want Belvoir dead. Only then will I believe that his mission has failed. And in order to exterminate the attacking forces, I have to surround them and thwart any escape attempt on their side. When they stop the train and attack it, a large force of ours should assault them from the back; and then, caught in a crossfire, they'll have no chance of surviving."

"How do you intend to do that?" asked the SS colonel, puzzled.

"By guessing the exact spot where they'll attack the train—and setting a trap for them," von Beck replied. "And that is the main reason why I convened this meeting."

"I don't believe in guesses," grumbled Standartenführer Liszt.

Von Beck's jaw tightened, but he managed to hold his smile. "Let's call that a very educated guess," he replied. "Anyway, we have the best expert to help us. Oberst Mannheim, will you enlighten us, please?"

The paratroop colonel, a thin, brown-haired man, strode to the map. He spoke very quickly, swallowing parts of his words, his hands and body perpetually moving. "We should try to place ourselves in the enemy's position, analyze his objectives and his limitations, his problems of logistics, tactics, access and retreat. I think that if we examine methodically all those aspects, we'll be able to narrow progressively the various options, and reach some solid conclusions. That's what I intend to do." He had a shrill, high-pitched voice, but on the whole gave an impression of reliability and thorough knowledge of the matter.

"Please proceed." Von Beck nodded courteously.

The colonel stood in front of the map, and with a somewhat theatrical gesture placed his hands, palms open and fingers spread, on both extremities of the map, which represented the western and eastern border regions of France.

"They won't attack here," he announced firmly. "First reason: too many concentrations of German troops in Alsace and Lotharingie in the East, and on the Channel coast in the west. Second reason: they must use several hundred people for the assault. There is no region in France where they have enough terrorists for an operation of that scope. Therefore, they have to bring them from all over the country, and mostly from the regions south of Paris, where the big terrorist bands operate. They will choose a place where it will be the easiest to bring the men, and from where they will be able to disperse in quick retreat in various directions." His busy hands jerked in a fan-like movement and came to rest in the center of the map. "Therefore, our first conclusion is that they'll attack in the center, somewhere between Amiens and Bar-le-Duc."

He paused, drew a deep breath and continued: "Second assumption: for obvious reasons they'll avoid the big cities and their immediate vicinity. That rules out Reims, Laon, Saint-Quentin, Amiens. Third assumption: they need a region where they won't be seen until the last moment."

"Mountains," quickly put in Standartenführer Liszt.

"No," Mannheim retorted. "Mountains are ideal for a small group of fighters who hit and run, and then disappear in the ravines. But for a large force like this one—and I estimate it between two and five hundred—mountains would become a trap. You can't make five hundred people disappear all of a sudden. They need a place where they won't be seen, but from which they could easily escape, using country roads, and even highways, if they are quick enough. What I have in mind is woods. A stretch of flat ground, covered with forest, as distant as possible from the big cities, with good access to country roads. Now, let us see which regions along the railroad correspond to those qualifications." He turned to the map and with quick, decisive gestures pointed to three spots: "Vitry-le-François—a ten-kilometer stretch; southeast from Laon—fifteen kilometers; Nesle, between Saint-Quentin and Amiens—ten kilometers." He looked around contentedly. "Now, if we try to narrow further . . ."

"I think we shall stop here, Oberst Mannheim," von Beck intervened, raising his hand. "Let us not stretch our luck too far. I suggest that we set our traps at all those three locations. You will divide your brigade in three roughly equivalent task formations. You'll have them move into those regions tonight. They'll stay camouflaged all day long, at about twenty kilometers from the railroad. In no case should any of them be spotted. Any reconnaissance near the railroad should be done by civilians. Monsieur Moreau here, from the Milice, will provide you with people who may wander close to the railroad, disguised as workers or peasants. I think that by the late evening, these observers will detect any unusual movement, and we shall know with a fair amount of certainty where the attack will take place. The unit assigned to that particular region will very cautiously surround the terrorists and seal their rear completely, so that when the attack takes place, they'll find themselves nailed between the train and the woods, on both sides of the railroad. You shouldn't let any of them escape. Any questions?"

There were none, so the meeting was adjourned. Standartenführer Liszt and Oberst Mannheim remained behind to work out the details of the operation with von Beck. Liszt looked closely, intently, at von Beck. "That idea of pinning them from both sides," he murmured slowly as a sly expression settled on his features. "It proves that you are a very bloodthirsty man, Herr Oberst."

The adjective struck him like a blow in the face. Bloodthirsty. He was on the verge of protesting, and then suddenly he realized that the man was right. He wanted to kill them all, to annihilate the entire group, and especially one man. He wanted him dead, at all costs, and he knew why. Not because of the Enigma. But because of this woman who slept in his bed, who drove him crazy—but didn't belong to him, and never would, for she was the woman of the adventurer, of Belvoir.

"I want Belvoir dead," he squeezed through clenched teeth, and there was such hatred in his voice that Liszt involuntarily stepped back.

Thirty kilometers away, the meeting in the Baron's villa adjourned as well. The *masquisards* unanimously decided to attack the train in the thick forest southeast of Laon.

On their way out from "*Le Rendez-vous des Amoureux,*" Henri pulled aside his comrades, Maurice and Raymond.

"You know what you have to do," he said quietly. "After the attack, your assignment is to take the Enigma to Rouen and hide it with the local people there, until we get orders from our Russian friend in Switzerland what to do with it. You have three cars, a good escort, and first-class papers."

Maurice looked at him, astonished. "I thought we promised to deliver the machine to the Baron."

Henri smiled wickedly. "He'll never see it, *mon petit* Maurice. His role in the operation is over. We get our instructions from Moscow, not from London."

Then he turned around and waved affectionately at the Baron, who stood on the porch. Belvoir smiled and waved too. "*Adieu,*" he murmured slowly. He knew he was never going to see those people again.

On his way to the Otto compound later that morning, Belvoir made one stop. He drove Bruno's Citrön to the gloomy workers' suburb of Pantin, close to the slaughterhouses of Porte de la Villette, where hundreds of head of cattle were daily sacrificed to satisfy the perpetual hunger of Paris. He reached the narrow *Canal de l'Ourcq*, whose dark and muddy waters lay still, rarely disturbed by the passage of a long, flat barge loaded with sand or cement and driven by a calloused, stern-faced sailor. Number 47, Quai de l'Oise was a dark brown two-storied building facing the canal. Belvoir parked the car farther down and walked along the canal, then crossed the street and stealthily climbed to the second floor. He knocked on the single door on the landing.

He heard a squeak, as if somebody were moving behind the door, holding his breath. He had no time to waste. "Open, Julot, this is the Baron," he said impatiently.

A long moment passed before a crack opened in the door. A suspicious, bloodshot eye peeped at him warily. "You're not the Baron. Who the hell are you?" the man asked in a raucous voice.

The Baron pushed the door, making the stooping man with the long black beard retreat in haste. "Oh yes, I am the Baron," he said casually. "You know my voice and you can see this is a disguise." The man called Julot examined him closely, patting his beard.

"I don't like your beard," the Baron went on. He explained patiently, "You see, *mon petit* Julot, a beard is something people remember. And in our profession, we'd better not attract too much attention, right? So if that gorgeous beard is genuine—and it is—I'd strongly advise you to shave it or change your profession."

"I grew it in the cooler," Julot mumbled defensively.

"Yes, Bruno told me you have just completed a stretch." Belvoir nodded and sighed. "That is entirely your fault and you know it. How many times did I tell you that explosives were definitely out of fashion? If you like breaking safes so much, you should devise a more sophisticated system—cracking the combination, or duplicating the keys. Explosives are so noisy, so indiscreet. . . ." While he talked, the Baron was walking around the untidy room, kicking with disgust old shoes, slippers and filthy stockings, bending to pick up a crumbled piece of underwear and put it aside. He raised a half-empty bottle of wine to his nose and sniffed it with apprehension. "As I thought," he said sadly. "Bad." Julot followed him with a dull stare. Finally the Baron turned and faced him. "Well, you didn't take my advice when I offered it to you. That's your affair. But now that you are in explosives, you can still be helpful. I have a small job for you."

"What job?" Julot asked doubtfully.

The Baron told him in detail what he wanted done. "Bruno will come to pick the stuff up tomorrow morning, all right?" He patted the ex-con on his back and slipped some paper money into his hand. "But before you start, go and shave, buy yourself some clean clothes and for Christ's sake, some decent wine."

He ran down the stairs, entered Bruno's car, and twenty minutes later reported for the afternoon shift in the Otto building. He showed his pass to the guard on duty and joined a group of workers who were transporting crates and boxes to the cellar.

In the late afternoon, while carrying a heavy case, he bumped against a German officer who was crossing the spacious lobby quickly on his way out.

He smiled sheepishly at the tall, blond German.

"*Entschuldigen sie mir, bitte.*" He mumbled his apologies with a pitiful French accent.

Von Beck hurried past him. For a moment he reflected that he didn't like the Frenchman's smile.

June 2, 1944, 2:50 A.M.–4:05 A.M.

AT 2:50 A.M. ON JUNE 2, HAUPTSCHARFÜHRER EGON Wepler, sergeant-major in the SS, put out his half-smoked cigarette and neatly replaced it in the flat tin box he always carried in the upper left pocket of his combat jacket. From the back window of the engineer's cabin of the locomotive, he beckoned to his men sitting on top of the coal and water tender to do the same. It took a minute or two before they noticed his signals. The night was pitch dark, and the pale moonlight that accompanied the train on the first part of its journey from Nancy had long ago disappeared behind the thick mass of dark clouds. Even if the clouds weren't there, he reflected, it wouldn't have made a big difference. The last hours before dawn were always the darkest and the most dangerous. He turned to the French engineer and his assistant, who were busily shoveling coal into the blazing furnace, like two black devils stoking the fires of hell. "You," he shouted in bad, clipped French. "Keep it on a steady sixty now, understand? Not one kilometer more!" The engineer nodded slowly and threw a glance at the speedometer. He shrugged. The 241-P locomotive, a monster weighing 130 tons and able to develop 3,300 horsepower could easily reach a hundred kilometers an hour. But the *boches* and their reasons, he said to himself; the freight they were carrying on this train was certainly most valuable, and necessitated extraordinary precautions. In the four long and bitterly humiliating years he had been driving German military trains, he had never piloted a convoy so heavily guarded. He wiped his flushed face, black from soot and sweat, and turned back to his furnace.

Egon Wepler patted the shoulder of his companion, young Corporal Stark, who nodded in understanding; the sergeant-major then climbed on the stack of coal in the rear of the locomotive, gripped the edge of the cabin's roof, and heaved his massive body on top of the cabin. The ice-cold, shrilly howling wind smacked his face and chest, carrying with it the thick, foul-smelling smoke that emerged from the engine's double exhaust pipes, protruding barely a few yards ahead. Wepler swayed heavily under the wind's impact, coughing to clear his aching lungs of the sickening smoke, and flung himself flat on the cold, sticky surface of the roof. He spread his body, to offer the least resistance to the wind, and firmly anchored his spraddled legs to the rear rim of the roof. He then adjusted a pair of goggles on his face to protect his eyes against the smoke and the hail of soot particles carried by the wind.

Stark, who had been watching him closely from the cabin's door, handed him the MG-34 machine gun and its box of ammunition. Wepler set the weapon in position on its bipod, fed the ammunition belt into the oblong chamber and snapped its cover shut. He carefully unhooked four wooden-handled grenades from his belt and placed them in front of him, stacking them tightly in the narrow space between the MG barrel and the ammunition box. That way he made sure they wouldn't budge. He shivered at the idea that one of them could roll on the slightly convex roof, fall of the train and explode on impact.

He had gone through those preparations once before, when the train crossed the first dangerous zone at Vitry-le-François. But nothing had happened and he had returned to the cabin at 11:30 P.M., to rest there peacefully until they reached the thick oak forest of Laon, a few minutes ago. They had left Reims at 2:35 and were scheduled to arrive at Laon at 3:25. The ambush lay in wait for them either in that dark forest, or after Saint-Quentin, sixty more kilometers and one more hour away. But he had a curious premonition that the assault would occur here, in the straight stretch ahead of them. He braced himself and stared watchfully ahead where the powerful projector, mounted on the locomotive's front like a cold Cyclops' eye cast, a dazzling beam of white light on the rails.

A few hundred yards behind him, in the ninth car of the train, SS Standartenführer Liszt looked at his watch and said to his chief of operations, for the second time since Vitry-le-François: "General alert!" No trumpet was blown and no drums were beaten. Silently, a few soldiers ran through the narrow corridors of the cars, shaking their sleeping comrades awake, whispering the order to the officers. The cars were plunged in total darkness. The soldiers, numb from sleep, took twice the needed time to assemble around the machine guns in the compartments, or to crouch in long lines in the central aisle, in anticipation of a swift exit by the doors. But this delay had been calculated in advance by the computing machine that was the cool mind of the Standartenführer. His men were read at exactly 2:50 A.M.

A few kilometers to the west, Oberst Mannheim, the Paratroop brigade commander, walked at that moment into the command post of his one-thousand-man-strong battalion, hidden in an abandoned farm five miles south of the railroad. He had just arrived from his rear command post at Creil, in the outskirts of Paris, which was situated at a roughly equal distance from the three danger zones. He had stayed there until the last moment, ready to drive immediately to the region where the attack took place. In the early evening, a growing flow of information from various sources had indicated that some unusual activity had been detected near Laon. But he had preferred to wait until the train was clear of Vitry-le-François before jumping into his car. Now, in the moist farm cellar that served as operations room, he bent over a big map of the region, covered with transparent celluloid. On the celluloid the operations officer had drawn with a red grease-pencil a large ellipse. Mannheim pressed the celluloid against the map. The ellipse comletely encircled an approximatly one-kilometer section of the railroad, at a point where it was crossed by a narrow dirt road. In this portion of the railroad, the tracks ran from east to west.

He pointed at the red circle. "So that is our line."

"Yes," the young operations officer confirmed, bubbling with excitement: "We have them completely encircled, Herr Oberst. We saw them come and take positions at both sides of the railroad, with the main force concentrated near the crossing with the dirt road. Maybe they want to use it as an escape route. We let them pass through our lines. They didn't suspect anything. Major Kruger has set up a secondary command post on the northern side"—he pointed at a small quadrangle at the opposite extremity of the ellipse—"and we have just issued a joint order to our people to start moving toward the railroad. The terrorists are going to attack the train any minute now—and they are completely encircled. Exactly according to plan."

Mannheim nodded coldly. "The mortars?" he asked.

"In position, zeroed in on the terrorists' concentrations, north and south of the railroad."

"That's fine." The colonel smiled dryly. "Let's move now and see some action."

In a cluster of young trees by the dirt road, barely a hundred yards from the railroad crossing, Henri checked his Thompson submachine gun. The Communist leader had just come back from a last tour of inspection. His men were ready. He had followed Maurice's systematic planning to the smallest detail. A detachment of ten men positioned at the western extremity of his sector was to blow the rails and stop the train. A similar detachment would attack the rear car. In the space between those two detachments, one hundred and sixty people, lying in position along the portion of the tracks where the train would be trapped, were to riddle it with grenades and automatic fire. After a few moments of preparation, the machine guns would concentrate their fire on the three first and last three cars, sparing the four communications cars in the middle of the train. He would then personally lead the assault on the train, at the head of one hundred people.

Some leaves rustled behind him. He turned sharply. His closest aides, Raymond and Maurice, crouched beside him, their weapons in their hands. "The men are ready," whispered Raymond, motioning to the indistinguishable dark mass lurking fifty yards behind. "We made a last arms check. Those Thompsons we got from England three months ago are first class."

Henri nodded. "You remember what you have to do," he whispered urgently. "Your part is the most crucial in the whole operation. Raymond, I want you to be the first to break into the Enigma wagon, ahead of your people. How many men do you have for the break-in?"

"Twelve."

"Fine. I'll be close behind you. You and your squad are responsible for killing everybody inside. No survivors. Nobody should be able to tell that the Enigma has been stolen."

"Yes, we know that," Raymond said. "We rehearsed that several times."

Henri turned to the Marseillais. "Maurice you move in immediately after the Germans have been killed. Your sapers blow an opening in the northern wall of the car. At this point you and Raymond get the machine, leave everything and split. Don't forget, I don't want you hanging around one more second. You jump to the other side of the tracks, carry the Enigma to the getaway car—and get the hell out of here. Don't worry about the rest. I'll stay behind."

He fell silent. The plan was bound to succeed. He estimated that five minutes after the beginning of the attack, Raymond and Maurice would be in the getaway car, the Enigma safely resting in its trunk. The getaway vehicle, a German staff car, had been stolen yesterday morning in Arras. It was waiting now by the dirt road on the other side of the tracks, concealed in the shadow of a tree, with the driver and another man already clad in German uniforms. They had all the necessary papers, duly signed and stamped. Nobody could detect the forgery. In three hours the Enigma would be in the safehouse in Rouen. He himself planned to stay behind just a few more minutes, to direct the complete demolition of the Enigma car, so that nobody would be able to notice, while inspecting the calcinated debris of the car, that the Enigma was missing. And then he would direct the quick retreat of his men by the duly rehearsed escape routes.

A muffled thunder rolled far away, somewhere to the east, its rumble growing closer and louder. He looked at his watch. It was 2:55. He trembled with anticipation and turned to his aides. "They are coming," he whispered.

Hauptscharführer Wepler didn't live to use his MG-34. He was still intently watching the railroad ahead when a tremendous explosion flung the huge locomotive upward and hurled it down again in a deafening crash. Wepler was catapulted high into the air and fell on his back with a sickening thud on the left side of the wrecked steel monster. His neck broke and he was dead before a burly *maquisard* materialized beside him and sprayed his chest with bullets.

The blast of the powerful charge transformed the locomotive into a twisted black carcass. But the monster died slowly, in a semblance of eerie agony. The locomotive lay on its right side across the blasted tracks. The explosion had shattered the connecting rods coupling the huge driving wheels, and the left wheels, no longer restrained by friction, weight, cranks and rods, furiously turned in the air as if trying to pull the train once again. The fire in the furnace still blazed intensely, the double exhaust pipes exuded their black smoke, while boiling water spurted in tiny geysers from the perforated boiler, enveloped in a cloud of hissing steam that wavered as a magic misty blanket over the locomotive. The mist was torn in one place by the powerful beam of the headlight, miraculously intact, pointing in a steep angle to the sky. And like the cry of agony of a mythological monster, the blocked locomotive whistle hooted shrilly, its high-pitched wail slowly subsiding as the pressure inside the steam engine gradually decreased.

The nerve-racking scream of the whistle provided a blood-chilling background for the sounds of the fierce battle that was waged around the immobilized train. The explosion that tore the locomotive from the rest of the train didn't overturn the cars, but it shook them mightily, totally disabling the train defenders for a minute or two. Henri's partisans launched their attack with deadly accuracy. The machine guns on both sides of the train barked in a grim chorus, and a hail of bullets struck the cars, shattering windowpanes, sowing death in the narrow aisles, buzzing in the compartments like angry, lethal bees. Several *maquisards*, oblivious of the danger of being hit by their own comrades, leaped forward and threw hand grenades through the compartment windows. A few of them used for the first time the weapon that had helped to stop the Germans in Stalingrad: they hurled bottles filled with a homemade mixture of sulfuric acid and potassium chlorate, nicknamed "Molotov cocktails," at the open doors and windows. The bottles exploded in a blazing yellow flame, setting afire everything around them. One of these cocktails exploded in the ninth car of the train, at the very feet of SS Standartenführer Liszt. In a split second, the Nazi colonel metamorphosed into a living torch. His horrifying, inhuman cries echoed in the car, while the stench of his burning flesh spread among his appalled aides. He died in screaming agony, his twisted body scorched and black, his lips drawn back, baring his teeth in a horrid rictus. A similar fate awaited the first soldiers who tried to jump out of the train through the cars' doors. The Molotov cocktails exploded in the open doorways, transforming them into walls of uncontrollable fire. In the first minutes of the attack, scores of SS soldiers met a terrible death, hit by bullets, shattered by grenades, burned to death by the devilish contents of the Molotov cocktails. The issue of the battle seemed certain.

And then the first MG machine gun stuck its black muzzle through a compartment window, and after it a second, a third, a fourth; soon there were dozens, all along the train, spitting fire in a desperate riposte. The machine-gun nests of the *maquisards*, lying exposed on the flat terrain, unprotected by any fortification, drew a heavy, accurate fire. A shout reverberated in one of the cars, soon repeated all over the train: "The smoke grenades!" In a few seconds, scores of such grenades were thrown out of the windows, soon enveloping the train in a cloud of impenetrable black smoke. Using to the full the few moments when the shooting of the Frenchmen lost its precision, SS soldiers feverishly jumped out of the train, hurled themselves forward and launched their counterattack. The narrow strips of land on both sides of the train became a bloody battlefield where Frenchmen and Germans engaged in fierce close combat, first exchanging automatic fire and hand grenades and soon throwing themselves on each other with drawn knives, brandished guns, and even bare hands clawing for the enemy's throat.

Henri led his men through the tangle of writhing bodies emmeshed in savage struggle. Neither the thinning ranks of his group, nor the cries of agony and the supplications for help affected his determination to get the Enigma. Like most of his men, he had been stunned by the deadly riposte of what he expected to be a trainload of clerks, staff officers and signalmen. Later he would regroup his men and lead them on a final attack on the enemy. But first, he had his mission to accomplish.

The bulk of his group quickly reached the Enigma car. It was strangely dark and silent. "Raymond!" Henri called urgently. His comrade jumped onto the first step of the car. "*Après moi!*" he shouted, and disappeared in the interior, quickly followed by a handful of partisans. Maurice crouched by the wooden steps of the car, surrounded by his sappers. Henri quickly dispatched several of his men to repel any attack of the Germans from the flanks.

All of a sudden, Raymond reappeared in the doorway. His face was a mixture of dismay and frustration. "Henri!" he shouted. "The car is empty! There is nothing inside!"

"What?" Henri roared in disbelief. Raymond slowly nodded. At that moment, an SS soldier jumped into the midst of the *maquisards* and emptied his Schmeisser at Raymond, who offered a perfect target, standing in the car's doorway. Raymond clutched his belly and fell, head first, amidst his comrades. Maurice dived instinctively toward the German, and the two men rolled on the ground. A second later, the Marseillais slowly got up, pulling his bloody knife from the slashed throat of the German. Henri didn't even glance at him. He looked, dumbfounded, at the dark doorway. One of

Raymond's men stuck his head out. "Henri, there is no machine here!" he shouted.

"Maybe it is in one of the other cars!" Henri mumbled uncertainly. But his men were already running back from the neighboring cars, deeply confused. "Nothing!" they reported, one after the other. "Not even a bloody *boche* inside!" cursed a partisan.

And suddenly Maurice was beside him again, pulling his sleeve, shouting in a voice filled with terror. "Look! Henri, look! Behind us!" Henri turned quickly. From the forest, illuminated by the multitude of small fires burning all along the train, approached a line of soldiers in steel helmets and combat fatigues, Schmeissers tightly pressed against their chests, firing short bursts at the *maquisards*. Some of the partisans manning the machine guns were already getting on their feet and running in panic toward the train; others were striving unsuccessfully to turn their weapons in the opposite direction.

"Paratroops!" Henri exclaimed and cursed. He quickly evaluated the situation. His men were trapped between the soldiers streaming out of the train and the paratroops emerging from the forest. At that moment, something exploded a few yards on his left. "Mortars!" Maurice shouted. "They are shelling us with mortars!" Henri felt there was no time to lose. "Roger! François! Frédo!" he summoned his aides. "Run to our men. Tell them to disengage immediately and to follow us. We'll try to cross to the other side of the train, join the others and escape through the woods. *Allez, vite!*" His men scattered among the fighting groups, shouting Henri's orders. He turned to Maurice: "Let's go!"

They bent low and crawled under the buffers and the couplers of the train to the other side of the tracks, their men closely following. Maurice was the first to emerge on the other side. "Oh, my God!" he gasped in despair. Henri knelt beside him, speechless. In front of them, another line of paratroops was coming from the woods. "We are completely encircled," he said in a muffled, broken voice, for the first time admitting defeat.

But when he turned to the men clustering behind him, he was again the determined, unwavering leader. "We have one chance," he said matter-of-factly. "A frontal attack, in a concentrated effort to break their line. Have your weapons ready. I'll lead the assault. When I get up on my feet, all of you follow. Don't stop shooting. Men with hand grenades, on my right and left." He jumped forward, brandishing his gun, and shouted hoarsely: *"En avant!"* With a savage roar, his men hurled themselves at the approaching paratroops.

They had no chance whatever. Machine guns joined in a murderous crossfire from every direction, pinning them to the ground. The SS and the paratroops closed on them from all sides, advancing in a hail of bullets, annihilating systematically the last pockets of surviving partisans. Maurice died slowly, his chest torn by several bullets. "Henri, the car," he rasped, a thin rivulet of blood oozing from the corner of his mouth. "Get to the car!"

Henri knew he would never reach the getaway vehicle. Instinctively, he darted back to the protective bulk of the train. He felt a jolt of excruciating pain as the bullets slammed into his left arm and leg, but he managed to cover the last few yards and dived under the train. He heaved himself painfully onto the main axle beneath one of the cars, and clutched it tightly, his legs hooked at the inner side of the wheels. He didn't know he had come back to the car that had been the objective of the whole operation. And there, clinging desperately to the underside of the Enigma car, clenching his teeth with pain, frustration and hatred, he watched the bloody massacre of his last companions. He couldn't know, at that dreadful moment, that only four *maquisards*, apart from him, would survive the hecatomb of the Laon forest.

At 3:45 A.M. the phone rang in the apartment of Rudolf von Beck. He grabbed the receiver. He hadn't slept that night, lying immobile in his bed, awaiting that call. Michèle, beside him, breathed regularly, too regularly perhaps. He doubted if she had been sleeping either.

"Von Beck," he said.

There was a lot of static on the line, then a faraway voice identified itself as an officer of the staff of Colonel Mannheim. With a ring of triumph, the paratrooper informed him of the total success of the operation. The terrorist band, he said, had been totally annihilated near Laon.

A large smile flourished on the lips of von Beck. "What about Belvoir?" he asked impatiently. "Did you find him yet?" After a pause he added: "Never mind, I am on my way."

He jumped to his feet and quickly dressed without looking even once at the bed behind him. Only when he was ready, neatly clad in his freshly pressed uniform, did he turn back and look at Michèle, who was sitting speechless in the bed, her bare shoulders shivering, her eyes wide with horror.

"I am sorry," he said, and despite his effort, his voice trembled with pain. "This is war. You shouldn't have gotten involved in it. Two of my people are waiting outside with orders to arrest you. Will you dress, please?"

He walked to the door. Something made him turn back again.

"I loved you, Michèle," he whispered to the immobile figure staring at him with her burning blue eyes in the semi-darkness of dawn.

He ran down the stairs. Schneider was asleep over the steering wheel of the Horch. He shook his shoulder and tried to smile. "To Laon!" he ordered in a clear, ringing voice, trying to sound cheerful and contented.

FROM THE DRIVER'S SEAT OF HIS BLACK CITOËN, PARKED ON the opposite side of the peaceful avenue Foch, Bruno Morel calmly watched von Beck's departure. He looked at his watch. It was 4:05, barely five minutes later than the tentatively set H-hour. He got out of the car and walked to a public phone booth. He dialed the emergency number of the Préfecture de Police. "*Allo oui*," a sleepy voice articulated slowly. "Police."

"This is the Voice of the Resistance," Bruno said unhurriedly. "We wish to inform you that highly explosive bombs have been planted in the Otto building at 23, square du Bois de Boulogne. The first one will explode at 4:15, the others at intervals of ten minutes each. *Vive la France!*" He slammed down the phone, entered his car and drove away. Five minutes later, as his car came down the deserted Champs Elysées, he heard the shrill wailing of sirens and saw three police cars darting in the opposite direction.

At 4:15 an explosion shattered one of the offices on the first floor of the Otto building. While police cars and German motorized *Feldgendarmen*—military policemen—converged at the little square, panicked soldiers and guards, many of them in their underwear, raced out in disorder. The police quickly surrounded the building and sealed the narrow street leading to the square.

The phone rang in the small apartment of Jean Rigaud, the chief explosives expert of the Paris police. "A bomb alert!" urgently shouted the voice of the officer on duty at the Préfecture. "23, square du Bois de Boulogne. Take the armored car and the bomb-disarming devices. The explosions have already started."

"*J'arrive*," said Francis de Belvoir, calmly replacing the re-

160

eiver on its cradle. He had been waiting for this call since
8:30 A.M., when he had broken into Rigaud's apartment at
ue Madame and easily overcome Jean Rigaud and his wife.
They now lay on the bed, safely bound and gagged. Belvoir
had spent the last half hour putting the final touches to his
new disguise. He had closely watched Rigaud during the past
wo weeks, and had carefully prepared a disguise that bore a
likeness to the police officer. He now threw a last look at his
reflection in the mirror: reddish-blond hair and a neatly
rimmed beard and moustache. The resemblance was only superficial, he admitted critically. But then, he assumed that in
he atmosphere of panic and confusion reigning at the square
de Bois de Boulogne, nobody would closely examine the face
of the police sapper.

Belvoir dressed quickly in Rigaud's overalls and police
képi, and went out. The armored police van was parked in
the street, in a reserved space right beneath the house. Belvoir
had barely come out of the building when the black Citroën
braked smoothly beside him. Bruno parked the car ahead of
the van and came out in a hurry. While getting out of the
car, he was fumbling with the buttons of his expensive
camel-hair overcoat. He took it off quickly and threw it on
the front seat of the Citroën. Under the beige coat, he too
was wearing police overalls. He opened the trunk of the Citroën, took out a police *képi* and put it on his head. Together
with Belvoir, he carefully lifted a big square object that was
resting in the trunk and carried it to the police van. Both
men also transferred some smaller parcels from the Citroën's
trunk into the dark-blue van. They opened the big armored
steel container that served for transportation of live bombs
and explosives, and put the objects inside. The whole transfer
lasted barely a minute. Both men jumped into the cabin of
the van. Belvoir started the engine and pressed the siren but-
ton, and the car darted forward in the gray light dawning
over Paris.

They reached the Otto compound in less than ten minutes.
The police officers manning the roadblock at the entrance to
the square recognized the car and urgently waved it through.
The Baron stopped the van at the very entrance of the Otto
building. French policemen, several German *Feldgendarmen,*
and quite a few soldiers stood in confusion on the opposite
sidewalk, staring sullenly at the massive edifice. A cloud of

black smoke came through a shattered window on the first floor. Splinters of glass lay on the deserted sidewalk.

Bruno and Belvoir swiftly alighted from the van, ran to its back and opened the rear double doors. They briskly dragged out the armored container and carried it toward the open entrance of the building.

"You there, just a moment!" a tall, stooping police captain shouted at them. "Wait!"

"We must go in, we are *l'équipe anti-démolition*," Belvoir shouted back.

The officer quickly crossed the street. He pointed at his watch. "Wait," he said again with authority. "Another explosion is due in one minute. You'll go in immediately after it. You'll have ten minutes."

He had hardly finished speaking when the explosion shook the building. It was stronger that time, and most of the first-floor windowpanes shattered and crashed on the pavement. Another cloud of smoke burst out of a window.

"Go in now, and good luck," the captain said.

Bruno and Belvoir hurried inside, carrying their large container. Once alone in the lobby, the Baron said: "Quickly now, we have less than ten minutes. Where did you plant the other bombs?"

"Four others on the first floor, two on the second," Bruno answered.

They opened the steel container, put aside the small parcels, and unwrapped the big square object that Bruno had brought in his car.

There it stood, looking like the real thing: the Enigma dummy.

While his Horch raced through the empty streets of Paris, von Beck stared woodenly ahead of him, his features grim and drawn, two bitter furrows descending to the corners of his tightly pressed mouth. He couldn't chase from his mind the image of the distressed face of Michèle and her horror-stricken eyes. He tried to brace himself and regain control over his emotions. He couldn't indulge in sentimentalism, he mused. He was a soldier and had an assignment to accomplish. She was a spy and he could do nothing about it. He tried to awaken the antidotes that slumbered in his subconscious, to convince himself that he had nothing to regret. He had succeeded, the Enigma had been saved, he had lured his formidable opponent into a death trap and destroyed him. He had every reason to be contented.

At the Porte de la Chapelle, by the northern exit of Paris, he spotted an open "Spezial" café, where a German officer could get a good meal. The prospect of a strong *café-filtre* and some fresh *croissants-au-beurre* was tempting. The food and drink could boost him, and he needed a boost pretty badly. He ordered Schneider to stop the car. He entered, walked to the brass counter, and ordered his breakfast. Four junior officers, merrily chatting beside the counter, jumped to attention and moved hurriedly aside. He absentmindedly returned their salute and hungrily bit into the crisp, golden croissant. On the counter stood an old-fashioned telephone. He decided to call his office; Brandner was on duty there, maintaining constant contact with Mannheim's command post. Maybe they had already identified the Baron's corpse. He needed a piece of good news.

He dialed his office, but there was no answer. He tried the other line, with the same result. He cursed inwardly, in growing irritation. Where the hell was Brandner? He wasn't supposed to leave the office at this crucial moment. He angrily dialed the Abwehr main headquarters at the Hotel Lutetia. The officer on duty might know what was the cause of Brandner's absence.

This time, the call went through immediately. He identified himself and asked his question. What he heard made his blood run cold. He rushed out of the café and jumped into his car. "Back!" he yelled at the astounded Schneider. "To the office, on the double!" While the car roared through the streets, he unfastened the stiff collar of his tunic and feverishly mopped his perspiring forehead. He tried to convince himself that this was only a coincidence, nothing else. But, deep in his heart, he already felt the bitterness of defeat.

Bruno and Belvoir hurried to the communications room in the Abwehr section on the second floor of the Otto building. The room was empty, deserted like all the other offices. The teletypes continued to clatter busily, however, printing the incoming information on the slowly rotating rolls of paper. Bruno and Belvoir rapidly substituted the dummy Enigma for the real one. They took the real Enigma and carefully carried it down. Just for an instant the Baron's eyes rested on the device that lay before him—that piece of wood, wire and steel that had already cost so many lives. And it wasn't over yet.

"It's up to you, Bruno," the Baron said. "You know what to do."

The big man smiled slyly. The Baron left him and again ran up the stairs to the second floor. Back in the communications room, he carefully unwrapped, one by one, the parcels he had brought with him. They were small, powerful bombs, equipped with very short time fuses. He set four of them around the room and one under the fake Enigma. On his way down he planted three more bombs in other offices. There was a last parcel of the same size in the steel container. He unwrapped it.

In a minute, Bruno was beside him. "Everything is all right," he reported. "Now let's get the hell out of here."

The two men dragged the steel container, too exhausted to carry it. The police captain sighed with relief when he saw them, but his eyes remained anxious. "Did you succeed?"

Belvoir shook his head. "We can't do anything," he gasped, short of breath. "The place is full of explosives." He turned away and, with Bruno, continued dragging the steel container to the van.

All of a sudden, a German military Horch came to a stop behind them in a strident screeching of tires. Colonel von Beck jumped out, his hair disheveled, his face taut.

"What is going on here?" he shouted, angrily glaring at the people around him. Another explosion echoed from the building. The police captain shrugged helplessly. In two strides von Beck was beside him. "Has anybody gone in or out of the building after the explosions started?" he asked quickly.

"Only the anti-demolition experts, sir," replied the police officer.

"Where are they?" von Beck bellowed. The startled officer nodded in the direction of the police van. Followed by the astonished stare of the soldiers and policemen assembled in the square, von Beck whirled and ran toward the two sappers, who were carefully lifting the steel container into the van. "Don't move!" he roared. "What have you got in that container?"

The larger of the two policemen stared at him in dismay. "That's the bomb container, sir," he said, nevertheless obeying von Beck's order and lowering the heavy metal box onto the pavement.

"Open it!" snapped von Beck, grasping the handle on the cover.

"I wouldn't if I were you, sir." The big man looked at him in terror. "There is a live bomb inside."

"Open it!" von Beck demanded.

The second policeman, a younger man with a reddish-blond beard, bent over the container and obediently unfastened the heavy cover. "What's inside?" von Beck insisted. "Show it to me."

Beads of sweat popped out on the forehead of the sapper. He looked for a moment at von Beck's angry face, then slowly reached inside the steel box. When he withdrew his hand, it was holding a cluster of dynamite sticks connected to a cheap clock that was regularly ticking. He held it forward for the officer to see. Von Beck peered over his shoulder into the container.

It was empty.

He hesitated for a second, then sighed. "All right," he muttered, defeated. "You can go."

For just another second the gray eyes of the sapper held his own in an oddly challenging gaze, then with a sigh of relief he put the bomb back in the container and snapped the cover shut. Both men quickly lifted the container into the van and climbed into the driver's cabin. Belvoir smiled wickedly at Bruno, put the truck into gear and drove away.

Von Beck stared after them uncertainly. Was there something familiar about the young sapper? A series of explosions broke the thread of his thought. He looked at the building. Thick black smoke erupted from two windows situated at the extreme left of the second floor.

"Damn it!" he said. "The communications room."

Oblivious of the danger, he ran into the deserted building and took the stairs two at a time. He reached the second floor and raced into the Abwehr section. On his left, another explosion shook one of the offices, but he didn't even look back. He hurried into the communications room. Everything had been completely destroyed. Radio sets, Morse transmitters and receivers and teletypes lay all over, broken to pieces, among furniture debris, half-burnt papers and chunks of plaster. In the middle of the room lay the remains of the Enigma—charred pieces of wood, twisted revolving drums, springs, broken type keys. He walked slowly inside and picked up a short piece of calcinated wire from the debris of the destroyed machine. He stood very still, pressing it hard and watching it disintegrate between his fingers.

The van had hardly moved a couple of hundred yards when it was forced to slow down and stop at a roadblock that barred access to the square. Bruno stuck his head out of the cabin's window. "Move that damn barrier," he shouted. "We have live bombs inside." Three of the policemen quickly started to push aside the fences stamped with the letters *P P*—standing for *Préfecture de Police*—while a fourth one, a short, fat man with merry black eyes, approached the van, peering inside. "Isn't that Jean's car?" he called happily. "Salut, Jean!"

Belvoir made a vague gesture with his hand and drove his elbow into Bruno's ribs. "For God's sake, tell them to hurry!" he whispered urgently. But the short policeman was already by the van, stretching out his hand for a handshake. "*Ça va*, Jean? How's the little wife?" Belvoir tried desperately to avoid the older man's stare, and mumbled a few indistinct words while feigning to scratch his face with his left hand. Suddenly the policeman uttered an exclamation of surprise. "Hey, you are not Jean! Who are you?"

He couldn't wait a second more. He slammed his right foot on the accelerator and the van leaped forward, shattering the last wooden fence that still barred the road. It dashed to the right and then up the avenue Foch. He could still hear the agitated shouts of the aging policeman: "That is not Jean Rigaud! Stop him! Stop him!"

"*Merde!*" Bruno exclaimed. He looked in the side mirror. Three black specks suddenly appeared behind the van, quickly growing in the mirror as they reduced the distance between them. "The bastards," he muttered. "German *Feldgendarmen*, on motorcycles." Belvoir pulled the siren switch while Bruno reached inside his overalls and withdrew a heavy handgun. It was a German Mauser 7.63, almost a foot long, with a big round grip. He fitted the chubby ten-round magazine in front of the trigger guard so that the giant pistol resembled a small submachine gun. "You said you would never use a gun," he snapped angrily at Belvoir. "Let's see what you are going to do with your bare hands against those killers." Belvoir ignored the remark. His face was grim, his eyes watchful while he drove the van through the maze of small streets between the Champs Elysées and the Seine in a vain attempt to shake off his pursuers.

"You must reach the boulevard Montmartre," Bruno said quickly. "Stop the van at the entrance of the Passage des Panoramas. It's an arcade pedestrian street, and cars can't get in. We'll run through the passage and get out at the rue Saint-Marc exit. There is another car, a brown Panhard, waiting for us there." Belvoir nodded. The van sped through the narrow streets, scaring the rare early morning strollers off the pavement, occasionally bumping against a garbage can or a vegetable-seller's cart parked in the street. Bruno loaded his Mauser. "Two more *boches*," he reported gloomily, checking the side mirror. One of the *Feldgendarmen*, looking like a messenger of death, his face protected by a steel helmet and black goggles, his Schmeisser hanging across his chest, approached. Bruno followed his movements closely. The German's right hand suddenly darted to his belt. "The sonofabitch wants to throw a hand grenade," Bruno said. With a swift movement he stuck the whole upper half of his bulk out of the window, turned back and aimed the Mauser, steadily holding it in his two hands. The gun barked twice. The German's hand froze in midair, and while his motorcycle overturned, the grenade rolled on the cobblestones and exploded. A huge flame engulfed the *Feldgendarm*. Bruno returned to his place. "That makes one less," he said matter-of-factly.

The van and its pursuers emerged in a wail of sirens and a roar of engines on the place de la Concorde. Two black Citroëns lurking by the wall of the Tuileries suddenly joined the race by trying to block the van in the middle of the huge square. "Gestapo," mumbled Bruno while Belvoir deftly piloted the vehicle onto the sidewalk surrounding Cleopatra's needle and past the improvised ambush. Belvoir again plunged the car into the labyrinth of small streets behind the Royal Palace, and finally rushed through the black-walled rue Richelieu and into the boulevard Montmartre. Bruno pointed to the right. "Les Panoramas," he announced. Belvoir noticed that the covered arcade was large enough for a Gestapo Citroën to speed through in pursuit of two running men. At the last second before reaching the arched entrance of "Les Panoramas," he sharply swung the steering wheel, took the van onto the large sidewalk of the boulevard and, once again turning to the right, slammed the front of the vehicle into the left pillar of the huge porch, completely blocking the entrance of the arcade. Bruno and Belvoir jumped from the immobilized van and hurled themselves into the big glass-roofed passageway. It was still early morning; the arcade was empty except for the traditional *clochard* asleep in a doorway with his empty wine bottle. They dashed past closed boutiques, bookstores, and haberdashery shops. Their running steps and the harsh gasps escaping from their aching lungs echoed in the emptiness of the arcade.

Suddenly another sound reverberated in the arcade—gunshots. Belvoir glanced back. The Gestapo had been quicker than the *Feldgendarmen*. Four men in civilian clothes, their raincoats swaying loosely on their shoulders, were running quickly toward them, shouting and firing. Two of them were getting closer, and the bullets whistled ominously in Belvoir's ears. "Let's stop them," Bruno rasped, flung himself to the right, rolled on the ground and came up crouching on his knee. He aimed the Mauser and fired twice. The closest man staggered, instinctively clutching his groin with both hands. "Good," said Bruno. At that very moment the second Gestapo agent fired three shots in quick succession. The former legionnaire swayed slightly and turned to Belvoir, his eyes expressing endless stupefaction. The Baron, oblivious of the gunshots, dived toward his friend. He grabbed the enormous bulk of his shoulders, trying to help him get up. And then he saw the small scorched holes in the overalls, his fingers touched the sticky warm liquid that oozed from Bruno's chest and he heard the hoarse whisper of his friend: "That's my end, Baron."

Slowly, peacefully, the big man fell, first on his elbows, then on his back. His legs spraddled grotesquely on the ground. Belvoir crouched beside him, amazed, unable to admit the loss of his friend. A bullet hit the pavement beside him, ricocheting with a strident, vibrating buzz. The sound brought him back to reality. He saw the second Gestapo agent, barely twenty yards away, raising his gun. Suddenly, he remembered Bruno's words on the Champs Elysées only a week ago: "There is a war going on, Baron. We can't get away from it." And then, with fierce determination, he grabbed his friend's gun, aimed it carefully, unwaveringly, and for the first time in his life shot his enemy dead.

"*Adieu l'ami*," he murmured, threw the gun and ran.

The brown Panhard was waiting behind the arcade, the key in the ignition. By the time his pursuers reached the rue Saint-Marc, he had turned the nearest corner and had disappeared in the crooked streets of the stock-market quarter.

Bruno Morel lay on the ground, his life slowly fading away. The *Feldgendarmen* and the Gestapo agents stood around him without touching him. They all understood it was too late. His eyes were closed, and a mortal pallor was setting on his face.

Another military car stopped by the arcade. Von Beck pushed his way through the small crowd and knelt by the dying man. He was deeply agitated. "Who are you?" he asked in French, in a low, barely audible voice. "What happened to the Baron? What did you do in the Otto building?" He repeated his questions two, three times in a row. He couldn't tell if the big man heard him. But then he slowly opened his eyes and looked at him. "Who are you?" von Beck asked again. "The Baron, where is the Baron?"

The man whispered painfully, "I am Sergeant Bruno Morel, First Regiment, Foreign Legion." His whisper became very low. Von Beck placed his ear to the lips of the dying man. They were moving in an effort to utter something. "Say it!" von Beck said forcefully. "Say it! What are you trying to say?"

He could swear that a note of pride rang in the deep voice, and a glint of triumph illuminated the big man's eyes when he finally whispered: *"Vive la France!"*

Bruno Morel was dead.

V

THE
SACRIFICE

By six o'clock in the morning Paris was hermetically sealed. Roadblocks were set on all the roads leaving the capital. Agents of the Gestapo, the Abwehr, the SD and the French police thoroughly screened every car and bus. At the railroad station, teams of policemen examined the papers of each passenger. Even the Seine wasn't spared. A motor launch of the Préfecture de Police systematically stopped every barge floating on the river, and eager officers checked every corner, prodding the cargo of sand, cement or coal with sharp steel spikes. The Baron had to be stopped.

At the Gare de l'Est, Paris's eastern railroad station, the security service inspected the papers of a French sergeant in the L.V.F.—the hated Legion des Volontaires Français. The L.V.F. was a five-thousand-man-strong collaborationist military unit. All its soldiers were volunteers who had joined the army to combat the "Bolshevist danger." They dressed in German uniforms and about 1,500 of them fought on the Eastern front, on Russian territory. Like the Milice, the Otto squads and other pro-German organizations, the L.V.F. drew most of its adherents from the scum of French society. In France, the L.V.F. soldiers were considered despicable lackeys of the Germans. Which could explain why the police officer who checked the sergeant's papers spat on the ground. But the sergeant, clad in an impeccable German uniform, the Iron Cross hanging on his neck, didn't react. He calmly produced his papers, certifying that he had spent a six-day leave in Paris and was returning to the front via Germany. He watched the agents who checked his bags with a slightly amused expression. Finally he was cleared, and walked purposefully to a second-class NCO car on the 7:25 Berlin Express.

The sidewalk in front of the main Otto building had already been swept clean, and a multitude of workers were busy repairing the damages inside when von Beck walked in, shortly past 8:00 A.M. Brandner was waiting for him in the lobby, which hadn't been harmed by the explosions. The young captain sighed with relief at the sight of his boss. "I have been trying to reach you since 6:00 A.M., Herr Oberst," he reported. "The phones won't stop ringing and there is a pile of telegrams lying on your desk."

"Well, I've been busy," von Beck said curtly. "I toured the roadblocks and the security barrages. I wanted to see for myself if they were really trying to capture the Baron."

"And, if I may ask . . ." Brandner started respectfully.

Von Beck's face formed a skeptical grimace. "They are trying," he said gloomily. "But they won't get him. He is too clever. He might be hundreds of miles from Paris already." He suddenly remembered something. "Did you get in touch with Mannheim's headquarters?"

Brandner nodded grimly.

"Well, say it!" von Beck flared impatiently. "Did they find anything?"

"No, sir," Brandner stammered. He had never seen the colonel in such a mood. "You were right. They checked all the terrorists' corpses in Laon. The Baron wasn't among them."

"Of course not." Von Beck shrugged and, in quick, nervous gestures, lighted a cigarette. "He was here, disguised as a police sapper, together with Morel. I saw him, but I didn't recognize him."

"Are you sure, sir? Maybe . . ."

"No maybe." Von Beck cut him off sharply and walked quickly toward the staircase. "I saw myself, fifteen minutes ago, the police sapper, the real Jean Rigaud. He had been bound and gagged during the night by Belvoir, who disguised himself in Rigaud's apartment. Rigaud recognized Belvoir's picture." He ran up the stairs among the hurrying workers, Brandner following close behind. "Damn it. We were looking for him in Laon, while he was here, in this very building, posing as a police sapper. But I still cannot understand what the hell he was doing here."

"The bombs, Herr Oberst . . ."

"The bombs! The bombs!" von Beck muttered mockingly. "This man is wanted by the French and German police, by the Abwehr and the Gestapo and who else. And you believe he would throw himself into the lion's den to plant some bombs? Any dilettante terrorist could have done it. No, he didn't come here to plant his bombs. He had some other reason."

"What a pity Morel died before talking, sir."

"Morel wouldn't have talked anyway," von Beck snapped. They reached the second floor. Workers were carrying pieces of furniture out of the damaged offices. In the first office on the left two masons were already at work, repairing minor damage to the wall. "I see they work very quickly," he remarked casually.

"They don't have to work too hard, Herr Oberst. There is very little work to do."

Von Beck stopped sharply. "What do you mean, very little? The police said they counted eighteen explosions. I saw the communications room myself. It was nearly destroyed."

"That's true, Herr Oberst. But the real damage is only there, in communications. In all the other offices the damage was superficial. Most of the bombs must have been quite small. The Otto organization has already resumed its activities, conforming to schedule. Arrival and shipping of goods will start again in half an hour."

Von Beck froze, his hand on the doorknob of his office. "You say that the damage was minimal?"

Brandner nodded eagerly. "Yes, sir. It looks like the bombs were not intended to cause damage, but to drive everybody out, and allow Morel and . . . and Belvoir to stay in the building for ten minutes, alone."

"And during those ten minutes they blew up the communications room," whispered von Beck. "Why the hell did they do it?"

He entered his office and slammed the door behind him.

The office had been spared. No bomb had exploded here. Von Beck morosely wondered if the Baron had shown him a special kindness. He walked to the table and leafed through the messages and telegrams. A smile curled on his lips. They were all congratulations. Congratulations for the brilliant Laon operation, where a huge band of terrorists had been totally annihilated and the Enigma machine had been saved. Von Beck's bitterness grew when he examined the signatures on the telegrams: the commanders of the SS, the SD, the Milice, even that butcher of the Gestapo, Kurt Limmer. All those murderers and torturers were proud of him now! And they were right, he admitted grimly, for it was he who had instigated that devious operation—to save the Enigma, but mainly to kill the Baron. Yet, the Baron was alive and well, and the twenty-eighth Enigma, Canaris's secret machine, had been blown to pieces. What had happened? Where had he gone wrong? Among the telegrams he saw a laconic one: "Hearty congratulations, Rudy." And the signature: "Canaris." He cursed under his breath. Canaris didn't know yet that their private machine, one of the guarantees of the success of their plot against Hitler, had been destroyed. But how? How had Belvoir learned about the existence of that machine? And why had he blown it up? It didn't make sense!

And then he remembered Canaris's words when he bade him farewell at "La Duchesse." "In this game of wits that is ours, you can never know who will outwit whom." Had the Baron outwitted him? Was that possible?

He quickly opened the two connecting doors and entered the communications rooms. It offered a sight of complete devastation. It had been sealed, according to his explicit orders. He couldn't let anybody find out that the Abwehr had used an unlisted Enigma. He walked now to the twisted table where the Enigma had stood. He knelt and carefully collected pieces of wood, wires, some type keys, a distorted electric rotor. He carried the debris to his room and packed it in a big paper bag. He went down the stairs and beckoned to Schneider, who was chatting cheerfully with a giggling German secretary in the shade of a chestnut tree.

"Sorry to disturb you," he said, "but I have to go to the Hotel Lutetia."

Schneider gave him a surprised look. He had never seen his boss so edgy. "*Jawohl, Herr Oberst,*" he said and hurried to open the door of the Horch.

The Abwehr's laboratory was situated on the fifth floor of the luxurious Hotel Lutetia, which housed all the other services of German espionage in Paris. An elderly, white-haired man in a white smock emptied the contents of the paper bag on a table covered with immaculate oilcloth. He listened intently to von Beck's instructions. "That presents no problem," he said finally. Would you like us to phone you the results?"

"No," von Beck said. "I'll wait. It's top priority."

"It will take a little while," the lab technician said uneasily.

"It's all right," von Beck replied. "I'll be in the building. I shall come to see you in half an hour."

He briskly walked out and descended to the third floor. He

walked around the corner and all the way down the long carpeted corridor. From behind the closed doors came a faint rattle of typewriters. One or two officers, hurrying by, slapped him on the back, congratulating him for his success. Every congratulation was like a stab in his heart. What did they know, for God's sake? Did they understand that he had failed in his main mission—to destroy Belvoir? How could they know that he had not been able to protect the most important Enigma of them all? And could anybody suspect the torment he felt that the woman he loved was imprisoned barely fifty yards away, having been arrested as a British spy?

He could feel his heart beating rapidly as he flashed his special pass at the armed guard whose desk barred the entrance to the west wing of the building. He passed the first five doors on his right; here were the quarters of undercover agents who came to Paris for debriefing and were kept in protective isolation, far from any indiscreet glance. The next ten doors were different. The original doors of the hotel rooms had been unhinged and replaced by iron doors equipped with special locks. The windows had also been removed and reinstalled, sandwiched between prison bars. It was a private prison, but a prison all the same, used by the Abwehr for detention of foreign spies for questioning. And here, behind one of those doors, was Michèle.

He beckoned to a guard, who followed him with his keys. He had never been so disturbed in his whole life. His heart hammered now, his mouth was dry, his hands and forehead perspired profusely. How would he meet Michèle now? How would she look at him when he entered her cell, a German interrogator coming to question his French prisoner? What would he ask her? "Where is your lover? What were his plans? What did he do in the Otto building?" Or maybe "Did you love me, Michèle?" He shuddered. How could he confront her and admit that he had used her, knowingly, as she had used him?

He approached the door and looked through the peephole. At first he recoiled; the girl sitting inside seemed so close. Her eyes were riveted on the door as if she were looking through it and straight into his face. He peered in again. She sat as he had left her in his room: immobile, strangely quiet, her bright eyes staring unseeingly in front of her. There was something hard and desperate and faraway in those eyes. And he knew then, with absolute certainty, that she would never talk to him, never look at him, only despise him for the abject role he had chosen to play: the police interrogator, the incarnation of brutal power, the enemy who comes to persuade her to betray her lover, her country. And what would he do to her if she refused to talk? Threaten her? Call in the Gestapo? The pain was unbearable. How he longed to touch her, to see her smile, how much he wanted to talk to her, to be with her in another place, another time, like two human beings who could love each other, who could wipe from their consciousness the fact that he was a German, and she a French woman destined for torture and death.

His throat contracted and he felt his eyes become moist. He clenched his teeth and turned back. The guard was waiting patiently, ready to insert his key in the lock. Von Beck shook his head. "No," he said in a low voice. "I changed my mind. I don't want to see the prisoner now."

And as he walked back through the deserted corridor, he realized he would never see her again.

"It was exactly as you suspected, Herr Oberst," the lab technician said eagerly. "It was an imitation. Nicely built, of the same wood, with type keys taken from a regular typewriter, wires, drums and plugs shaped to resemble the authentic components of the Enigma. But on the whole it was a very rudimentary imitation that couldn't stand any close check."

"Would you say it was intended specifically to provide debris that would look as if it came from a real Enigma?"

The white-haired German considered the question before answering. "Yes," he said finally, "you may be right. The machine as a whole wouldn't have fooled us for a moment, of course, but its charred debris could induce anybody to believe that those were the remains of an authentic Enigma."

"Thank you." Von Beck shook his hand and hurried away. Another piece had fitted into the puzzle, and yet he couldn't see any pattern. Belvoir and Morel had undoubtedly substituted their dummy for the real Enigma in the communications room. They had then blown it to pieces. But what did they do with the real Enigma? They didn't take it out of the building. And yet, it had vanished. Where was it? A terrible suspicion gnawed at him: could it be that Belvoir had succeeded in stealing the twenty-eighth Enigma? But how?

Back in his office, Brandner was waiting for him with a slovenly dressed lieutenant who had nervous hands and sparse, greasy hair. Von Beck looked at his aide inquiringly.

"This is Lieutenant Kreski of Manpower, Otto organization," Brandner explained. "He knows Morel; he was employed here."

There was something unpleasant in Kreski's subservient manner. He clicked his heels, bowed deeply, and with a sticky smile took a photograph from the thin yellow file he held in his hand and gave it to von Beck.

Von Beck looked at the picture of the big face, the boxer's nose, and the slightly sarcastic smile. He sat behind his desk and lit a cigarette. "Yes," he said, "that's the man. Any criminal record?"

Brandner answered that quesion. "A very long record, sir. I checked that with the police. Bruno Morel was a well-known criminal. On my request the police have been intensively questioning their informers about Morel, since early this morning. Information is still coming in, but the most important intelligence is that Morel was very close to the Baron, who had once saved his life." He added quickly: "I know it was not in the Baron's file, sir. They kept that relationship pretty secret. People were afraid of Morel. Only after he died were they ready to talk."

Von Beck slammed the desk furiously. "And they call themselves police! If we just had known about Morel we could have captured the Baron weeks ago! And those idiots didn't know about it! The only piece of information missing from their bloody file was the most important one!" He jumped from his place and strode around the room.

When he finally calmed down, he turned to Kreski: "You say he worked here?"

"Yes, sir. Since 1941. And it might interest you to know that about a month ago, on May 4, he recommended one of his friends for a job in the compound. A man named Duclos. He didn't report to work today."

Von Beck's mind feverishly analyzed the new pieces of information, connecting them in a series of inductions that pointed to an inevitable, disastrous conclusion. "Do you have a picture of this Duclos?" he asked quickly.

A smile flashed again on Kreski's colorless features. "Yes, sir." Von Beck grabbed the second picture from his outstretched hand and examined the face it reproduced. He tried to imagine the features in the photograph without the wire-rimmed glasses and the black moustache. Yes, this could be Belvoir. "This explains the twenty-eighth Enigma," he murmured to himself.

The two junior officers looked at him questioningly.
"Leave me alone," he snapped.

Dusk was already settling on Paris, but von Beck hadn't
moved from his place. For hours he sat there alone, deeply
immersed in thought, refusing all phone calls and the trays of
food that a worried secretary brought from the canteen. He
felt he had all the elements in his possession, and yet he
couldn't pierce the devious scheme of his foe. The building
was deserted now; the repairmen had finished their work by
noon and the various branches of Otto had resumed their
routine activities. Only the communications room remained in
its state of utter devastation. Von Beck had grown used to the
perpetual muffled clatter of the machines; the deathly stillness
that now reigned around him stirred in him an odd feeling of
unreality.

He tried to put some order to his thoughts. There was no
longer any doubt in his mind that the Baron had outwitted
him; while he believed that he was outwitting the Baron, the
Baron was outwitting him. Belvoir had found out that he had
read his file, and was familiar with his methods. Therefore,
he had let him believe he was using his characteristic methods
once again, while cunningly setting up his devious scheme.
Belvoir knew that he would expect him to introduce an agent
in his vicinity, therefore he had sent Michèle to him. It was
clear now that, from the start, the Baron had wanted him to
discover the double role of Michèle, to let her see the false
document and to set a trap for him. It was a fantastic diver-
sion, for he had cold-bloodedly sacrificed an entire network
of the Resistance. And all that time, while he, von Beck, was
busy setting his ambush, the Baron was preparing his real hit.
He had discovered the twenty-eighth Enigma. And he had
stolen it. But how?

The ingenuity of the Baron's plan, von Beck admitted with
admiration, was in stealing the secret, unlisted machine. Neither von Beck nor Canaris could ever admit openly that this
Enigma had been stolen; they couldn't admit that it had ever
existed. If the SS or the Gestapo found out that Canaris
possessed his own Enigma, they would be confirmed in their
suspicions that he was busy ploting against the Führer. That
would mean the scaffold for Canaris. And for him too. The
only way for him to save their necks was to keep secret the
theft of the Enigma. And to find it.

He smiled bitterly as he thought of the Baron. Yes, this

brilliant adventurer was indeed the man he had wanted to become in his faraway youth. His mistake was in underestimating his cunning. He thought he knew the Baron. Well, if he did, could he guess how he would take the Enigma out of France?

Belvoir didn't take the Enigma away before he substituted the dummy for it. So the device must have remained in the building. He must have removed it by a different way. But how? Nobody could walk out of the building, past the guards, with such a heavy object. There was no way to take something out of the compound. No way at all, unless. . . . He froze in mid-thought. Oh, God, of course there was a way! So daring, and yet—so simple! Could it be true? He grabbed the phone. With trembling fingers, he dialed a few numbers and asked several questions. Then he ran out of the building, shook the napping Schneider and shouted savagely: "To the Bourget airport, quick!"

Half an hour later he took off in a special plane. Below him, Paris slipped into darkness.

It was a quarter to four in the morning, and in the Hauptbahnhof, the main railroad station of Berlin, a group of porters had just finished unloading the special freight train from Paris. Military lorries were loaded with the crates and cases stamped "Otto organization" and were dispatched to various destinations all over Germany, to distribute the loot from France. Soon there was almost nobody left in the station, except four elderly soldiers who were standing guard over a few crates still left by the tracks. It was a cold, damp night and a heavy gray mist lay over Berlin, giving the sleeping city an eerie appearance.

Steps echoed on the stone floor of the deserted warehouse. Three men appeared on the platform. Two of them were porters. The third was younger, formally dressed in a black suit, a Spanish cape and a wide-brimmed hat. He approached the sergeant in charge. "I am the Spanish vice-consul," he said with a heavy accent. "I have come to take delivery of a crate that was sent to us from Paris." He handed the soldier a sheaf of papers. The sergeant attentively read the official documents. They had been dispatched from the Otto offices in Paris, and certified that a crate, containing a piece of antique furniture, had been sent by General Horst Wulff, military commander of Gross Paris, to the Caudillo of Spain, Generalissimo Franco, as a token of friendship in memory of their close cooperation during the Spanish Civil War. The present was sent via Berlin, as required by military regulations.

The officer checked the number on the voucher. The bright disk of light produced by his flashlight danced briefly on the head of crates, then focused on a middle-sized case. "Here it is," he said. "Will you please sign here?"

The vice-consul signed the release slip with a flourish. The two porters bent over the crate.

"Just a moment," a new voice said. A shadow detached itself from one of the stone pillars of the platform and slowly approached through the gently swaying mist. The blurred silhouette gradually metamorphosed into the tall, upright figure of a German officer, carrying colonel's insignia on his epaulets. In his right hand he was holding a submachine gun. He spoke softly: "I am Oberst von Beck from the Abwehr, on special assignment." He aimed the weapon at the small group of people. With his left hand he flashed his papers in front of the sergeant, while still covering the others with his Schmeisser. He went on, in the same soft voice: "Will you please, all of you, leave me alone for a moment with that Spanish gentleman?"

The soldiers and the porters docilely obeyed.

Their footsteps died in the distance. Far away, the sad wail of a locomotive whistle broke the stillness of the night. The two men stood still, enveloped by the mist, their eyes locked.

"Alone at last, Monsieur le Baron," said von Beck mockingly.

The Baron bowed coldly. "A brilliant piece of deduction, Colonel," he said.

Von Beck nodded. "Yes. It took me a little while to realize that the only way for you to take the machine out of France was by using us. All you had to do during those ten minutes you spent in the building was to pack the Enigma in a crate and carry it to the storage room, with the goods that were to be dispatched on the same day. You had prepared the crate and the documents beforehand. You were in the Otto building several times, weren't you?"

The Baron didn't answer. He was looking around, calculating his chances of escaping. And for the first time in his life he felt there was no way out.

"I presume you have a plane ticket for a flight to Madrid this morning, and this crate has been listed already as diplomatic cargo. I believe you used a roughly similar way to steal the gold of the Gestapo."

The Baron remained quiet, his face devoid of expression.

"Well, I am sorry for you, Baron, but this seems to be the end of the road." Von Beck couldn't suppress the note of triumph in his voice.

Belvoir spoke. "If you want to do something, do it. Let's not waste my time or yours."

Von Beck cocked his weapon and took one more step toward the Baron. Instinctively, Belvoir took off his hat and looked at him. That was the way the colonel saw him—a gray-eyed adventurer, clever, daring, but most of all, proud. He felt the trigger's cold touch under his curled finger. He needed just a sign of weakness, an imploring word, a glint of panic in the gray eyes, an attempt to escape—so that this romantic image he had built and cherished in his imagination, the image of the man he had longed to become, would be shattered. But Belvoir did not move, did not flinch, did not ask for mercy.

And von Beck could not press the trigger. He wanted this man dead. And he could not kill him.

In a rage, at the very last moment, von Beck sharply shifted the gun's muzzle and squeezed the trigger. The slugs tore through the wood and the cardboard, crippling the Enigma machine, perforating the delicate revolving drums, slicing the thin wires, shattering the keyboard, turning the most precious secret of the Reich into a smoldering piece of useless debris.

"The girl won't be delivered to the Gestapo," he said slowly.

Then he turned and walked away into the thick white fog, leaving behind him the one man he could not kill, Francis de Belvoir.

"I'LL TAKE THE CALL IN MY OFFICE," GENERAL BODLEY SAID.

He returned the file he had been consulting to the cabinet and locked it, then walked into his office and closed the door. His secretary had been instructed never to inquire about the identity of those who called the head of M.I.6 on his direct line. He picked up the phone. "Bodley," he said guardedly.

"I am back in London and I want to see you."

He was speechless for a second, when he recognized the deep voice with the slightly sarcastic tone. "We thought you were dead," he said dryly. "We had lost all contact with you."

"Sorry to disappoint you, but I am still very much alive."

Bodley hesitated for an instant. "Well, let's meet, by all means," he said uncertainly. "But right now I am terribly busy. Let's say in a few days, all right? Where are you? When did you arrive?"

Belvoir ignored the questions. "I want to see you today," he said. "My mission failed and I'll tell you why. There is a traitor in your service, a double agent. I was betrayed even before I set foot in France. The Germans knew all my moves in advance. I was nearly caught, more than once."

There was a long silence on the line. "Look," said Bodley finally. "May we pick you up at 10:00 P.M. sharp, at the corner of Shaftesbury and Piccadilly?"

The line went dead.

It was the same unmarked limousine that had left him here ages ago. The driver stopped the car, but didn't budge from behind the wheel, fixedly staring ahead. Belvoir got in. The driver did not say a word and drove carefully north and out of London. The drive lasted more than an hour. Belvoir recognized the gently sloping Chiltern hills, and the small

Buckinghamshire town of Dunstable, heralding the rich pastures and lush hunting grounds stretching between Bicester and Bedford. They passed through the drab outskirts of Bletchley, where ungraceful factory chimneys loomed over the ugly blocks of workers' small houses. Belvoir's eyes missed nothing, and his memory was as good as ever. He expected the car to reach the estate of the Duke of Bedford, at Woburn Park, when suddenly he saw a discreet sign on the side of the road. It read: Bletchley Park.

The car penetrated along a narrow access road into what looked like a military camp. Belvoir had never seen such intensive security in his life. The place was surrounded by three barbed-wire fences. Watchtowers equipped with powerful projectors had been erected at regular intervals along the fences, and the powerful beams of the searchlights were permanently sweeping the narrow strip of land adjacent to the outer fence. Triangular signs hanging on the barbed wire announced the presence of minefields. The second fence was patrolled by soldiers walking watchdogs; the inner fence was electrified. The car had to stop at three roadblocks before it was finally cleared and admitted to the compound.

In the clear moonlight, Belvoir noticed a few wooden huts spread on a rather neglected lawn. The car moved past them and up the driveway, until it came to a stop in front of a brightly illuminated red-brick Victorian mansion. It was an extremely ugly and pretentious edifice, two stories high, with gabled roofs, long sturdy chimneys, and a tasteless ornate facade.

Belvoir alighted from the car. A stocky, heavy-boned staff sergeant came out of the arched porch. "Mister Belvoir? Will you follow me, please?"

Bodley was waiting for him in an oval sitting room incongruously furnished with graceless modern armchairs, a metal-framed table and a thin, threadbare rug. He came forward to greet him, neat and erect as ever, his white moustache manicured to perfection, the piercing eyes glowing with their cold blue flame. He didn't shake hands.

"I guess you don't like the house," Bodley said in an effort to be casual. "Well, it's hideous, really. One of those Victorian monstrosities that we had to use, unfortunately, for . . ."

"I didn't come to discuss country-house architecture with you, General," Belvoir cut him off bluntly. "I have other things on my mind, as you might guess."

"Yes," Bodley said quickly. "Yes, of course." Belvoir suddenly realized Bodley's clumsy attempt at small talk was a desperate effort to conceal his nervousness.

"I gather you remember our phone talk of this morning," Belvoir pressed on.

"Yes," the head of the M.I.6 said. "I couldn't speak to you over the phone. But now I can tell you. You were right. There was somebody here who betrayed you and reported to the Germans."

"So you got him!" Belvoir exclaimed angrily. "I knew that somebody very highly placed in London betrayed me!"

"Yes." Bodley was very pale, very taut. "We got him."

"Who is he? Somebody from S.O.E.?"

Bodley's expression didn't change. "He is here, in this house. Let me take you to see him."

He led Belvoir through a maze of corridors, past offices bustling with activity. Officers and civilians ran in and out of the rooms, talking excitedly. Belvoir caught a few sentences, but couldn't understand what they were saying; the conversations were interspersed with enigmatic codewords. In any case, he was in no mood for listening. His face was deeply flushed and a deadly fury raged in his heart. How long he had waited, how much he had sacrificed for this moment, for his encounter with the traitor. He felt he could strangle him, make him pay for all the tortured and murdered Frenchmen, for the death of his only friend, for the use of an innocent girl who was now in the hands of the Abwehr.

The head of M.I.6 stopped by a closed door. He breathed deeply. "Calm down," he said, as if he perceived Belvoir's anger. "He is inside."

He opened the door and entered, momentarily blocking the room from Belvoir's sight. The Baron quickly followed him. The room consisted of a tiny vestibule, totally bare and unfurnished, with another door in the opposite wall.

There was nobody inside.

Bodley turned to him slowly. His face was inscrutable.

"Here you are with the traitor," the head of M.I.6 said. "I did the reporting to the Germans."

Belvoir gasped with astonishment. "You?" His eyes were wide open with shock and disbelief. "You?" he repeated.

But Bodley didn't behave as a traitor. "Come," he said with disconcerting softness in his voice. "I think I owe you an explanation."

Belvoir followed him, his mind in turmoil. Opening the

second door of the small vestibule, they entered a large hall. It was the biggest communications center the Baron had ever seen. Scores of technicians, most of them equipped with ear-phones, were bent over sophisticated radio sets. They were carefully inscribing the messages received. Soldiers and of-ficers were dashing between the tables, carrying sheafs of ra-dio messages. In two elevated glass booths in the back of the room, behind rows of telephones, sat the supervisors.

"Look!" Bodley said and pointed to the middle of the room.

Belvoir looked and froze, thunderstruck.

In front of him, on a separate table, he saw it.

The Enigma.

An officer sat behind it, gently typing on the keyboard var-ious messages that were piled on his right. And the decoded messages were coming out of the machine, on an oblong sheet of paper.

"The Enigma," Belvoir said in awe, and repeated the name again and again. As if suddenly awakened from a dream, he darted among the soldiers, pushing aside anybody who stood in his way, until he reached the decoding device. He bent over it, his unbelieving eyes examining it closely. There was no doubt. The wires were plugged into their sockets, the in-dented disks were slowly turning, and the little Gothic letters on the tiny plaque at the left side of the contraption spelled it clearly: Enigma. He ran the tips of his fingers over the smooth wooden surface of the box. The operating officer, a lieutenant, raised his eyes, glanced at him indifferently, shrugged and resumed his typing.

Bodley touched his shoulder. "Come," he said, "let's have a little chat."

He followed the general out of the room, his mind unable to shape a coherent thought. The general led the way up a winding, narrow staircase, until they reached the upper land-ing. A sergeant stood on guard near the small access door. "It's all right, sergeant," Bodley said. They got out on the roof. Belvoir looked around him. All over the roof, on the gables, and the domes, a multitude of radio aerials glistened in the moonlight. They were of all kinds—intricate webs of delicate wire, large concave discs facing different directions, rod-shaped antennae gently swaying in the night wind, evil-looking red-and-white poles crossed with crooked, steel-spike bars, looming in the dark like futuristic totems.

Bodley gestured toward the steel forest. "The biggest eavesdropping center in the Western hemisphere," he chuckled dryly. "There is almost no message the Germans send over the air that is not intercepted here. With those devices our people are able to detect the faintest murmur a transmitter flashes on the Continent."

Belvoir listened, slowly regaining control over his reactions.

"And the one and only purpose of this huge listening system," the general went on, "is to feed the machine. The small machine that is the most jealously guarded secret of this country today. The Enigma. Thanks to it, we are going to win the war."

"You mean you had the Enigma in your possession for a long while?" Belvoir asked, astonished.

"Since 1939, as a matter of fact," Bodley said conversationally. "Would you like a cup of tea?"

The unique advantage of the dining room that served now as an officers' canteen was its spacious veranda, overlooking the park. The night was crisp, but not cold, and the perfumed fragrances of spring gently wafted in the country air. General Bodley carefully placed his empty cup on the stone balustrade.

"The Enigma was stolen from the Germans by some Polish agents," the head of M.I.6 said quietly. "They concocted a very sophisticated plan and carried it out remarkably. They faked a car accident near Danzig in which an Enigma of the German Army was supposedly destroyed. The Germans, who had just started to use the machine, never suspected that the device was actually stolen. One of our people received the Enigma from the Poles in Warsaw, and succeeded in bringing it to this country barely a week before the World War started."

"And you've been using it ever since," Belvoir put in.

"Yes, and with tremendous success. For almost five years we have been decoding the top secret messages of the German High Command. We call the information so obtained the Ultra secret. And I may tell you that this is indeed our ultrasecret weapon. Thanks to the Enigma, we read Göring's orders to the Luftwaffe—and we won the Battle of Britain. The R.A.F. was ready whenever Göring's planes attacked. The same way, we read Rommel's messages—and we won the Libyan campaign."

"Then why the hell . . ." started Belvoir indignantly.

Bodley anticipated the question and raised his hand. "As I

said, this is our best-kept secret in this war. But we had to share it, of course, with our Allies. A certain American general—I won't tell you his name—unfortunately disregarded the strict security precautions while using the Enigma information. He carried out several successive attacks on the Germans in Italy, which convinced them that we knew their secrets. They opened an urgent inquiry, immediately ordered the application of tight security measures, and suspended the use of the Enigma. German field security suspected that we might have gotten the machine, or that we built one and succeeded in breaking their codes. We were cut off from our main source of information."

"When was that?"

"About three months ago. With the invasion of Europe approaching, we desperately needed the invaluable Ultra information. The introduction of the V-2 rockets, Hitler's vengeance weapons, convinced our government that we had to act quickly. We had to convince the Germans at all costs that we didn't have the Enigma." Bodley sharply looked at Belvoir. "At all costs," he repeated forcefully.

Belvoir lit a black cheroot. His hands were steady. "And then you decided to send somebody to France, to steal the Enigma."

"And that somebody had to fail," Bodley pointed out. "Your mission, and your failure, were the best proof the Germans needed to be convinced that the Enigma was safe, and that they could use it without fear. You saw it functioning now. Since day before yesterday the air is again full of messages."

Contained anger flashed in Belvoir's eyes. "That's why you sent me, and not one of your team."

Bodley sighed, but his gaze didn't waver. "You were expendable," he said matter-of-factly. "You would have been posthumously decorated and pensioned."

"When you let me know, through your network in Paris, that the operation was called off, you intended to deliver me into the hands of the Gestapo, right?"

"Yes. We expected you to break during interrogation and to disclose the details of your mission. As I said—your failure was all we wanted. You had to be sacrificed."

"But you sacrificed also several Resistance networks!" Belvoir exclaimed scornfully.

Bodley thought a moment. "You know," he said quietly, "during the Battle of Britain we decoded, by means of the

Enigma, Göring's order to the Luftwaffe to destroy Coventry. We had about five hours time—enough to evacuate the city. It was a terrible dilemma. Should we evacuate Coventry, saving the lives of hundreds of our citizens—and thus reveal to the enemy that we had the Enigma? Or sacrifice all those lives and win the war?"

"And you chose, of course, the second solution."

"The Prime Minister chose it on my recommendation."

"For God's sake," exploded Belvoir, "what kind of inhuman machine are you? Don't you care for human lives? All those innocent people, dead to serve your spy games!"

Bodley suddenly turned away and stared into the night. His voice was oddly strained. "Five hundred fifty-four people were killed in Coventry. My wife was among them. My only daughter was maimed, condemned to a wheelchair for the rest of her life. I condemned her when I made my decision."

For a long moment Belvoir stood very still. Then he turned and walked into the house.

Bodley followed him, again looking his calm, imperturbable self. "You will get the balance of your payment, of course," he said briskly. "From our point of view, you accomplished your mission in the best possible way."

"I almost succeeded in blowing it." Belvoir smiled bitterly. "For a short while, I had the Enigma."

Bodley looked at him in dismay. "Tell me about it," he asked.

The night was almost over when Belvoir finished his story, in the small sitting room where Bodley had received him on his arrival at Bletchley. "Incredible," Bodley murmured, and added in wonder: "You are a brave man, Belvoir."

Belvoir disregarded the remark and got up to leave. "By the way," he asked, "how did you inform the Germans about my moves in France?"

"Oh, that?" said Bodley lightly. "We captured their radio team in London years ago. Their main operator is one of our agents. We use them quite a lot for feeding the German false information."

They left the porch. Belvoir asked: "May I have my money today?"

Bodley glanced at him in slight surprise. "What's the hurry?"

Belvoir hesitated, but finally he made up his mind. "I don't mind telling you. I am going back there."

"France?! What for?"

Belvoir shrugged. "It's personal," he replied coldly.

For the first time that night, Bodley smiled. "It's the girl, isn't it? Don't worry, this time I shall not report you to the Germans."

He escorted him to the car.

Far away to the east, the dawn filled the sky with a pale gray light. "You'll get your money by tonight," the head of M.I.6 said. "But I doubt that you'll get there as easily this time."

For he knew something that Belvoir didn't. He knew that at this very moment, the largest armada ever assembled was sailing through the troubled waters of the Channel, toward the beaches of Normandy. Thousands upon thousands of Allied soldiers were making their final preparations before they jumped from their ships and planes onto the soil of occupied France. This was June 6, D-Day—the day of the landing in France, which could be the beginning of the end.

Belvoir looked at him closely. Before the car moved, he leaned out of the window and said to Bodley in his slightly ironical voice: "Don't you worry, General. I'll get there all right."

There was a curious note of respect in Bodley's voice when he said slowly: "Yes, I guess you will." And surprising even himself, he added: "Good luck, Baron."

Baron? Belvoir looked suspiciously from the already-moving car to detect any hint of mockery in Bodley's face.

But there was none.

EPILOGUE

AFTERMATH

After the successful landing of the Allies in Normandy on June 6, 1944, Hitler's opponents in the High Command of the German army decided to act.

Admiral Wilhelm Canaris was one of the main ringleaders of the attempt on Hitler's life that took place on July 20, 1944. That day Count Klaus von Stauffenberg planted a highly explosive bomb in the Wolf's Lair, Hitler's Eastern Headquarters. Hitler escaped death by a miracle. His revenge was terrible. Most of the ringleaders of the generals' dissident group, who called themselves "*Die Schwarze Kapelle*"—the Black Orchestra—were massacred. All the three senior officers whom von Beck encountered at "La Duchesse" restaurant in Paris met ghastly deaths. Field Marshal Erwin Rommel was forced to commit suicide by poison. General Karl Henrich von Stülpnagel was less fortunate; he tried to kill himself in his cell in the Berlin Plötzensee prison, but failed, and shortly thereafter was strangled to death by order of the Führer. Other leading German generals were hanged or beheaded by medieval ax, one of the Führer's favorite instruments of execution. Canaris himself wasn't put to death immediately. He was kept in prison until a few weeks before the final collapse of the Reich. On April 9, 1945, at dawn, he was hanged, naked, on a gallows erected in the Flossenbürg concentration camp. Following explicit orders from the Führer, the hangman used a thin piano cord in order to prolong the death convulsions of the man who had rebelled against his madness.

Rudolf von Beck didn't play an active part in the July 20 plot. After his showdown with the Baron in Berlin, Canaris ordered him back to Paris to cover up the traces of the destroyed twenty-eighth Enigma. In the following weeks he was employed at minor tasks in the Hotel Lutetia. He never again went back to the prison wing on the third floor. He tried to erase Michèle from his memory, but her image was too fresh, too vivid; sometimes the pain was unbearable. After the July 20 plot failed, he suspected Canaris had kept him out of it on purpose, in order to protect him in case something went wrong.

He became strangely indifferent to the dramatic change in the course of the war. Something deep inside him had snapped on the second day of June, and he followed with passive interest the advance of the Allies throughout France. When the second armored division of General Jacques-Phillippe Leclerc liberated Paris on August 25, he docilely surrendered to the Free French and marched to captivity through the rue de Rivoli, with other officers of the Commandment of Gross Paris.

While walking in the crowded streets, his hands on his head, between two human walls of delirious Parisians, shouting and spitting on the prisoners, he didn't notice a badly maimed Frenchman in civilian clothes, painfully elbowing his way through the crowd. Had he noticed him, he wouldn't have recognized him. The invalid was Henri, the Communist leader who directed the attack on the German train in the forest of Laon. That terrible night, which had cost the Resistance some three hundred lives, had left Henri a bitter man, obsessed with revenge. He had survived the massacre by a miracle, and after the main German forces had been evacuated from the battleground, had succeeded in crawling into the forest, where he was discovered two days later by an elderly woman collecting mushrooms. He was brought to an isolated farm on the outskirts of Laon, where a doctor attended to his wounds. But it was too late to save his left leg. After he recovered, he reappeared at the secret meetings of the Resistance in Paris, leaning heavily on his crutches and preaching to his comrades a merciless fight against the Germans.

One day before the liberation of Paris, he saw the poster plastered on the walls of the city by Colonel Rol, the head of the Communist underground: "*A chacun son boche*—Let everybody kill his own German!" And today, clutching his old 7.65 Long pistol in his right hand, which also held his crutch, he was determined to get his *boche*.

He didn't recognize the features of the tall, handsome blond colonel who walked in the column of prisoners. All he saw was the image of the German conqueror, the enemy who had made his beloved city suffer, and who had massacred his comrades. He limped through the crowd, past the man who escorted the prisoners, and stood in front of the German. He pushed his right crutch against the pavement and raised his gun. For an instant his eyes met those of the German officer. He was briefly taken aback by the lifeless look he saw there.

He fired. The bullet pierced Rudolf von Beck's forehead, and the German officer collapsed on the cobblestones, his arms outstretched, his eyes staring unseeingly at the limpid blue sky of a free Paris.

Nobody stopped Henri. He slowly limped away, forever denied the knowledge that he had avenged those who died in the forest of Laon.

Otto Brandl, the man after whom the Otto organization was named, succeeded in escaping to Germany on August 12, a few days before the Allies captured Paris. In the last few months before his escape, he had succeeded in smuggling and concealing huge portions of his fabled treasure over the world. Gold, diamonds, jewelry, paintings, foreign currency were stowed away in hideouts in Germany, France, Portugal and Argentina. Parts of the Otto treasure were found soon after the fall of the Reich; others kept appearing as late as 1949. There were securities worth 60 million francs in Lisbon, a seventeenth-century Gobelin tapestry in Munich, a crate of solid silver plates in Fürstenfeldbruck, fifteen paintings of Manet, Corot, Sisley and Renoir in a farmer's house at Pfarrkirchen. But most of the treasure was never found.

As for Otto himself, he was arrested in Munich by the U.S. Army on August 6, 1945, and imprisoned in Stadelheim jail. The next morning he was discovered dead, hanging from a beam in his prison cell.

General MacAlister, Victoria Cross, K.B.E., died shortly after the war of a heart attack.

General Bodley resigned from active duty after V-Day and served as "M," the head of the Secret Intelligence Service, until 1955. He resigned the same day as Winston Churchill and spent the last five years of his life with his invalid daughter, in a modest cottage he bought in Sussex. He never set foot in Coventry again.

After the astounding escape of Michèle Lemaire from the Hotel Lutetia on June 29, 1944, nobody ever heard of her or of the Baron de Belvoir again.

Nobody except old Louise Lemaire, who regularly brings flowers to Bruno Morel's grave at the peaceful Père Lachaise cemetery.

But she, of course, would never tell.

Author's Note

THE FOREGOING EVENTS ARE NOT AS FICTITIOUS AS THEY might seem. The Enigma coding machine really existed and was one of the most closely guarded secrets of the Reich. However, the Polish Secret Service succeeded in getting hold of an Enigma machine in early 1939; a week before Germany attacked Poland, the precious machine was flown to England. Thanks to the Enigma, British Intelligence decoded top-secret German messages during the whole war. The information so obtained was known as "Ultra." The Ultra secret was not cleared for publication until 1974, when F. W. Winterbotham revealed it for the first time in his best-selling non-fiction book, *The Ultra Secret* (Harper and Row, New York, 1974).

The team of highly skilled technicians who decoded the Enigma messages was based, as I pointed out, at Bletchley Park, in Buckinghamshire. In order to protect the Ultra secret, which Churchill called "my most secret source," very tight security precautions were taken. The most dramatic was certainly the decision not to evacuate Coventry. Countless schemes and methods were used in various ways to cover up the source of the information supplied by Ultra. Nevertheless, at certain moments during the war, the suspicions of the German High Command were aroused. It is conceivable that in an effort to lull the Abwehr at a decisive moment, Francis de Belvoir was sent on his mission.

It is a fact that the Ultra messages played a crucial role in the Battle of Normandy and in the final collapse of the Third Reich.

M.B.

Elba House
Sandy Lane
Barbados 1977

About the Author

Michael Barak is a pseudonym for a well-known Israeli author who served as press secretary to General Moshe Dayan during the Six Day War and later, as a paratrooper, crossed the Suez Canal into Egypt during the Yom Kippur War. He is the author of *The Secret List of Heinrich Roehm,* also available in a Signet Edition.